The Bargainer Series

A Beggar's Bargain

The Bargainer Series

A Beggar's Bargain

Jan Sikes

Fresh Ink Group
Guntersville

A Beggar's Bargain

Copyright © 2024
by Jan Sikes
All rights reserved

Fresh Ink Group
An Imprint of:
The Fresh Ink Group, LLC
1021 Blount Avenue #931
Guntersville, AL 35976
Email: info@FreshInkGroup.com
FreshInkGroup.com

Edition 1.0 2024

Covers by Stephen Geez / FIG
Cover art by Anik / FIG
Book design by Amit Dey / FIG
Associate publisher Beem Weeks / FIG

Except as permitted under the U.S. Copyright Act of 1976 and except for brief quotations in critical reviews or articles, no portion of this book's content may be stored in any medium, transmitted in any form, used in whole or part, or sourced for derivative works such as videos, television, and motion pictures, without prior written permission from the publisher.

Cataloging-in-Publication Recommendations:
FIC014090 FICTION / Historical / 20th Century / Post-World War II
FIC045020 FICTION / Family Saga
FIC014030 FICTION / Historical / Romance

Library of Congress Control Number: 2024901925

ISBN-13: 978-1-958922-77-4 Softcover
ISBN-13: 978-1-958922-78-1 Hardcover
ISBN-13: 978-1-958922-79-8 Ebooks

ACKNOWLEDGEMENTS

Stories can come from the strangest of places, and the idea for A *Beggar's Bargain* came from a song by The Damn Quails entitled "Fool's Gold."

It is a piece of fiction, written from the author's imagination. It features real locations in Missouri, but the events described and characters developed are purely fictional with no intent to depict reality.

I would like to thank Brenda Tindill Isenbletter for her outstanding help in my research on the area around Everton, Missouri. She put me in touch with several local folks who shared their knowledge of and stories of the area. Brenda helped me gain access to old newspapers via microfiche at the Dade County Library in Greenfield, Missouri. That proved to be invaluable.

Thank you to the residents of Everton, Missouri, who opened their hearts and minds to me. I am forever grateful, as their willingness to share helped shape the story in a believable way.

A big thank you goes out to my beta-readers, the Story Empire authors who encourage and support me, and my wonderful critique partner, my sister, Linda Broday.

Thank you, Fresh Ink Group, for taking a chance on this story.

PROLOGUE

With a heavy heart, Layken Martin clutched a spray of purple asters and wild bergamot that grew along the banks of a Missouri creek. Blinking back tears, he removed his Army hat and uniform jacket and wiped the sweat from his brow. He kneeled beside two simple gravestones in Sinking Creek Cemetery, marking the life and times of his parents, Jacob and Nancy Martin. It had come as no shock that Jacob had only lived a few short months following Nancy's death.

They'd lived simple lives with nothing much to show for their time on earth except a two-hundred-acre farm and one son.

He placed the flowers between the two headstones. His quiet voice trembled. "Mom, Dad, I promise you I will do my best to carry our legacy forward. No matter what it takes."

Never had Layken felt so alone, not even during the big war when entrenched on the battlefield in France. At least there he had comrades.

Now, for the first time in his life, he had no one. And to top it off, the family farm had fallen into ruin.

The letter from his father informing him of his mother's death reached him in France, two months after the fact. Then, a letter from the local reverend arrived two days later telling him of his father's death.

The dilapidated state of the place where he'd grown up left him reeling when he arrived home three days ago. His aged parents had fought their own private war with the elements while he was away.

Casting a glance at the cloudless sky, he cleared his throat and continued. "I'll make the land produce again."

His father's words in that final letter hung fresh in his mind. *Promise me you'll never lose the farm, son.*

He crushed his hat in his hands. "Mom, I wish I could have been here to help you and Dad." His throat clogged with unshed tears. "I'm here now, and on both your graves, I vow to do my best."

Restoring the farm to its glory days wouldn't be easy, yet he looked forward to the hard work in quiet solitude, away from gunfire, bombs, and screams of agony that haunted him.

He sat back on his haunches, tuning into the lilting birdsong drifting down from the white oak and elm trees and the gentle cascade of water over rocks in the creek. This was a good place to be buried, to find rest and peace. And in his heart of hearts, he knew his weary folks had found both.

After a while, he stood, brushed off his pants, and squared his shoulders, feeling sure Jacob and Nancy Martin had heard him.

They'd be watching.

And he wouldn't let them down.

CHAPTER 1

Every single day since Layken Martin had returned home after his discharge from the Army, he'd prayed for a miracle.

But none came.

He stood in the pasture next to the old farmhouse and scooped up a handful of dry Missouri dirt, then let it trickle through his fingers, as sweat ran down the middle of his back. Squinting against the blistering July sun, the sky gave nary a sign of a cloud that might bring relief to the dried, cracked ground that hadn't produced a decent crop in two years.

The struggle to make anything grow in the middle of a drought, only to have it taken over by weeds, had killed his father's spirit and, finally, his body.

The stress of falling deeper into debt pounded the final nails into Jacob Martin's coffin.

Layken tucked in his nicest clean shirt and tightened his belt. He smoothed back his military cut, brown wavy hair, and placed his prized fedora on his head. Dread snaked up his spine and lodged in his throat.

Layken hated admitting defeat.

Hated begging even more.

But he'd made a promise. Not only a promise to his mother and father, but to the land itself. He loved every square inch of the two-hundred-acre farm surrounded by ancient walnut trees, black oak, cottonwood, sweet gum, and silverleaf maple trees. Embedded in his soul, the spirit of the land and his connection with it had kept him going when he lay sleepless on foreign soil.

A letter crinkled in his shirt pocket as he climbed into his father's 1937 Dodge pickup. After spending hours yesterday cleaning spark plugs and tuning the engine, he prayed like hell it would start.

The farm, the old pickup, and an ancient Farmall tractor were the three things he'd inherited when his parents died. Well, that and a debt.

And now, based on the letter in his pocket, he stood on the brink of losing it all.

Then what would he do?

He couldn't—no, wouldn't let that happen.

When the old pickup started, he breathed a sigh of relief.

That alone had to be a good sign, right? A cloud of dust followed him down the dirt lane to the narrow blacktop leading to the nearest town of Everton, Missouri, that barely surpassed three hundred folks.

Jaw set in a firm line, he once again mentally counted the cash in his pocket. Only fifty dollars left from his last army paycheck. That was all he had to his name. He'd have to hold back a little to keep gas in the old truck and buy seeds for planting. The rest he'd offer up as a show of good faith.

Twenty minutes later, he came to a stop in front of the First Bank of Missouri on Main Street. The building could benefit from some serious updating. It showed its age with a ragged awning barely hanging over the entrance and a large crack in the front window.

He pushed through the door that jingled a bell announcing his arrival and removed his hat.

A woman perched behind the teller's window glanced up, the rotating portable fan beside her ruffling her gray hair. "Can I help you, sir?"

He cleared his throat and pulled the letter from his pocket. "Yes, ma'am. I'm here to see Mr. Williams."

She motioned toward a door labeled Bank President. "Go on in, I reckon."

Layken knocked on the door before turning the knob.

"Yeah. Who is it?" an irritated voice called out.

"Mr. Williams, it's Layken Martin. I need to speak with you."

"Well, come on in, then."

A blast of cool air dried the sweat on Layken's forehead when he opened the door.

An overweight, balding man wearing suspenders and thick eyeglasses sat behind an ancient wooden desk. A rare air-conditioning unit jutted from the small opening cut in the wall. "Don't stand there gawking and close the damn door before you let all the cold air out." He motioned toward an empty chair. "Have a seat."

Layken gently closed the door and slid into the nearest chair, resting his fedora on his knee while he removed the letter from his shirt pocket. "Sir, I received this letter from you yesterday, and I'm here to negotiate for more time." He passed it to the banker.

Mr. Williams glanced at the letter and tossed it aside. "What kind of negotiation do you have in mind?"

"For starters, I have forty dollars I can pay you today as a show of good faith. If you can see your way clear to give me more time, I'm sure I can make a partial crop before winter sets in."

The overweight man hooked his thumbs in his suspenders and leaned back. The chair groaned under his weight. "Forty dollars, huh? That's all you've got?"

Layken nodded. "That's all."

"Sorry, that ain't enough. Your daddy owed this bank nine hundred dollars when he died, and now there's interest added to that. Reckon you inherited that debt with the farm. Now, your loan is in severe default. We can't keep the doors open if we let every Tom, Dick, and Harry go without paying their debts. Surely, you can understand that."

"Yes, sir. I do understand. Got plans to plant peanuts right away. Hear tell they're selling for twice the amount of sorghum or wheat. I'm doing my best." He picked at a hangnail.

"Peanuts? Are you crazy? No one around here grows peanuts. Hell, they probably won't even grow in Missouri soil. Besides that, it's too blamed hot to plant a crop."

"Sir, I promise I've done my research. I believe they will grow. I'm willing to bet the farm on it."

Williams squinted. "You know, you ain't the only one around here with these troubles. Nevertheless, the bank has its rules and regulations. If you can't pay at least a hundred today, I'm afraid I'll have to start foreclosure proceedings."

Layken fought against rising bile, wishing he'd had more than coffee for breakfast. "I've only got forty dollars. Sir, I swore an oath to my father I'd never lose the farm. He was a customer at this bank his whole life and always paid his debts."

"That is true. But it doesn't change the fact that you aren't paying the debt now. Why, we barely know you, son. You were gone so long folks around here forgot about you."

Shifting on the hard wooden chair, Layken struggled to tamp down rising anger. "Yes, sir. It's true, I was gone, fighting the Germans and Japs, trying to save our country." He gritted his teeth. "That oughta count for something."

The older man peered over the rim of his glasses. "No need to get bent out of shape. I'm just doin' my job." He reached into his top drawer and fished out a cigar, offering one to Layken. "Smoke?"

"No, thanks." Why couldn't the man understand his situation? "I give you my word. If you can see fit to give me a grace period on this loan, I'll find a way to pay it off—even if it means selling part of the acreage." He leaned forward. "I've got time to get seeds in the ground and produce a partial crop before winter sets in. I'm sure of it."

While Williams struck a match and lit the stogie, Layken glanced around the small office. A cheap print of a snow-covered mountainside hung lopsided on one wall. Other than that, there was no decor. It was as if the man had nothing personal to display.

The banker blew out a smoke ring and pushed his glasses up on his nose. "You know, there might be one other alternative."

Layken perked up, a glimmer of hope rising. "I'm willing to do anything to save the place."

"You ever been married?"

"No. But I don't see what that has to do with anything."

"It might have everything to do with the situation you're in." He flipped ashes off the end of the cigar into a large ashtray.

Layken fidgeted with his fedora and waited for him to continue.

"I've been courting the Widow Jones. You remember her, don't you? She taught you in grade school."

"I remember her. She was my math teacher." He and the other kids made jokes about her being a crone because of her sharp nose and tongue.

"You see, I asked her to marry me, but she said she's never gonna marry me so long as my daughter lives under my roof."

"I don't mean to be rude, Mr. Williams, but I don't see the bearing on my situation."

"At least, hear me out." The man blew out another smoke ring.

"I'm listening." Layken chewed the inside of his cheek.

"My girl ain't been the same since her mama died. She ain't touched in the head or anything like that. She's just different. But I ain't gettin' no younger, and I'm tired of being alone. I want to get married."

Layken's heart pounded erratically. "I don't mean to be disrespectful, but I fail to see what any of this has to do with me."

"What if I make you a deal? You come from good stock. Everyone around these parts thought highly of Jacob and Nancy Martin. They came to church most every Sunday."

"They were great people," Layken agreed. "But none of this is making any sense."

"It's simple. Marry my Sara Beth, give her a home, and I'll postpone payment on your debt for two years. That should give you enough time to get on your feet and get your farm back producing."

"What?" Layken leaned forward, swallowing hard. "Did I hear you right? You're offering your daughter to me in exchange for two years of grace on the loan?"

"Yep. That's about it in a nutshell. I need her out of my house. There ain't another eligible bachelor anywhere in this county. You're a nice-looking young man from a good family. She could do worse. So, what do you say?"

Layken sat back and blew out a deliberate breath. Surely, he was dreaming, or the sun had made him delirious. This couldn't possibly be real. "I'm speechless. The very last thing I need is a wife. I don't even know your daughter."

"She would've been a few years behind you in school. But my Sara Beth is smart, and she's kind most of the time. She can get a mean streak now and again." The banker chuckled. "But can't all women?"

"Mr. Williams, this is not a solution I'm willing to consider." Surely, the banker must be off his rocker. What kind of man gives his daughter to a stranger?

"Then, I guess you leave me no choice but to foreclose."

Layken jerked to his feet, struggling to find his footing. "I really wish you wouldn't. If you could only see your way clear to give me more time."

"I offered you a solution. It's the best I can do."

"Sorry I took up your time, sir." Layken opened the door, jammed his hat on his head, and darted out of the bank.

The temperature difference almost knocked him to his knees as the sun's relentless rays hit him.

What in the holy hell happened in there?

He stumbled to the rusty pickup and climbed in, resting his forehead on the steering wheel.

No.

Everything inside him screamed in protest, and his temples throbbed as a massive headache formed. His stomach growled, and the local diner across the street called to him. He still had fifty dollars. He needed a meal and a cup of coffee. He could spare a dollar.

A man couldn't think clearly on an empty stomach.

As with most places in Everton, Mom's Cafe didn't have the luxury of modern air conditioning. Fans stirred the stifling air, mixed with the aroma of cooked bacon.

With hat in hand, Layken slid into a booth.

The waitress, a rotund lady with gray-streaked hair pinned in a bun and wearing an apron, greeted him. "What can I get you today?"

"I'd like the breakfast special and coffee, please."

The woman laid silverware on the table and nodded. "Be right back with that coffee."

Layken stared out the front window as the streets of the tiny town came to life. The bank was in his direct view. He rubbed his temples and tried to digest what the banker had said. Surely the man was off his rocker.

It didn't add up. Something must be terribly wrong with Sara Beth Williams. Hell, something must be wrong with him for even thinking about it.

He took a sip of the black coffee that appeared before him.

Sure, someday he'd find the perfect woman and start a family, but that wasn't now, and certainly not with a stranger he'd never even met.

No. It was a preposterous proposal.

Still, two years to get the farm back up to par and making a profit would ease the burden.

He ate mindlessly once the food arrived and pondered his options.

When the waitress checked on him, he fished for information. Maybe this woman knew the banker's daughter. "Sure is hot, ain't it?"

The lady nodded. "One of the hottest summers I can remember. You're that Martin boy, aren't you?"

"Yes, ma'am."

"A pity about your folks. They were good people. We all knew when your mama died, your daddy wouldn't be far behind her. Sorry for your loss."

"Thank you. Say, do you know Sara Beth Williams?"

"Sure. Everyone knows everyone here, and if you stick around long enough this time, you will, too."

"What can you tell me about her?"

"She took her mother's death hard. Ain't been the same since, ramblin' around in that big ol' house. Her daddy won't give the poor girl the time of day. It's a true pity." The woman pierced him with a stare. "Why are you askin'?"

"Her name came up in an earlier conversation."

"Folks 'round here don't cotton much to her kind. She's a sad, unfortunate soul, bless her heart, and that's all I'm gonna to say."

What in the Sam Hill did that mean?

A sad, unfortunate soul.

That could aptly describe him.

"Her kind? What does that mean?" His headache spread from his temples down the back of his neck.

The woman pursed her lips and stared at him for a long minute. "If you don't know, reckon it don't mean nothin'. Got work to do." She hurried to another table, leaving Layken with his thoughts again.

He finished his meal, left money on the table, and walked back outside and across the street.

He paused, one hand on the pickup door, then turned on his heel and strode back inside the bank.

Without asking for permission, he opened Mr. Williams' office door.

"Sir, I've reconsidered your offer."

CHAPTER 2

"That didn't take long." Mr. Williams chewed on the end of the cigar that had long since gone out.

An intense loathing for the man enveloped Layken as he dropped into the same chair he'd vacated earlier. He didn't bother removing his hat. "I have some questions."

"Shoot."

"I only have forty-nine dollars to my name. Because my mom and dad's health failed the past few years, the house is in need of repairs. I'm going to need money to survive until I can get a full crop harvested. I can plant one small field now, but it'll be spring before I can go full force."

"The day you marry Sara Beth, I'll give you two hundred dollars as a dowry. That'll have to do."

He must have taken leave of his senses to continue this cock-eyed negotiation, but Layken Martin was a desperate man. The words that fell out of his mouth seemed to have a mind of their own, and his voice sounded like that of a stranger. "That should do."

"Look. I want my Sara Beth to be comfortable. I trust you'll see to it that she has what she needs."

"To the best of my ability. Can she cook?"

"She's a damn good cook. Necessity is a great teacher."

Layken cleared his throat, his jaw aching from clenching it so hard. "I can assure you there won't be a marriage bed. She'll have her privacy and her freedom."

"That will be between you and her. None of my business."

Again, Layken questioned what kind of man could give his daughter to a virtual stranger so casually. His heart went out to the young girl, suddenly wondering how young. "How old is your daughter?"

"She's of age. Turned twenty last month."

Layken nodded, still questioning his sanity. All of this was wrong, yet he remained sitting in the chair as if glued to it by some invisible force. "I'm sure your daughter will want a say in this arrangement."

The banker leaned back and hooked his thumbs in his suspenders with a satisfied smirk. "She'll do what I tell her."

The words carried a sharpness that grated on Layken's already frayed nerves. His jaw tightened even more, coming dangerously close to cracking a tooth from the force. "I guess the only other question is when do you want the marriage to take place?" His heart rate rose to a rapid crescendo, and he wiped sweaty palms on his pants leg.

"Tomorrow ain't too soon for me."

"I want to meet Sara Beth first." Not that it mattered much, but still.

"You can meet her at the courthouse over in Greenfield in the morning at ten sharp. I'll call the judge. He's a friend of mine."

"I've got some stipulations of my own before I agree to this cockamamie proposal." He leaned forward on the edge of the chair and met the banker's haughty stare. "No buttin' into our business. Ever. No backing out on our deal. I'll do what you ask, but if it doesn't work out, I insist on the option to ask for an annulment."

"Fair enough." Williams slipped his thumbs out of his suspenders and rested his elbows on the desk. "There ain't nothin' wrong with my girl if that's what you're thinking. She's pretty enough and slender like her ma. I'll stay out of your affairs as long as you keep your end of the bargain."

"I will." Layken stood. "I guess that's that, then."

"Shake on it."

Layken's hands trembled violently as he slid into the pickup, inserted the key in the ignition, and turned it.

Nothing happened.

"Dammit," he muttered. "Don't be difficult now, Lucy." Where his father had come up with that name for the old pickup, he'd never know.

When he turned the key again, it only made a clicking noise.

He got out and raised the hood. After adjusting the battery cable connections, he tried again.

Thank God, this time, it turned over.

After he slammed the hood, he backed out onto the street and steered Lucy toward home.

"Holy hell, man, what have you gotten yourself into?" It didn't matter that he said the words out loud. No one could hear him.

But not for long.

A wife. That had been the farthest thing from his mind when he'd left for town that morning.

All the way back to the farm, he rolled the proposal around in his brain. What woman would want to walk into a farmhouse that had sat vacant for months with a man she'd never met? He had lots to do before ten tomorrow morning.

While he'd swept out the worst of the dirt on the inside of the house, he'd been mainly focused on tuning up the pickup and clearing tall weeds outside to eliminate the threat of snakes.

But now, he had to make the place presentable for Sara Beth.

It's the least he could do.

He strode into the house and went straight to his parents' bedroom. It was exactly the way they'd left it.

When he returned home a few days ago, he'd taken his old room.

Now, he looked around and tried to imagine the bedroom through a woman's eyes. Faded chintz curtains hung limp in front of a four-paned window. The wallpaper around the window frame was peeling, and someone had spread a thin chenille bedspread over the bed. The whole feeling of the room was one of sadness and disappointment. After a while, he gave up and moved to the kitchen.

He'd let Sara Beth sort out the bedroom. He didn't have the heart to sift through his folks' things.

With a sink full of soapy water, he set about putting the kitchen into some kind of order. He could hear his mother's famous words: *We may not have much, but we can be clean.*

Soothing sounds from nature filtered through the open windows and screen door. Birds chirped and fluttered from tree to tree. Varmints rustled through the underbrush. The familiarity of it all soothed his frayed nerves.

"It'll be like having a roommate. Maybe she'll even help me put this old place back together." As was his habit, he talked aloud to himself when worried.

And he was plenty disturbed.

He enjoyed being alone, and something told him Sara Beth probably did, too. He'd make it clear this marriage was in name only, to appease her father—to give Layken a chance to save the ancestral farm.

Would she have a car to drive? Or would she even know how? Many women chose not to learn, especially in a small town where everything was within walking distance.

Add that to his list of questions for Sara Beth.

Two hours later, his job finished in the kitchen, he stood back and admired the result of his efforts. The light brown linoleum flooring responded to his industrious mopping—nothing he could do to hide the bare spots or the rip beneath the square oak table where he'd shared thousands of meals with his parents.

While the cabinets showed years of wear, the stove was in good shape, and his father had purchased the electric icebox only a couple of years back. Faded yellow curtains with pink tulips on the border flapped in the window. He'd helped to hang them. He swallowed past the lump in his throat.

His mom's electric mixer sat on one corner of the cabinet, and, for a brief moment, he could visualize her there in her apron, mixing up a chocolate cake, his favorite. He blinked hard and blew out a slow breath. He'd done his best.

After a long minute, he moved into the living room and switched on an electric fan in the corner, turning in a full circle.

He didn't want Sara Beth thinking he was a slob. He wasn't. The military had made sure of that.

Try as he might, he couldn't look at the familiar room through a stranger's eyes. It held too many fond memories for him—sitting around the radio, listening to Jack Benny and laughing out loud, watching his mother crochet doilies to sell or trade in town, and his father with his head back snoring.

They'd had him late in life. It seemed they were always old from as far back as he could remember.

He picked up stray magazines and papers and then decided to keep the magazines.

Sara Beth might enjoy looking through them.

He searched for a way inside himself to come to grips with the strangeness of it all.

It was like getting the house ready for special company.

Only she wouldn't be a visitor. She'd be his wife.

That had a permanence to it—even if it was only a beggar's desperate bargain.

CHAPTER 3

Sara Beth stood in a shaft of evening sunlight splashing through the living room window. Violent trembling shook her from head to toe, and she almost dropped her pet rabbit. Getting a better grip, she drew herself up to her full five-foot-three height, every swear word she knew running through her head.

"You did what?" Her voice trembled as she tried to find words. "No! I won't! You can't make me."

"Now, Sara Beth, hear me out." Homer Williams paced the length of the living room. "It's time you had a husband. Time you did something besides wag around that useless rabbit you insist on keeping. This is for your own good."

"My own good?" Her teeth clamped together so hard she was sure they might break. Hot, angry tears welled up. "You know that's a lie. It's all about you, dear Father."

He whined, "Now that's unfair."

"No, it's always been about you. I've been a thorn in your side since the day I was born. I couldn't be the son you wanted. But this is the lowest of lows, even for you."

Homer Williams slapped his daughter, sending her reeling. "How dare you speak to me like that? If it wasn't for me, you and your mother wouldn't have had nice things, a decent place to live, and plenty to eat, even when our country was in the worst depression in history. I won't tolerate any disrespect, young lady."

She regained her footing and brought a shaky hand to her stinging jaw. Her reply barely rose above a faint whisper. "Thank you for providing us a home. I'm sorry I've been such a burden."

With Cuddles tucked under her arm, she sprinted up the stairs to the sanctuary of her room.

"You'd best pack up what you want to take with you," Homer called out. "Once the ceremony is over, he'll bring you here to fetch your things."

Under her breath, she muttered, "Then you'll be rid of me for good." She ran a hand over the bunny's soft fur. "Oh, little Cuddles, what has my father done to us?" The tears she'd fought so bravely to hold back fell in torrents.

And now she understood the message from the tarot cards earlier that day. While many believed the Death card predicted a physical demise, her mother had explained it simply meant the end of a situation. And the Knight of Cups that followed must indeed represent Layken Martin.

Her determination to embrace the tarot cards and gemstones her Gypsy mother had taught her to use not only embarrassed but angered her father. To avoid his wrath, she kept them hidden away, wrapped in the colorful silk scarf her mother had inherited from her grandmother.

But she'd not been immune to the gossip and whispers in town. Folks believed her mother to be a witch and that she'd passed it on to her daughter.

If her situation weren't so dire, she'd laugh out loud. What she wouldn't give to place a curse on the man who called himself her father— if only she knew how. And on the gossipers, too, especially Widow Jones. That was the reason she wouldn't move into the house until Sara Beth was gone. She'd as much as told her and her father so.

She was past caring anymore. "To hell with them all," she ground out.

Her heart pounded at the horrifying idea of being forced into a marriage contract. What if Layken Martin was abusive?

Her heart froze. What if he was like her father?

Indeed, if he agreed to this arrangement, there must be something wrong with him.

Maybe he was disfigured or crippled.

She sucked in a sharp breath. What if he was a decrepit old man? She hadn't had the presence of mind to ask his age, or any other questions for that matter. Now, she was kicking herself. She needed some answers.

With her emotions in a jumble, she dropped onto the bed and stared up at the ceiling, tears trickling out and running inside her ears. The possibility of any man pawing around on her, trying to take her virginity, made her stomach heave.

Cuddles curled up against her side. She stroked the bunny's head and whispered, "What if he hates you? Too bad if he does." The soft bunny was all she had left, and she vowed to keep and protect him. To hell with this Layken fellow.

The bunny's nose twitched as he snuggled closer.

When the front door slammed, there was no doubt her father was on his way to see the Widow Jones, quite sure he couldn't wait to deliver the good news. They were two of a kind and deserved each other.

But what did she deserve? She'd always believed a kind gentleman would fall in love with her and sweep her off her feet. But that was only a young girl's dream.

How her mother had ever tolerated the selfish man she called her father, she'd never know. Maybe her only way out was to die. A sob broke loose from her throat. "Oh, Mama. But why did you have to leave me?"

She reached for Cuddles and went in search of the ancient groundskeeper who'd been her friend and guardian since birth. She spotted his battered straw hat through the kitchen window as he methodically watered the blooming rose bushes that grew in the garden at the back of the house.

Seymour King jerked upright when she slammed the back screen door.

A frown creased his brow. "Child, what's wrong?" He removed his hat, wiped sweat away, and lumbered over to a nearby garden bench. "Come here."

She dropped down next to him, her tears falling freely. "It's my father again. Only this time, he's done the most vile thing." Her voice broke. "He's making me marry a man, a stranger. I don't know what to do."

The white-haired man put a gentle arm around her slender shoulders. "He's what? Slow down and start at the beginning."

"He's made some bargain with a man named Layken Martin to marry me tomorrow. He wants me gone." A sob caught in her throat. "So he can marry Widow Jones."

"Now, if that don't beat all." He clicked his tongue. "If that don't beat all."

"What am I going to do? Maybe I should run away. But where? And how?" The words tumbled out fast and furious. "I've got no money for a train ticket. And besides that, where would I go?" She clenched her teeth. "I'd never ask Father for a penny."

Seymour rubbed his stubbled chin. "Layken Martin. I remember that boy. Grew up here. Was always polite. Come from a decent family. They had a farm outside town."

She grew silent and swiped at her nose. Cuddles hopped onto Uncle Seymour's lap. "Grew up here? Why don't I remember him?"

"Woulda been a bit older than you. Been gone away a few years to the Army. I heard down at the store yesterday that he was back. That old farm's been vacant since his folks passed. Got his work cut out for him."

She sat up straighter. "So, you think I need to go through with it?"

"Don't see as you got much of a choice. You can't stay here." His rheumy eyes met hers. He grazed her red face with a gentle fingertip. "Your daddy go and hit you again?"

She nodded and lifted her head. "Won't happen anymore."

The old man shook his head. "If only your mama hadn't up and gone away. She'd never stand for it. Tell you what, girl, I promised her on her deathbed that I'd look after you the best as I could. I aim to keep that promise. You marry this Martin boy, but if he so much as speaks harshly, much less lays a hand on you, you come and find me." He gazed unsee-ing over her head, his voice calm yet hard as granite. "You come and find me. You hear?"

She nodded, her throat constricted. The unspoken promise gave a measure of comfort.

They sat in silence for a long minute. Then she got to her feet and placed a kiss on his weathered brow. "Thank you, Uncle Seymour. Guess I better go get packed up."

"Reckon you better. Try to think positive. At least you'll be away from your daddy."

She gathered Cuddles. "I'm going to miss you something awful." She trudged back inside.

Trapped like the proverbial rat in a trap, she resigned herself to whatever fate lay ahead with a tiny glimmer of hope that life would give her a break.

Upstairs, she retrieved a trunk from her closet, numbly filling it with her most precious memories, her mother's journals, jewelry, and photographs. She wouldn't leave behind anything she treasured. Her clothes would go on top to protect those memories. She ran her fingers lovingly over the smooth wood of the thumb piano her mother had given her on her tenth birthday.

Plucking out an ancient melody, the strains of the music floated around her like a cocoon.

She only hoped that this man who would be her husband show her some semblance of kindness. If there really was a God up there, like the preacher said on Sundays, surely he would grant her that much.

Or maybe overnight, the world would come to an end the way Reverend Horton hollered about the last time she went to church. It would at least spare her from having to face tomorrow.

It would be a welcome relief.

Following a sleepless night, the morning dawned exactly as it had every other day—like nothing in the world was different or out of sorts. Yet everything was.

Sara Beth bathed and brushed her hair until it shone. Wasn't much she could do about the circles under her red-rimmed eyes or the bruise on her cheekbone.

She slipped into her favorite powder blue dress with a chocolate brown stripe running through it that matched her eyes. She methodically braided her long brown hair into a single strand down her back.

The thought of breakfast made her stomach do somersaults.

She stayed in her room with the door closed until her father called out. "Sara Beth, you need to get on down here and fix breakfast. We leave in an hour."

"I'm not hungry," she replied.

"I don't give a damn. Get down here and fix me some breakfast."

She blew out a resigned sigh and, with Cuddles under her arm, dragged herself down the stairs. For two cents, she'd poison his eggs.

But she was no murderer.

Without a glance in his direction, she donned her apron and pulled a cast-iron skillet off the hook.

After a while, he followed her in. "You look nice, Sara Beth. Remind me of your mother."

"Don't bother with flattery. I'm not up for it, sir."

Homer Williams whined, "Now, Sara Beth, don't be that way. You'll see this is best for everyone. No one loses."

It took all her composure not to spit out a biting retort, but she didn't want to go to her wedding with another red handprint or bruise on her face.

What would her husband think? Would he care? Add a matching one to the other cheek?

She methodically fixed breakfast, then fed Cuddles. "I'll be waiting upstairs."

"You're not going to eat?"

"Not hungry."

"You better not faint and embarrass me."

In a voice so quiet it barely raised above a whisper, "And it's always about you."

Homer Williams got to his feet and laid a hand on her shoulder. "Eat. I insist."

She shrank under his touch. "I can't. You wouldn't want me throwing up on my new husband, would you?"

Her father blustered, "Of course not."

"Then let me be. I'll be waiting upstairs."

With her tears spent and emotion dried up, she picked up Cuddles and stumbled back up the stairs to her room.

The sooner this day was over, the better.

At least then, maybe she'd know what lay in store for her.

If it was intolerable, she would plan how to escape.

And escape she would, one way or another.

CHAPTER 4

Layken had worked into the wee hours of the morning sorting, straightening, and cleaning. It helped to keep his hands busy. Lord knew his mind was awhirl. Of all the scenarios he could have imagined, none rivaled what was about to occur.

As the sun peeked over the horizon, he boiled coffee and scrambled eggs, then carried his breakfast outside to soak up the silence. He dropped into a cane-bottom chair next to the wall, stretching his long legs out in front of him.

Being an only child, he'd learned early in life to enjoy solitude.

He contemplated his future wife as he ate. She was also an only child. No doubt, she too valued silence.

He'd make damn sure she had plenty of that.

The day was setting itself up to be another scorcher. He scanned the tree line as far as his eye could see.

Near the aging barn, a mama deer scampered out of the brush, a spotted fawn close on her heels. He watched the pair nibble leaves on a bush. Unless he moved, they had no clue he was anywhere near, or at least didn't see him as a threat.

Animals were lucky. Even though they had to endure nature's harshness from time to time, they never had to worry about a bank foreclosure, or money, or planting seeds, or the scruples of other men that caused wars.

Something rustled beyond the tree line, and the two deer took off like a streak of lightning.

Layken stood and rolled his shoulders. He ambled back inside to prepare for the makeshift wedding.

After he cleaned his dishes, he moved to the one bathroom in the house. He stopped dead in his tracks. In a matter of a few hours, he'd be sharing that one bathroom with a woman. That was something he'd never contemplated.

He ran hot water in the sink, then lathered a shaving brush with soap and covered his face. Until he went into the Army, he'd used nothing but a straight razor to shave. But the military issued razors with removable blades. He unscrewed the handle, tossed the old blade, and inserted a new one.

Not that it mattered what he looked like for this farce of a wedding. Yet, something inside him said he should make the effort.

By the time he got into Lucy and nosed it down the lane, his insides were nothing but a giant ball of nerves.

He arrived at the Dade County Courthouse in Greenfield ten minutes early.

For two cents, he'd turn around and drive right back to the farm. But then what? Williams would make good on his promise to take it. That was a fact.

Despite his trepidations, he could only imagine what Sara Beth must be going through. How awful to be given to a stranger, a man she'd never met. His loathing for the obese banker grew by the minute.

Williams had both of them in a trap, with only one way out.

Inside the small courthouse, a sign pointed upstairs to the judge's chambers. The coolness of the semi-dark interior did little to calm the raging storm inside him.

Apprehension and dread grew with each step.

The door that led into the judge's chambers was open, so he didn't bother to knock. A gray-haired man wearing spectacles glanced up at his approach.

"May I help you?"

Layken removed his hat and cleared his throat. "I am meeting Homer Williams and his daughter here this morning."

"Oh, yes." The judge shuffled a stack of papers. "You're a few minutes early." He pointed toward a worn leather chair. "Have a seat. I'm sure they'll be along shortly."

Fighting the urge to run, Layken perched on the edge of an oversized chair.

At some point, he became aware that he was holding his breath and sucked air into his lungs.

Tall shelves crammed with leather-bound books covered the entire wall behind the judge's desk. He wondered if there was a clear precedent in one of those law books for ending a marriage entered under duress.

Footsteps echoing off the wooden stairs brought him out of the chair.

Homer Williams bustled through the door, wearing a smug grin. Ignoring Layken, he greeted the judge. "John, thank you for agreeing to see us on such short notice."

The judge stood and shook the banker's hand. "Only for you, Homer."

Behind Homer Williams, a young girl moved soundlessly, as if she could will herself to be invisible by not making a sound.

Layken stared at her. Yes, it was rude, but this situation didn't seem to call for manners.

He took in her slight build, delicate features, and simple braid that hung down her back. Williams hadn't lied. Sara Beth was far from ugly. Maybe a little on the plain side, but pretty in an honest way.

She kept her eyes glued to the floor.

He wished she'd at least acknowledge him. The magnitude of what both of them were being forced to do shook him to the core. And clearly, from her demeanor, it did her as well.

She carried a slight bundle under one arm, and for a moment, Layken surmised it might be her worldly belongings. Then it wriggled, and two bunny ears popped out.

The comic gesture almost brought a laugh.

Williams snapped, "Come on up here, Sara Beth. The judge ain't got all day."

The banker pointed at Layken. "You, too. Get on up here. Let's get this over with. I've got things to do."

Layken moved closer to the judge's desk, as did Sara Beth. Still, she refused to look at him. Not that he blamed her.

The judge stood, jerked his robe off a hook, and slipped into it. He cleared his throat. "Okay. It is my understanding that you two are here to get hitched. Is that correct?"

Homer bellowed. "Of course, that's it, John. Why else would I have asked you to perform the ceremony?"

"Just making sure. These two don't seem like most couples I see in front of me."

Layken moved closer to Sara Beth. He didn't miss a tear that slid down her cheek. It took all his effort not to gasp out loud when he spotted the bruise on her cheekbone. He ground his teeth. It was as if he was violating the young girl. But it wasn't him' It was her father.

When he found his voice, he spoke low. "Yes, Judge. We're here to be married."

"Sara Beth?" The judge prodded.

She nodded without raising her head.

"Then let's get on with it." The judge shuffled papers on his desk, drawing one out. "I've got the marriage license here. I'll need you both to sign it. But first, I'll get the formality over with."

Homer reached between Layken and Sara Beth and tried to grab the bunny from her. "You don't need this damned rabbit right now."

She didn't answer her father, but half-turned and clutched Cuddles tighter.

He growled, "Do what you're supposed to, or else."

Sara Beth raised her head. "I'm ready."

Layken strained to hear the whispered words. When the judge glanced at him, he nodded.

"It seems this is an unusual circumstance. It's none of my business, but if it's all right with the two of you, I'm going to skip all the normal Bible reading and wedding malarkey." He took a step closer. "By the power vested in me by the State of Missouri, I pronounce you man and wife." He stared at Layken. "You may kiss the bride."

Layken would swear the man's eyes glittered for an instant. He cleared his throat. "No, sir. I'd rather not."

"Fine." The judge reached for a pen. "Then both of you sign here."

Layken scrawled his name on the line the judge pointed to, then passed the pen to Sara Beth.

Her hand shook as she slowly wrote her name.

Homer Williams let out a whoop. "Hot damn! Hot damn!"

Sara Beth stepped aside, her face an undeniable mask of pure sorrow.

Fighting rising anger toward the man who claimed to be a father, Layken frowned at him. "I want to make one thing clear, sir. You stay out of my business and honor your promise. I will take care of your daughter."

Williams blustered. "I have no interest in your business. You keep your end of the bargain, and we'll be fine." He turned back to the judge. "Now, John, I'm getting married next week, and you're invited to the wedding. It's going to be a grand affair."

The judge threw back his head and laughed. "I bet it is, Homer. I'll be there." With a wave of his hand, he dismissed the three of them.

Layken followed Homer Williams and his daughter down the stairs.

Outside, Homer withdrew a wad of money from his pocket that he pressed into Layken's hand.

Angling away from the despicable man, Layken carefully counted the bills.

"It's all there, like I said." Homer didn't attempt to hide his irritation. "Now, you go take Sara Beth to fetch her things. I have to get to work, but I want all of her things gone before I get home."

Facing the man again, he stuffed the money into his pocket. "They will be." How he got the words through gritted teeth was a mystery. He'd never wanted to hit a man so badly in his life.

But it would be a mistake.

As far as he was concerned, he'd be happy not to lay eyes on the self-centered man again until he had the money to pay off his debt.

Homer lumbered off toward his shiny Chrysler.

Layken called to him. "Mr. Williams."

The man stopped. "What?"

"You need to know you are not welcome in our home—ever. Don't bother to visit."

Homer waved over his shoulder in dismissal.

Layken focused on Sara Beth. "I'm sorry. I hope that didn't offend you. Believe me, I didn't want this any more than you. But I promise on my sweet mother's grave, I will not hurt you."

When she met his gaze, fear swam in her chocolate brown eyes, and her bottom lip trembled.

"Just give me a chance. That's all I ask."

She gave the slightest hint of a nod.

His heart broke for her. She reminded him of the beautiful doe he'd watched earlier that morning—skittish and wary.

No doubt, he would have to work to earn her trust.

He placed a hand on her elbow and steered her toward the pickup.

CHAPTER 5

Sara Beth stole a covert glance at the man, now her husband, driving the rusty pickup that rattled over every bump. It was a far cry from the smooth ride of her father's Chrysler.

She clutched Cuddles and sat close to the door putting as much distance as possible between them.

His strong jawline spoke of a quiet sort of pride. He had kind eyes, which she found particularly comforting. And he hadn't raised his voice when he'd issued the strong warning to her father. The muscles in his arms told her he was no stranger to hard work. But he was a bit too lean. Perhaps he hadn't been eating much.

When he shot her a glance, she quickly swiveled toward the window.

"What's your bunny's name?" He drawled.

"Cuddles." Her heart thudded. She prayed he wasn't about to insist that she make him into a stew.

"Is Cuddles a boy or girl?"

"Boy."

"Seems pretty special to you."

Cuddles chose that moment to hop out of Sara Beth's arms and onto the seat. She reached for him. "Sorry."

"Sorry for what?"

"He got out of my arms."

"So?"

"So, my father would have tried to toss him out the window."

Layken rubbed the bunny's long ears, then angled toward her. "Let's get one thing straight here and now. I'm not your father. I'm nothing like him. From what I've seen, he's a poor excuse for a man. He should be ashamed of the way he treats you."

Surprised at his declaration, she whispered, "Thank you."

Steering the pickup onto the side of the road, he pulled to a stop and twisted around on the seat, resting one arm on the steering wheel. "Sara Beth, look at me."

She forced herself to meet his steel gray-blue eyes.

"You need to hear from my perspective why I agreed to this forced marriage. My family settled here in the 1800s. They cleared the land by hand, planted crops, fought natives and outlaws to keep it, and built a home. I am the sole heir to that land. When I returned from the Army only a couple of days ago, I discovered my father left me a debt when he died. Your father threatened foreclosure."

"If you didn't marry me," Sara Beth interrupted quietly.

"Yes. That's about it. So, I see this as a partnership. We're in it together. I want you to know you're free to do whatever you want. I am not your husband except on paper."

Her chin quivered, and she fought against hot tears. "I won't be any trouble to you, Mr. Martin."

"Layken. I'm not Mr. Martin to you. I'm Layken, and you're Sara Beth to me."

"Layken," she repeated his name, letting the sound of it roll off her tongue. "This is all so awkward."

"For me too. But let's start as friends. I make no demands on you. I will not share a marriage bed with you. You'll have your own room, your privacy. And as I said before, I promise I will not hurt you. I only want to rebuild my farm and pay off the debt." He put the pickup in gear and let off on the clutch. "Let's go get your things."

Random thoughts raced through her mind. Her cheeks flushed at the idea of a marriage bed, and she breathed a sigh of relief that Layken would not expect that of her. Her insides started to untangle the slightest little bit.

She reached for Cuddles again and continued gazing out the window as a hot breeze snatched wisps of her hair from the braid.

When they reached Everton, she directed him to the two-story house she'd called home all her life.

No longer would she think of it in that way. It was simply a structure she'd grown up in and had nothing more to offer her, except there was still Uncle Seymour. As she remembered the old man's promise, something told her she would never have to ask for his help.

Layken Martin would treat her kindly.

Sara Beth opened the front door and stood aside for Layken to enter. She tried to see the luxurious home through his eyes. To her, it had become a prison where she had to walk on eggshells after her mother died.

Layken jerked off his hat and turned in a full circle, letting out a soft whistle. "Nice." He shuffled his feet on the plush carpet. "You need to know where I'm taking you is not anywhere near as fancy as this."

She lifted her chin. "I don't care. None of this means anything when you aren't wanted."

"I suppose that's true. Just thought I'd warn you. My home is a simple farmhouse that has stood for almost a century."

"I don't need fancy. I'm sure it's lovely." She put Cuddles on the sofa and pointed up the stairs. "The trunk is in my room. I'm happy to help you carry it down."

"That won't be necessary. Show me where."

She climbed the stairs for what might be the last time with no emotion other than relief.

With Layken close behind, she opened the door to her room and pointed to the trunk at the foot of her bed.

He picked it up with ease. "Is this all?"

"That's it. I'm not taking anything my father can throw a fit over or accuse me of stealing. Only what's mine and my mother's."

Layken nodded toward the door. "After you."

While he carried the trunk out and loaded it in the back of the pickup, she gave the house another glance and picked up Cuddles.

On second thought, she entered the kitchen and reached for her apron that hung on a hook next to the pantry. She couldn't stomach the idea of her new stepmother wearing it.

"Sara Beth," Layken called out from the living room.

"In the kitchen." She stared out the window, hoping to see Uncle Seymour going about his chores.

Layken walked up behind her. "Looking for something?"

"Someone." She folded the apron and tucked it under her arm. "Our groundskeeper, Uncle Seymour. I was hoping to tell him goodbye once more."

"Want I should go look for him?"

"He's probably running an errand for my father. I said my farewell last night. I'm ready to go."

She didn't miss the way Layken held the door for her, then closed it behind him. That small gesture told her a lot about this man, now her husband.

"I'd be happy to bring you into town anytime you want to visit."

Tears threatened to fall. "You'd do that for me?"

"Of course. I'll have to come to town now and again for supplies. You can ride along with me anytime."

She climbed in the pickup, and Layken closed her door.

He started the engine and backed out of the driveway. She watched until the house and her entire life up to this point faded from sight.

On the way to the farm, Layken chatted about his plans to put in crops as soon as he could get a piece of ground plowed. He'd work on repairing and sprucing up the barn and house through the winter.

At one point, he grew silent. "Sorry. I'm rambling on and on. You haven't said a word."

"Just listening and thinking."

"Want to share your ideas?"

"Not until I've seen the place. But I might have some ideas to make life a little easier."

"Hey, I had a thought." Layken glanced toward her. "Do you drive?"

"No. My father never saw the need for me to learn." She rubbed her pet rabbit's head. "But I'd like to."

"Then I'll teach you. You can learn the way I did, in a pasture where there's nothing you can hit or hurt."

Sara Beth smiled for the first time. "You'd teach me? Seriously?"

"Sure. You need to know how to drive." He tapped his fingers on the steering wheel. "I might need to send you into town on errands. Or what if I get hurt, and you need to go for help? It's several miles to the nearest neighbor."

Her heart thudded with excitement. She could learn to drive. That was one more step toward independence.

Damn the narrow-minded men like her father who treated women as if they were worthless and kept them suppressed. He'd never tried to hide his disappointment that she wasn't the son he wanted.

Things were changing for women in America. The war had forced many to leave their homes and take jobs for the first time in their lives. She'd read all about it in the weekly newspaper.

She longed to be an independent woman who didn't need a man to provide for her. But in the meantime, Layken Martin appeared to be a far cry from the domineering, controlling man she called father.

Maybe God had seen fit to rescue her and provide a chance for a different kind of life.

Layken's words echoed. *Just give me a chance.*

That honest request, simple and plain, went straight to her heart. She could honor his plea.

Sara Beth sat straighter and took in the countryside, peering anxiously for a glimpse of her new home.

It brought a heaping measure of comfort to think Layken might genuinely listen to any ideas she had. No man had ever done that.

And she'd show him she could be an asset. Perhaps in some small way, she could help him regain control of his farm.

She reflected on the tarot cards she'd drawn two days ago. As they had predicted, life as she'd known it had died.

Uncle Seymour once told her the importance of always being ready for a new door to open. Is that what had happened? Perhaps. Time would tell.

She glanced at Layken and smiled to herself, then focused on the green countryside.

A foreign emotion washed over her. She struggled to name it, then settled on hope.

Hope for something better, for freedom, and a purpose.

CHAPTER 6

Layken made a left turn off the blacktop onto his property. They rumbled over uneven ground, and Sara Beth bounced on the seat, clutching the side of the door to stay intact.

"Do you have cows?" She leaned out the window for a better view.

"My dad did. During the depression years, he'd slaughter one and share it with folks that didn't have anything to eat."

"How kind of him." By now, she was fairly hanging out the window.

It struck Layken how childlike her curiosity came across. And the way she held onto the pet rabbit as if it were her lifeline reminded him of traumatized children he'd seen clutching a stuffed teddy bear during the war.

Yet, her father had said Sara Beth was twenty. She'd either been sheltered or deprived. And, after what he'd seen of Homer Williams, he'd bet on the latter.

When he rolled to a stop in front of the house, Sara Beth didn't wait for him. She opened the door and eased out with Cuddles tucked tightly under one arm.

He followed her as she stepped onto the wide front porch. "I love a big front porch. It could use some rockers or a porch swing."

Layken glanced around. "You're right. It doesn't look very inviting right now. I remember it having a porch swing at one time. I'll look for it. Might be stored in the barn." He appreciated how Sara Beth didn't point out the peeling paint or dirty windows.

Sara Beth raised her eyebrows. "How long have you been back?"

"Only a few days. Mostly, I've been tuning up Dad's old pickup and clearing out weeds from around the house. Don't want snakes." He opened the front door. "But I did a little cleaning up inside yesterday."

"It's so quiet." She followed him with slow, dragging steps.

"That's one of the things I love about it. All I hear are birds and animals wild in nature."

In the living room, Sara Beth stopped and turned in a full circle. She pointed to the radio, and a brief sadness flitted across her face. "I've wanted one of these forever, but my father said it was a waste of money. It wasn't like he didn't have the money. He never wanted me or Mama to enjoy it."

"I have some great memories of my folks gathered around listening to Jack Benny or the Grand Ol' Opry. Sometimes the shows would come in clear, and sometimes not, depending on the weather. But the baseball games were the highlight." He swallowed past a lump in his throat.

She started to touch the radio console and drew back. "Have you turned it on since you've been home?"

"No. To be honest, I haven't. I want you to try to feel at home here. It's okay to touch anything you want." He pointed toward the hallway. "Let me show you to your room."

He tried to read the expressions that crossed her face. Fear seemed to have taken a slight backseat to curiosity. In his opinion, that was a good trade.

He led Sara Beth down the hallway and pushed open a door. "This is it."

"What a lovely open room." She stepped inside and deposited Cuddles on the bed.

"Sorry. I haven't had a chance to clean it out." He motioned around the room. "Honestly, it was too painful to go through my folks' stuff. I'll find you some boxes. Feel free to pack it all up."

"Are you sure? This seems almost sacred." She reached for a tintype photo on the dresser and rubbed away the dust with her thumb. "Who is this?"

"That would be my great grandparents. They were the original owners of this place. They passed on long before I was born."

"They have kind eyes, like you."

Layken cleared his throat. "I'll go fetch your trunk. The bathroom is the next door down on the left."

Sara Beth continued to hold the photograph as if she desperately needed something filling her hands. "Thank you."

When he returned with her trunk, she was standing exactly where he'd left her. The signs of curiosity he'd seen earlier had vanished. She turned doe eyes brimming with unshed tears toward him.

While he wanted to comfort her, he didn't dare. Instead, he pretended not to notice and set her trunk down at the foot of the bed. "Like I said, please make yourself at home. What's mine is now yours. Don't be shy. And you don't have to ask my permission to do whatever you want."

She whispered, "It's all so hard."

"I know. Really. I understand." He stuck his hands in his pockets. "But we'll get through it."

"I wish I could believe that."

"You don't have to believe it today. All you can do is put one foot in front of the other. Once you're settled in, maybe it won't hurt so much." He shifted nervously. "I'll go see if I can find you some boxes. There may be some down in the cellar."

Hating like hell to walk away and leave her, it was the best thing—no, the only thing— he could do. He glanced down at his wedding clothes. Best to change into work clothes before going in search of boxes.

After changing clothes and before heading out, he glanced into Sara Beth's room to see her sitting on the edge of the bed petting Cuddles. He'd give her all the time she needed to adjust.

Deciding to explore the root cellar first, he opened the wooden trap door outside the kitchen and shined a flashlight down into the dark, cool space.

He'd heard many stories about his great-grandfather digging the cellar by hand to protect his family from storms and, at the time, from marauders. Over the years, it had turned into a storage area but was still a safe place to go in case of a tornado.

The beam from the flashlight reflected off shelves with jars of random canned goods. More times than he could count, he'd stood on the steps and taken jars his mother passed to him. Would the food still be safe to eat? Maybe he'd ask Sara Beth to take a look at them.

He found the string in the center of the space that turned on a single overhead light bulb. It had been an exciting day when he'd helped his father run electricity to it. It provided a significant improvement over candles or flashlights.

He located a stack of empty cardboard boxes in a corner, shook out any spiders hiding in them, and hauled them up.

Sara Beth hadn't moved from the bed. Layken dropped the boxes next to the door. "Found some boxes."

She met his gaze, a mix of confusion and fear swimming in her coffee-colored eyes. "Okay."

"Are you hungry?" Layken leaned against the doorframe.

"Maybe. I don't really know."

"Did you eat today?"

She shook her head. "Too wound up."

"How about I fix us something? You can start getting settled in."

Clutching Cuddles, she got to her feet. "Will you show me the kitchen?"

"Of course. Come on." He motioned toward the door.

She followed with her apron draped over one arm.

To break the silence, Layken chatted about his mother. "She could make the best pies. Blackberries grow wild all around here, and she'd pick them fresh. I can almost smell them just thinking about it. Did your mother cook?"

"Yes, and she taught me a lot. But after she died, I had to do it all. I like to cook and try new things."

"Good. Down in the root cellar, I found some jars my mother canned. I don't know if any of them are still good, but maybe you wouldn't mind taking a look at some point."

"I'd be happy to."

They stepped into the kitchen, and she let out a soft sigh. "I like this room. It feels like a lot of love passed through here."

"It did." He swallowed hard and pointed toward the pantry. "I've got a few staples in there, but as soon as you can, make a list of what all you need, and we'll stock up."

Cuddles wriggled out of her arms and hopped across the kitchen floor, his nose twitching. Sara Beth scooped him up. "I'm sorry. I'll try to keep him in my room."

"I told you this is your home. Cuddles is welcome here, wherever he wants to go. Please don't apologize."

"It's a habit."

"One I hope you'll find easy to break."

"If he makes a mess, I'll clean it up, but he's good about going to the bathroom outside."

"A trained rabbit." He let out a short laugh. "Now, that's something I could have never imagined. But then all of this is beyond anything I could've conjured up."

A smile graced Sara Beth's delicate face, taking the focus off her red-rimmed eyes. "Neither could I. Thank you for trying so hard to make me feel at ease here. Why don't you let me make us some food? Doing something normal for the first time today would feel good."

"If you're sure." Pointing toward the refrigerator, he continued. "I have some beef tips I picked up in town. Might make a good soup."

"Go on and do whatever you need to. Leave it to me. I'll have us something to eat in no time." She slipped the apron over her head.

Layken left her rummaging through the refrigerator and strode toward the barn.

He'd look for the porch swing. It had to be around here somewhere. And if something that simple could bring Sara Beth joy, he'd do whatever he had to.

An overwhelming need to be alone, to avoid the kitchen, engulfed him, and he could be pretty sure Sara Beth longed for the same.

He liked that she was making a valiant effort to accept this as her home.

After all, they'd be stuck together for two years unless he could find a way to pay off the debt quicker.

But then what would Sara Beth do? She certainly couldn't go back to her father's home. He wouldn't want her to go back to the home she'd just left and the self-centered man who called himself her father. Plus, he had to wonder what Widow Jones had against the girl.

Time would answer all those questions.

Layken could hear his mother's sweet voice saying, *Worry about crossing that bridge after it's built.*

For now, they would find ways to live together in peace.

For now, he could be a friend to Sara Beth.

And for now, that was enough.

CHAPTER 7

Sara Beth watched her tall husband stride with purpose toward a barn that desperately needed a coat of paint. Finally, she was alone. Alone in a strange house, strange kitchen, strange world, so vastly different from anything she'd ever known.

Perhaps she'd taken for granted the comforts her father had provided. Nevertheless, she would try to keep a good attitude and help out however she could.

She sincerely appreciated the efforts Layken had taken to make her feel at home.

What's mine is yours...

Obviously, he was trying to make the best of a difficult situation.

She rummaged through the refrigerator and found enough ingredients to make a simple soup. However, it was apparent she'd need to make a shopping list.

Once she had the meager supply of vegetables chopped, she ran water into a pan and struggled to light the stove. She was beginning to wonder if it even worked when a burner sprang to life under the match she held to it. An odor she couldn't identify filled the air.

But no matter. She had a fire and ingredients for a meal. Once the water boiled, she dumped in the vegetables and beef tips, added salt and pepper, and settled the lid over them.

While it cooked, she searched for ingredients to make either biscuits or cornbread. When she opened a container of cornmeal, bugs crawled around inside. She quickly put the lid on and shuddered. The flour appeared to be okay, and she decided on biscuits.

Sweat ran down her face and dripped onto her dress. A slight breeze rustled through the open door, and she stepped into the opening for some relief from the heat.

It was easy to tell where a garden had once been planted. With a little work, they could make it ready for a crop of root vegetables that would have time to grow and help sustain them through the winter. She wished she'd paid more attention to the things Uncle Seymour had taught her about planting.

A fenced pen with a lean-to in one corner must have provided shelter for animals at one time.

They needed animals. Maybe some goats or a cow for milk. And what was a farm without a dog or pigs or sheep? For sure, they needed chickens for fresh eggs as well as meat. She'd ask Layken what he preferred.

While she gazed out, lost in her thoughts, Layken made his way from the barn toward the house, carrying a large load and balancing a ladder on his shoulders.

Her first instinct was to rush to help him, but she stayed rooted. He was obviously a man accustomed to hard work and might not take kindly to a woman's offer to help. The last thing she wanted was to aggravate him after he'd shown such kindness.

He disappeared around the corner of the house, and a heavy thud followed a few minutes later, shaking the house.

Unable to curb her curiosity, she gathered Cuddles and hurried through the living room and out the front door.

She gasped at seeing a porch swing and set the rabbit on the wooden planks.

"I found it." Layken brushed away cobwebs. "Needs a coat of paint. When I go to town I'll see about buying some. It's not the only thing around here that needs freshening up."

"Need my help?" She kneeled and took one of the rusty chains in her hands.

"I can manage. Wouldn't want you getting your hands dirty."

She pushed to her feet and put a hand on one hip. "I take offense to that, sir. I don't mind getting my hands dirty. Despite what you may think of me, I am not spoiled."

Layken pushed his hat back. "Sorry," he mumbled. "Trying to show respect."

"Look. As you said, we are in this together. I want to be useful."

"All right then. Can you lift one end while I secure it?" He set a ladder in place and lifted one side. "Something's smelling good."

"I'm making soup and biscuits. Cornmeal had weevils. I'll dump it out for the birds later." She struggled to lift the swing.

"They'll appreciate it, I'm sure."

As she lifted, he pulled, and together, they hung the porch swing on large metal hooks embedded into the ceiling.

Sara Beth gingerly sat on one corner and pushed the swing with a slight foot. "This is nice. A good place to cool off in the evenings."

Layken folded the ladder and stood back. "Glad you like it. Mom used to have a couple of rockers, but I don't know where they are."

"Thank you for the effort of getting the swing up, Layken. I'm going to make biscuits now. Then we can eat."

She scooped up Cuddles and hurried inside. Layken's kindness touched her deeply. She'd proven more than once she was built of stronger stuff than folks thought. She'd do her part.

Her mother's soothing voice echoed in her head. *Sweet Sara Beth, life is hard. Only the strong survive it. You have a strength you don't even know of yet. One day you'll be forced to find and use it.*

That day had arrived.

She stifled a sob and soon had her hands covered in flour as she kneaded dough and formed it into round shapes. Thank goodness for the butter she'd found in the refrigerator. The biscuits would be flaky.

When Layken returned to the house, Sara Beth had the biscuits ready for baking.

After several attempts to light the oven only to have them fail, she sat on the floor next to the stove, her head in her hands.

"May I help you?" Layken's deep voice vibrated in his throat.

"I can't get the damn thing to light. It keeps blowing out my matches. Sorry about swearing. I don't make a habit of it."

Layken chuckled. "You don't have to apologize, although you did shock me. Here." He took the matches from her and kneeled. He turned the knob and held the match toward the back of the oven as fire sprang to life.

"I don't know what I was doing wrong. It's certainly not my first time to light an oven."

"It's probably your first time to cook with propane, and it responds differently than gas."

"Oh, so that's what I was smelling when I lit the top burner?"

"You'll get used to it."

"Thanks. Food will be ready in about thirty minutes." She got to her feet and brushed herself off.

Layken scooted a chair out from the table and sat. "I feel the need to make a budget. Are you good with numbers?"

Sara Beth sat across from him. "I am. And happy to help. Where can I find paper and pencil?"

"Mom kept some in an end table drawer in the living room. I'll go look."

Cuddles hopped across the floor and laid his head on Sara Beth's foot. She reached down and petted him.

When he returned, Layken had a tablet and pencil in hand. "Found them." He sat back down and slid the paper and pencil across to her. "Let's divide it into two columns. One for necessities and one for wants."

She nodded and drew a straight line down the middle of the paper. "Good approach."

Layken leaned back and rubbed his chin. "First, we need to take care of ourselves, mainly food and maybe a few basic medical supplies."

"I spotted the garden plot out back. We have time to grow vegetables before winter. Maybe plant things we can store, like carrots, potatoes, onions, and such? What do you think?"

"Good idea. I won't be of much help with that yet. I've got to get seeds in the ground to try and make a crop right away. But I'll be happy to haul water to keep it alive until it rains if need be. You ever planted a garden before?"

"No, but I've helped Uncle Seymour plenty of times. He's good at making things grow." She swallowed past the lump in her throat at the memory.

"Okay. So, vegetable seeds. Let's put that on the necessity side. We also need some chickens. That's what we built the enclosed pen next to the house for. It needs a few repairs, but I have everything for that in the barn. I can take care of that right away."

Hope bloomed in her heart. "Chickens would be good. And what about a goat or cow for milk? I noticed the fenced area with the lean-to."

"I don't think I can afford to buy or feed a cow, but maybe a few goats. They're usually cheap and eat about anything. Hardy animals."

"Goats are perfect. That would give us milk. I'll make a list of food staples this afternoon. In the newspaper last week, President Truman made a call to all the American people to have two days a week without meat or eggs. He said it was to stave off the coming food shortage for the winter. Looks like beans and cornbread will be popular this winter."

"Well, I can't speak for the rest of the country, but I can speak for us. We will have to watch our pennies. I'm a good hunter, though, and there's plenty of wild game in the woods." He propped his elbows on the table. "Put paint on the wants side of the list. Every building on the place needs a good coat, but it's not a necessity. I have to make the money stretch until I can get a crop in and harvested. And the sooner, the better."

"How much do you need to hold out to buy seeds?"

"My dad was stubborn and set in his ways, which is one reason he got so far into debt. Even in a drought, he insisted on planting corn and sorghum because that's what he'd always done. But it wouldn't grow. I've done some research, and I want to try growing peanuts. Do you know they sell for almost twice as much as sorghum?"

Sara Beth chewed the end of the pencil. "What I know about farming, you could fit in the end of this pencil. Will peanuts grow here?"

"I believe anything will grow with water. Rain is essential. But some things require less water than others, and peanuts is one of them."

"So, how much to buy seeds for planting?"

"I think maybe twenty dollars will do it. That'll leave us enough to last until I can harvest the crop. Peanuts only take around a hundred and twenty days from planting to harvest. I should make a decent profit from one planting."

They continued adding to the lists until the aroma of fresh-baked biscuits filled the kitchen.

While she'd never heard of anyone growing peanuts in these parts, she believed Layken had looked into it thoroughly. Just because it wasn't the way things had always been done didn't mean it wouldn't work.

She quietly admired that about him. That he would dare to break out of the mold told her much about his character. And it was something she understood.

It wasn't easy to go against the grain.

A man who is brave enough to try new things often reaps greater rewards. Or loses everything.

Was she brave enough to embrace this new way of life with a stranger?

Maybe she was, and maybe she wasn't, but what choice did she have?

At any rate, she'd do what she could to help him succeed. Then what? What would happen to her once he repaid the debt?

She could almost hear Uncle Seymour telling her to take it one day at a time.

Live for today—plan for tomorrow.

That's what she'd do.

CHAPTER 8

A loud knock on the front door startled Layken as they finished the last bite of their meal.

"Better not be Homer Williams," he muttered under his breath and strode toward the living room. He opened the screen door to find his nearest neighbor standing on the front porch. "Mrs. Grover. What a surprise. How are you?"

"Heard you were back. Also, heard a rumor in town that you got married, so brought some things." She lifted a heavy basket and peered around him. "Can I meet your bride?"

He relieved her of the load. "Of course. Come on in." The rotund woman bustled past him. "Mrs. Martin. Oh, Mrs. Martin," she called out in a singsong voice.

"She's in the kitchen. You didn't have to bring us a gift."

The woman hurried through the living room toward the kitchen. "Oh, it's nothing. Just a few things I thought you could use, having been gone so long."

Layken wished he had time to warn Sara Beth about the pushy woman, but he had a feeling she was no stranger to obnoxious people.

Sara Beth stepped out of the kitchen, carrying Cuddles. "Mrs. Grover."

"Oh, it's you." The woman's mouth flew open.

"It's good to see you, ma'am."

"You're Layken's new bride?"

With a broad smile, Sara Beth flashed a nervous glance toward Layken. "Yes. I suppose I am. How are you and your family doing?"

Again, the woman blustered. "They're all fine. But you married Layken Martin?"

"It would seem so."

"Well, I'll be. I'll just be."

Layken cleared his throat. "Mrs. Grover brought us a gift." He carried the basket into the kitchen and set it on the counter.

"Oh my. You didn't have to do that, but we sure do appreciate it." Sara Beth joined Layken in unloading the bounty.

Mrs. Grover stood in the doorway. "It's not much. There's a few things from the canning I did last fall."

"Fresh eggs!" Sara Beth gingerly transferred the eggs to a bowl. "We were just discussing the fact we need to get some chickens. You wouldn't happen to have any you'd sell?"

"No. But I heard old man Mallory down past the mill has some."

Cuddles chose that moment to hop across the floor. The older woman put her hands on her hips. "I think it's a downright disgrace having a rabbit in the house. In my opinion, they belong in a stewpot."

"And you're most certainly entitled to your opinion, ma'am." Layken leaned down and picked up the rabbit. "Cuddles is Sara Beth's pet."

Ignoring the conversation, Sara Beth straightened her spine and finished emptying the basket. "Oh, and you baked a pie. This is lovely."

Layken leaned against the counter, trying his best not to grin. His new wife was proving she could stand her ground. "Mrs. Grover, can we offer you something? Maybe a glass of tea?"

"Oh, no. I've got to get going." She stared up at Layken. "Your folks were fine people."

"Yes, they were. Thank you for being a good neighbor."

"I'm happy to see you back. Your mama would sure be glad. Maybe you can bring some life into this place again."

"That's my goal, ma'am."

She stepped toward Sara Beth. "And you. Don't be doing any of that hocus pocus stuff around here. I expect you'll bring my empty jars back."

Sara Beth offered a quick hug, choosing to ignore the derogatory comment. "Thank you. Of course, I'll return the jars."

With the empty basket dangling from her arm, Mrs. Grover waddled out the front door.

"You handled that like a pro." Layken set Cuddles on the floor, and the rabbit hopped across the floor.

"I'm accustomed to pushy people. I can promise you she won't stop until everyone for miles around knows we got married. They may be offering condolences rather than congratulations."

"Let them offer whatever they want. This gift will help us maintain until we can get to town for supplies."

"That it will." Sara Beth placed the jars of canned vegetables in an empty cabinet. "I don't think you know what I mean. Folks will feel sorry for you, marrying the town witch."

"Town witch? What are you talking about?"

Sara Beth faced him, her jaw set. "People believed my mother was a witch, and that she tricked my father into marrying her. And they think she passed her skills down to me."

Layken studied her for a long minute. "A witch, huh? Maybe you could conjure up some rain."

"I wish." She sighed. "You don't know how many times I've wished I could work magic spells. Especially on my father and Widow Jones."

"So, that's why the good widow wouldn't marry your father until you were out of the house?"

Sara Beth nodded.

He let out a chuckle. "That rumor might work to our advantage. Especially after I produce a crop of peanuts when everyone else's fields are drying up."

"I suppose you're right. So you don't believe rumors?"

"Nope. Never have. Folks around here do love juicy gossip."

"Without a thought of what their gossip might do to someone's life."

"At any rate, these canned goods will help out. Mrs. Grover meant well. She and my mom were good friends and often had canning parties together."

"I appreciate her kind gesture." Sara Beth pointed to the pie. "Care for a slice? Looks like blackberry."

"My mouth has been watering since you set it out. I'll boil coffee to go with it. Then I'm going to get busy plowing. Gotta get the ground ready for planting pronto."

Sara Beth moved around his mother's kitchen with ease, as if she'd always been there. He hoped she'd find comfort in settling into this new life. But it might take time. After all, she'd only been there for a few hours.

A witch.

The absurdity of the claim almost made him laugh out loud, but he didn't want his new wife to think he was crazy. While the coffee boiled on the stove, he looked over the list they'd started.

If he played his cards right, he might come up with a winning hand.

Sara Beth put the eggs away in the icebox. Layken returned to the table and concentrated on their list. It made her feel good that he'd dismissed the preposterous witch rumor.

While they were still strangers, he'd gone above and beyond to help her relax into their situation. And he'd defended Cuddles. That alone said a lot.

She looked forward to learning more about the man with whom she'd be sharing a home. Besides saving the family farm, what were his other goals in life? Or did he have any?

A handsome man with his chiseled profile, steel-gray eyes, and wavy brown hair surely must have girlfriends.

Did Layken Martin have secrets? Of course, he did. Didn't everyone?

Would he ever feel comfortable enough to share his? Or would she ever feel secure enough to share her own deepest desires and longings?

The aroma of coffee filled the kitchen, and she hurried to get saucers for pie. She looked forward to baking her own pies soon. Once she got settled, she'd take the time to gather blackberries and rhubarb that grew wild.

"Coffee's ready." She poured a cup and set the pie and coffee on the table.

Layken pushed the list aside.

Between mouthfuls, he asked, "Do you know how long it's been since I had blackberry pie?"

"No. But guessing from how you're devouring it, I'd say it's been a long time."

"I used to dream about Mom's pies when I was overseas."

Sara Beth savored the tart sweetness. "What was it like?"

"What? Dreaming of pie or being overseas?"

"Being in a foreign country."

"Different, for sure. Not only the languages but the cultures, too. I was first stationed in Southern France, then, the Philippines."

"I can't imagine. I've hardly ever been outside Dade County. Did you join, or were you drafted?"

Layken swallowed a bite. "I joined up before I got drafted. I hated to leave Dad to work the farm alone, but figured I didn't have much choice."

"I read in the newspapers that most soldiers returned home when the war ended. So, why did you stay, or am I being too nosey?"

"I enlisted when I was twenty, in 1942. I signed up for five years. That ended two weeks ago. I could've mustered out early and almost did when the folks died, but I had made Captain and felt obligated to stay."

"I'm sorry. I'm talking my fool head off."

"Don't apologize." Layken laid his fork on the empty saucer and downed the rest of his coffee. "You can ask me anything you want. But right now, I'm going to see if I can get the old tractor fired up and do some plowing before dark." He paused at the door and turned around. "Please, make yourself at home."

Sara Beth sat still for a long minute after the screen door slammed shut.

She couldn't imagine being in a foreign country, although she'd read everything she could get her hands on about many places beyond Missouri.

After she'd cleared away the dishes, she drifted down the hall to her bedroom. HER private space. She let that reality sink in.

But before she entered, she walked past the bathroom to Layken's room and stopped in the doorway. No surprise that the room was neat and swept clean.

Fighting the feeling of being an intruder, she returned to her room and opened one drawer and then another. She packed Mrs. Martin's clothes in a box, and the mister's in another. Perhaps Layken might be able to wear some of his father's things if he wanted.

Before opening her trunk, she went to the kitchen for a wet dish towel to clean away the dust and cobwebs while Cuddles napped on the bed.

As she worked, she let her tangled mind unwind. In one simple day, her entire life had changed. She had a lot of new things to learn. How she wished she could talk to Uncle Seymour.

After two hours, the bedroom sparkled.

She stood back and surveyed the space. The bed needed to be nearer to the window to catch the breeze.

Tugging and pulling, she finally moved the iron-framed bed where she wanted it.

Next, she scooted the chest of drawers and the night table to sit against the now blank wall.

Finally, it looked fresh and new in her eyes. With her trunk emptied and clean sheets stretched on the bed, she blew out a long, slow breath and picked up Cuddles, who had ignored her cleaning and rearranging efforts.

"I think this will work." She stroked his velvet ears. "What do you have to say, Cuddles?"

The bunny twitched his nose.

She twitched her nose back at him and went to sit on the front porch as the sun lowered in the sky.

"What a beautiful view." She set the rabbit on the seat beside her and pushed the swing back and forth with her toe.

The slight breeze lifted tendrils of hair that escaped from her braid and tickled her neck. In the distance, a mourning dove cooed, and a cardinal tweeted.

A sense of peace washed over Sara Beth Williams Martin.

Her first full day as a married woman was coming to an end.

For half a second, she wondered if her father missed her. No doubt, he didn't.

The chugging of the tractor grew louder as Layken neared the house. Would he be hungry or expect supper on the table?

What were his nightly routines?

A blush crept onto her cheeks when she remembered his casual mention of a marriage bed or lack thereof.

Relief that he wouldn't expect or demand it added to the peaceful feeling.

However, if Sara Beth had learned one thing about life, it was that peace often disappeared as quickly as it came. She shuddered, remembering the way her father's attitude had changed toward her immediately following her mother's death. Almost as if he had no more connection to her—as if he was no longer her father. She'd never understood it.

Night sounds in the country came alive as cicadas sang, and animals rustled through the brush.

Day one of her new life drifted into history.

What new challenges would the next day bring?

CHAPTER 9

The next three days passed quickly, with Sara Beth settling into a daily routine of cooking, cleaning, and working on the garden plot. She'd struggled with guilt when Layken insisted she put the only fan in the house in her bedroom at night.

"What about you?" she'd asked.

"I'm used to sleeping in conditions a lot worse and hotter than this. I don't need it."

In the end, she accepted, thankful for the cool air the fan provided. And the noise helped mute the sobs that she'd been unable to stifle that first night. She'd never felt so alone, forsaken, and forlorn, despite Layken's kindness. She fell asleep each night dreaming about her beautiful mother laying a cool hand on her brow.

While Layken plowed the field, she pulled weeds and hoed the garden. Then, in the evenings, Layken repaired the chicken pen and stretched a string so she could make straight rows in her garden. Her back ached, and her hands were blistered. Yet, somehow, it brought her joy.

For the first time since her mother died, she had a purpose. She was useful—and appreciated. Her confidence grew.

As the sun peeked over the horizon on the fourth day, she set plates of eggs and biscuits on the breakfast table while Layken poured coffee.

"I'm going into town this morning. Want to ride along? We can pick up all the things you need for the kitchen and the garden. It's time to get the peanut seeds and more kerosene for the tractor."

"I'd like that." She placed a plate of dandelion leaves on the floor for Cuddles. "And let's stop by Mr. Mallory's and see about getting chickens."

"That was on my mind, too, now that I've got the coop repaired." He took a sip of coffee. "Sara Beth, I haven't told you how much I appreciate all your hard work. You've made some serious headway in the garden. And the blackberries you picked yesterday will make downright delicious preserves."

"And another pie." She dipped her biscuit into the eggs. "I hesitate to say anything, but I thought I saw a boy in the woods when I was out picking yesterday. He disappeared so fast it might have been my imagination."

"Or an animal."

"That's why I didn't say anything last night. Don't want you thinking I was starting to see things that weren't there."

"The woods are thick and full of game. But if you see it again, let me know, and I'll take a look. With the depression and war, it's not unlikely that someone could be camped out." He finished the last bite on his plate. "And if they're on my land, I want to know."

She nodded. "Do you think we might try to get a few goats soon?"

"I'll ask around." He stood and took his plate to the sink. "Whenever you're ready, let me know. I'd like to be there when the stores open."

"Give me thirty minutes." She loved that he showed her consideration instead of ordering her around as her father had done.

"Take all the time you need. I'll load up the empty kerosene cans." He settled his fedora on his head and whistled on his way to the barn.

She had the dishes cleaned, dried, and put away in no time. Then she stepped out onto the front porch with Cuddles under her arm as Layken dropped the metal cans into the back of the pickup. "I'm ready."

Layken opened the pickup door for her, then closed it. Driving down the long dirt driveway, he pointed to the field on his right. "That's the field I'm planting first. It gets the morning sun and a little shade from the trees in the evening. With any luck, I'll have a few seeds in the ground before dark."

She gazed in the direction he pointed at the freshly turned dirt. "What about water?"

"I've got some ideas. Have to think it through first, though."

"I like that about you."

"What's that?" He focused on dodging some of the deeper ruts.

"That you are a thinker."

He laughed. "Reckon I've always been that way. I find that life goes a little easier if I think before I act."

"Except for getting married." She clutched Cuddles and held onto the side of the door to keep from bouncing off the seat.

"Wasn't much to think about. Your father didn't give me a choice."

"Are you regretting it yet?"

His eyes crinkled in the corners when he turned to face her with a smile. "Sara Beth, you're making a good partner. You're not afraid of hard work, and you haven't complained once. So, no, I'm not regretting it."

"Thank you."

"No thanks needed." He turned onto the smooth blacktop. "Look, I know this isn't easy, but if you hang with me, I think we can make a go of this. Then you'll be free to do whatever you want."

"That's frightening."

"What? Freedom?"

"I don't know what I want. For years, I've thought I wanted to move away from here and live in a big city where there are movie theaters to attend and fashionable clothes to buy."

"I'm sensing a but."

"But now I don't know. It's a big scary world."

"You have lots of time to decide."

She stared out the window, lost in thought. She meant it. Reading about the world was one thing, but experiencing it was another. "I'd like to pick up a newspaper today if that's okay."

"Of course it is. I've noticed you like to read. How about you see if they have any new books in the store? We can afford one. I'm glad you chose not to pack up my mom's books and magazines. She was a reader, like you."

"Wish I could have known her. I think I would have liked her."

"She was a strong, resilient woman, but she was always old. Even when I was a boy, she seemed old. I thought it strange they had me so late in life. I'm sure I was an accident."

She glanced down at the list in her hand and changed the subject. "If we can't afford to get everything today, that's okay. I have the essentials marked with a star."

"I'm sure we can get all of it. You aren't nervous about going into town, are you?"

"Not a bit. People can say what they want. You?"

"You'll soon learn that I could care less about what people say or think. But I won't tolerate any disrespect shown to you."

"I can take care of myself." The last thing she wanted was for Layken to feel like he had to defend her.

"Of that, I have no doubt. Still…"

Sara Beth pointed at a farm they were passing. "Look. Goats. Can we stop on the way back and see if they'd sell us a few? We need a milk goat."

"Sure." Layken steered around a curve. "That's the Becker place. I went to school with their son."

"It's funny that I've lived here all my life, but don't really know many people outside Everton."

"I guess that's the downside of being a city girl and the banker's daughter. I'm sure I'm not the only one who has had to deal with Homer Williams."

Her cheeks burned. "I really wish he wasn't my father. He's not an honorable man."

"There are some things you can't change or control."

They grew quiet, and Sara Beth fought against hot tears that threatened to fall. As far as she was concerned, she no longer had a father. She would not let that man cause her one more minute of grief.

She straightened her spine and lifted her chin. Oddly enough, she was grateful that her father had forced Layken to marry her. At least she was out from under his demanding heavy hand and curses.

And she'd do her very best to help her husband make a go of the farm that meant so much to him.

Layken glanced over at Sara Beth in time to see her swipe angrily at her eyes. He hated that the thought of her father could still upset her, but it was understandable.

She'd only been his wife for four days. Surprised that it brought a comfortable feeling, he let that thought settle around him.

While he pondered life's changes, a glimmer of hope bloomed— Hope that he would save the farm and that it would prosper again. He hadn't even known he needed help. But having another pair of hands made a difference. And he'd be lying if he said he hadn't enjoyed regular meals again. Homer Williams told the truth about that part. Sara Beth was an excellent cook and seemed to enjoy it.

He'd never let her know he'd heard her crying in her room at night. She'd work through her grief. And that was it, pure and simple. She'd lost her mother, father, and the only home she'd ever known.

And he'd make sure they got everything on her list today. Plus, the chickens and maybe some goats. With any luck, the truck would be loaded down on the way back to the farm.

"Would you be okay with me dropping you at the store while I get the seeds and fuel?"

"Of course. I'm in as big of a hurry to get in and out of here as you are. I can only imagine the gossip."

"I told you gossip doesn't bother me. Don't pay any mind to it."

"I'll do my best."

A few minutes later, Layken pulled to a stop at the only general store in Everton. He handed her some bills. "I'll be back soon. Don't forget to get a new book, if they have one."

Sara Beth nodded and stepped out of the pickup, clutching Cuddles. She turned and waved before disappearing inside the store.

Layken drove away, vowing to be back as soon as possible. With the feed store only a couple of blocks away, it shouldn't take long.

"What can I help you with, young man?" A grizzled white-haired man leaned against a wooden counter inside the feed store.

The mixed smells of fertilizer and seeds tickled Layken's nostrils. Everything the store stocked had always intrigued him, including belts for tractors, plows, discs, and kerosene.

He took off his hat. "I need to buy fifty pounds of peanut seeds, some vegetable seeds, and kerosene."

"I ain't got no peanut seeds here. I can get some ordered in. Otherwise, you'll have to drive over to Springfield."

Damn! He hadn't counted on the store not having them. "If you order, how soon can they get here?" It would mean another delay.

"Well, that depends."

"On?"

"On if there's a truck heading this way anytime soon. If there is, I can have them in by next week."

Layken scratched his head. "You sure they have them over in Springfield?"

"Purty sure."

"Any way you can find out? I'd hate to drive all the way over for nothing."

The old man grabbed a cane and hobbled around behind the counter. "I swear nobody has any damn patience anymore. You young folk want everything right now."

"I don't mean no disrespect, sir, but I've got to get the seeds in the ground as soon as possible."

"You crazy? No one around these parts grows peanuts. This is corn and wheat country."

"Yes, sir. I know. I want to try something different." He thumbed through the packets of vegetable seeds while the man fumbled through a card index.

Finally, he pulled out a yellowed card and dialed the number. "Slim? Howdy. This is Jake over at Everton Feed. How are things over there?"

"Uh-huh. Same here. Say, you got any peanut seeds in stock?"

Layken laid the seed packets on the counter and listened, trying to be patient.

"Uh-huh. Yep. I know. I told him so. These young folks think they know it all."

Fighting the urge to jerk the phone away from the dithering man, Layken gripped his hat and breathed.

"Okay. I'll tell him. Thanks."

Before he could cradle the receiver, Layken asked, "Well?"

"Says he has some but says it's the wrong time of year to plant 'em."

"Yes, sir, I know. But I don't have a choice."

The old man squinted. "Ain't you that Martin boy?"

"That's me. I'm in kind of a hurry. Need to fill up my kerosene cans, then get on over to Springfield."

"I knew your daddy real well. A fine man." The old man didn't move.

"Yes, he was. The kerosene?"

"Over there in the back." He crooked his thumb. "Help yourself."

Layken sprinted out to the pickup, grabbed the five-gallon cans, and then hurried to the back, where he found a pump. He filled them to the brim, then stopped by the counter to pay.

"That'll be three dollars."

"Thank you, sir." Layken tossed the bills on the counter. "And thanks for calling over to Springfield for me."

He didn't wait for the mumbled reply. He stuck the seed packets into his pocket, lugged the cans back to the pickup, and headed back to the general store to pick up Sara Beth.

There was no sign of her when he parked, so he hurried inside.

He spotted her near the back of the store. What he didn't miss was the whispering between two shoppers.

"The nerve of her to trap that poor Martin boy. You do know she's a witch. Probably brewed up some spell to put on him."

A tall woman wearing a bonnet nodded. "And how dare she bring that infernal rabbit into the store where we buy food."

"Ladies."

Both women blustered at his sudden appearance.

"It's a lovely day, isn't it?" Layken tipped his hat and hurried to Sara Beth's side. "Looks like you made a haul."

"Got pretty much everything we had on the list. Now, I can set up the kitchen proper. Did you get what you needed?"

"Partly. I'll tell you when we're out of here." He carried the rest of the purchases to the counter.

Once they paid the cashier and boxed up their bounty, Layken carried it out to the truck.

Sara Beth got in, and he closed her door, then hurried around to the driver's side.

"Thanks for that in there. I was doing my best to ignore them."

"I'm glad I walked in when I did."

"Me too, but I wasn't going to let them get to me." She settled Cuddles on the seat next to her. "What did you mean by partly getting what you need?"

"Got kerosene and vegetable seeds, but gotta drive to Springfield to get peanut seeds. Didn't have any here."

"Oh, that's a long way."

"No choice, though. I'll drop you off at the house first."

"The chickens?"

"I almost forgot. Let's go find Mr. Mallory now."

By the time they reached the farm, they had a dozen laying hens, plus their other purchases.

"Sometime soon, I'll go see Becker about a few goats," Layken said as he unloaded crate after crate of chickens into the coop while Sara Beth made sure none escaped. "I'm grateful Mr. Mallory had extra feed he was willing to sell us. I'll pick up more in Springfield." He closed and latched the door to the chicken coop.

Then, with arms full, Layken followed Sara Beth into the kitchen.

He dropped his load on the table, then jerked around when she shrieked.

"What is it, Sara Beth?"

"Someone's been in here." She turned to face him, wide-eyed.

CHAPTER 10

"What do you mean, someone's been here?" Layken glanced around the kitchen, puzzled by Sara Beth's obvious distress.

"The biscuits. I left them on a plate on the stove. And look." She pointed. "The plate's empty."

"Maybe we have mice. Or a raccoon might have gotten in."

"I don't think mice could carry off eight biscuits. Raccoons would have eaten them there, and crumbs would be all over the stove." She brought a hand to her mouth. "I think someone came in while we were gone."

Layken took off his hat and scratched his head. The last thing he wanted was for Sara Beth to feel afraid. "I don't see how that's possible. There are no close neighbors. We're not exactly close to the road."

"What if it was the person in the woods? Maybe they're starving."

"I'll check to see if anything else is gone." Layken frowned and strode into the living room, then to the bedrooms. He couldn't shake the uneasiness as he hurried back to the kitchen. "There doesn't seem to be anything else missing."

"Some of the eggs Mrs. Grover gave us are gone."

Layken looked over her shoulder. "Shit! That gives me an unsettled feeling. I won't leave you here alone while I go to Springfield." He couldn't.

65

Sara Beth closed the icebox door and turned to face him. She put her hands on her hips, and her brown eyes flashed with determination. "I'll be fine. All they took was food. I have lots to do. You go on."

"You sure? I don't like this." Taking a step back, he stared out the back door.

"I'm sure."

"You ever shoot a gun?"

"No, and I don't intend to start now. I'm telling you I'll be fine. I have a strong feeling someone was desperate. And, if they come back, I fully intend to feed them proper."

Layken had to admire her surprising tenacity. "You have a big heart, Sara Beth. The least I can do is help you put things away."

"That isn't necessary. You go on to Springfield and hurry back."

Layken jumped at a loud knock on the front door. His heart hammering inside his chest, he motioned to Sara Beth. "Stay here."

Before he could get to the door, another knock came.

"Coming," he yelled. While he'd never felt threatened in this home, times had changed. For a brief moment, he wished he had his rifle handy. Maybe he should put it over the fireplace where his father always kept it.

He paused at the screen door. "Can I help you?"

An elderly black man stood on the porch, hat in hand. "I'm lookin' for Miss Sara Beth Williams. Am I at the right place?"

Sara Beth flew into the living room. "Uncle Seymour!"

"Yes, ma'am. I do hope I'm not intruding."

"Of course not." She hugged him. "I'm so glad to see you. I've missed you somethin' terrible."

Uncle Seymour cleared his throat. "Yes, ma'am. Me too."

"Come in." She turned to Layken. "This is my Uncle Seymour. Remember me telling you about him?"

Layken offered a hand. "Of course, I remember. Sorry about the less-than-hospitable welcome. We discovered some food taken while we were in town."

Seymour gave him a quizzical look. "That's a shame." He shook Layken's hand. "Seymour King's the name."

"Come on in. I've heard a lot about you."

Sara Beth ushered Uncle Seymour inside. "Did you walk from town?"

"Yessum."

"We came from that way. Wish we'd seen you. Could've given you a ride."

"I took a shortcut through the woods."

"You must be thirsty. I have some tea in the icebox." She hurried to the kitchen.

The genuine affection between the old man and girl was evident. Layken motioned to the couch. "Have a seat."

"That's all right. Don't want to mess anything up."

"Nonsense. This ain't Homer Williams' house, Seymour. Make yourself at home."

Seymour cleared his throat. "Am hoping this can be more than a visit, sir. The Widow Jones fired me this morning. Got nowhere else to go."

"Well, you can most certainly stay here." Layken dropped into a chair and pointed again to the couch. "Please. Have a seat."

The older man eased down, sitting on the edge, hat in hand. "Thought you might have some work. Did some sharecropping back in Mississippi."

Layken ran his fingers through his hair. "I could sure use some help, and that's a fact." Another pair of hands would ease the workload. "Ever planted peanuts?"

"Peanuts?"

Sara Beth hurried in with glasses of tea. "Layken thinks he can make more money growing peanuts than wheat or corn. And I agree."

Seymour accepted the glass from her. "I know a thing or two about growing most things." He took a long drink from the cold glass. "Wouldn't ask for much. Maybe a bed and meals."

She raised her eyebrows. "What are you talking about, Uncle Seymour?"

"Widow Jones fired me this morning. Everything I own is outside in that wagon. Lookin' for a place to stay, at least for a little while, 'til I can figure out what's next."

"I've already told him I could use his help, Sara Beth." Layken took a sip of tea. "This house is small, but there's a room in the barn where my dad's hired hand stayed. Might need a little sprucing up."

"I'd be grateful."

"That horrible woman. I swear her and my father are two of a kind. A match made in heaven." Sara Beth sat on the sofa next to Seymour.

"Or hell." Uncle Seymour chuckled.

Sara Beth laughed. "That too. I guess they'll be gettin' married this weekend."

"She's already changing everything around the house that reminds her of your mother."

"Hmph. Glad I'm not there."

Layken cleared his throat. "Seymour, now that you're here, I don't have to worry about Sara Beth while I go on into Springfield. You couldn't have showed up at a better time."

"Happy I did, sir."

"Tell you what." Layken stood. "I'll show you to the room in the barn and leave it to you and Sara Beth to settle in."

The old man got to his feet and handed his empty glass to Sara Beth. "Thank you for the refreshment. It hit the spot."

Sara Beth took the glasses into the kitchen, picked up Cuddles, and followed the men to the barn. Her heart swelled with gratitude for how Layken accepted her guardian without question.

No doubt, she had married a good man.

She listened to the conversation between the men as they walked. Uncle Seymour pulled a wooden wagon loaded with his belongings over the rough ground.

"This place has been in my family since the early 1800s." Layken swept his arm wide. "My ancestors came in here with bounty land grants from the War of 1812."

Seymour ambled, pulling the heavy load. "It's a fine place. Sure is."

They reached the barn, and Layken tugged aside a sliding door.

It took a minute for Sara Beth's eyes to adjust to the dim interior. It was her first glimpse inside the barn, and the sturdiness impressed her. From the outside, it seemed more rundown.

A mouse scurried across the dirt floor. A yellow tabby cat dashed out from under a crate and soon had the mouse in its mouth.

"I didn't know we had a cat." Sara Beth bent over and called to the cat.

Layken laughed. "I didn't either. They've always come and gone around here. Never tried to tame one. Need 'em to do their job." He pointed toward the back left corner of the structure. "The room is back there. It's got runnin' water and a potbelly stove. Can't say much about what shape things are in. I haven't looked."

"It'll be fine." Seymour smiled, showing teeth yellowed from tobacco. "I'm much obliged."

"I'll make sure you're comfortable." Sara Beth laid a hand on the old man's arm. "I can't tell you how happy I am that you are here."

"That makes two of us, little girl." Seymour lumbered toward the back of the barn.

"If you two are okay, I will go on into Springfield. Want to be back before dark." Layken took a step toward the door, then turned. "Sara Beth, anything you need to help Seymour, feel free to use it."

"Thank you. I will."

She watched until Layken was gone, then strode across the barn to catch up with her friend. "Let's see what we've got. I've never even been out here. Been so busy around the house, I hadn't even thought to explore the barn."

Uncle Seymour squinted. "You look happy."

"It's a funny thing. I was so scared to come here, but Layken has been nothing but kind to me. I'm starting to get used to not being bossed around and handed demands or walking on eggshells, so I don't get hit. He's never so much as raised his voice to me."

"That's real good. Had a gut feelin' it would work out." He pushed open the door to reveal a small room with one window, a bed, a toilet, and a stove. A chintz curtain hung limply over the dirty window.

"Needs a good cleanin' for sure. But seems dry and sound."

"Come with me back to the house. I need to put away the things we bought in town, and then we'll make this room livable."

"Now, don't you worry none about me. I've stayed in lots worse places."

"Nonsense. No reason I can't help make it comfortable."

"You've always had such a big heart, little girl. So much like your sweet mama."

Sara Beth's eyes misted. "She did have a big heart. I sure do miss her."

"Didn't mean to make you sad. Someday, when you're ready, I can tell you stories about your mama you might not know."

"I'd love that. For now, let's get back to the house and get cleaning supplies." She headed toward the door, then stopped and called, "Kitty. Kitty." A soft meow answered, but the cat stayed hidden.

She liked that the cat had shown up. Maybe it would stick around and be some company for her old friend.

While they headed back to the house, she couldn't resist the urge to scan the tree line, looking for any sign of the food thief.

All she glimpsed were birds and butterflies flitting among the trees.

To have Uncle Seymour here with her filled her heart to overflowing. He was family—much more than her so-called father.

Cuddles snuggled under her arm as if he could read her thoughts.

"This is a downright purty place." Uncle Seymour followed her gaze.

"Yes, it is. And even though I didn't think it possible, I'm already starting to think of it as home, and I've been here less than a week."

"You didn't have any other choice. Glad it's working out."

"Me, too, Uncle Seymour. Me too. And for the record, I'm glad Widow Jones fired you."

She matched her steps with the slower ones of the man who meant so much to her.

"Reckon it was for the best."

Life had put all three of them in situations with no choices.

Forced to play a hand with cards they couldn't see, Layken, she, and Uncle Seymour would win.

She knew it deep down. How? And at what cost?

No one could answer that.

Working together as a unit would make each of them indestructible.

And everyone knew only the strongest would survive.

CHAPTER 11

Sara Beth chattered all the way back to the house, thrilled to have Uncle Seymour back in her life. She pointed out the newly acquired chickens and the garden plot.

"So, once I get the purchases from town put away, we'll get your room in order."

"Don't go to no trouble. I can take care of myself."

She paused and touched his thick shoulder. "I know you can. But please allow me to help. I want to."

Uncle Seymour stopped outside the back door. "In the morning, I can help you plant your new garden. I know a few tricks to make things grow."

Her heart soared. "Oh, that would be wonderful. You always kept our gardens looking so beautiful." She passed Cuddles to Uncle Seymour. "I want the same here, but I know it will take a while. Layken said this place sat vacant for over a year after his folks passed on."

He stroked the wiry white bristle on his chin. "Didn't get a chance to tell him, but I have a few buckets of paint in the wagon."

"Oh, that's wonderful. I'd like to use some right away to paint the porch swing." The thought of making it look new again brought a surge of excitement. "There's so much to do. I want to hurry it all up."

"Anything worth doin' takes time. If I've learned nothing else in my many years of living, I've learned that much." He held the door open, then followed her in.

Sara Beth unloaded the boxes while Uncle Seymour placed things where she pointed.

Soon, she gathered cleaning supplies, left Cuddles in her bedroom, and the two hurried back to the barn.

"It's interesting that the barn floor is dirt, but someone took the time to put down a wooden floor in this room. Maybe it was the man who worked for Mr. Martin." Sara Beth swept while Uncle Seymour moved the sparse pieces of furniture away from the wall for her.

"This'll make a right fine place to spend my nights." He moved the bed back and made way for her broom. Then, with a rag and vinegar, cleaned the small window and slid it open, propping it up with a stick. Sweat dripped down his face. "This'll catch a nice breeze."

Once she'd finished cleaning the floor, she stood back and wiped her brow with a dusty hand. "All that's left is cleaning your toilet, and then we can move you in."

"No." He scratched his chin. "I can move myself in, and you can go about your own chores. You've done enough."

Sara Beth laughed. "All right. You win. I'm going back to the house to find bed covers."

It took a few minutes to find spare bed linens. By the time she returned, Uncle Seymour had put away what few clothes he owned into the drawers of an ancient oak dresser and nailed his lucky horseshoe over the doorway.

It struck her how little he had brought with him. Yet he'd said it was all of his possessions. Once again, anger flared toward her father. This man had faithfully worked for the family for as long as she could remember, and he had nothing to show for it—a wooden wagon filled mostly with tools.

She bit her lip and turned away for a moment before she passed the bed covers to him. "Here you go. I found an extra pillow and a few towels, too."

"I'm obliged to you, little girl." He laid the covers on the small bed. "Now you're done out here, and so am I. What can I do for you?"

"I was thinking about the root cellar. Layken said there were jars of canned goods down there, but didn't know if they were still any good. Maybe you could bring them up."

Uncle Seymour put on his hat and followed her out without a backward glance at the small room. "I can sure do that."

They worked together over the next two hours. He laboriously carried jars up, and Sara Beth examined them. Any with mold or bulging lids went into one of the boxes she'd emptied earlier. The others, she set on the counter.

"This is the last of 'em." The old man wiped his brow and huffed. "It's a sight cooler down there than it is up here. You need to know there are some empty jars down there. Someone has been into the food."

She glanced up. "I'm not surprised. It's been vacant. And someone took biscuits from the kitchen right before you came. I hate to think of somebody out there hungry."

Seymour nodded. "Me too. We'll keep an eye out for them. I found some shriveled-up potatoes we can cut and plant. Long as a piece has an eye, it'll grow."

Sara Beth pulled a chair out from the table and pointed. "Rest while I pour you a glass of tea. I have lots to learn about growing things."

He accepted the cool glass. "I'll teach you everything I know."

She dropped into a chair across from him. "You've never told me. How did you meet my mama?"

"They was traveling through Mississippi. Reckon it was about 1926. You know, folks shunned the Gypsy caravans. Thought they was all thieves. It was common for the black folk to offer them food and a place to camp."

"She camped on your family's place?"

He nodded. "I was sharecropping. A hard livin' if ever there was one. When it came time to leave, she asked if I'd like to get out of the field and go with them. It wasn't a hard choice."

"How old were you? She must have been a young girl."

"She might've been seventeen or eighteen. I was already close to my fifties and plumb wore out from working the fields. We had some sort of instant kinship. She read the cards for me, and they all said to go. Didn't have a clue where either one of us would end up. A short time later, she met your daddy, and they married. Part of her agreement to marry Homer Williams was that I could stay."

"What about her folks? My grandparents?"

"Her mama and daddy had done passed on. Never knew them."

"I wonder what they would've been like? I never had any grandparents. My father's folks were dead too."

"If her parents were anything like her or you, they were good decent folks." Seymour finished his tea and stood. "We're burnin' daylight. I'll carry these jars out and start a compost spot away from the house."

"Compost?"

"A place where you dump discarded food to let it rot, then mix it in with the dirt. Makes a rich fertilizer."

Sara Beth sighed. "See. I have so much to learn."

He laid a rough, calloused hand on hers. "Maybe that's why I'm here. A man needs purpose."

While Seymour carried out the tainted jars, Sara Beth glanced around the fully stocked kitchen and breathed a contented sigh.

Choosing to cook the chicken she'd bought in town, she drew water and set it to boiling, then slipped her apron over her head.

Chicken and dumplings was one of her specialties, and she looked forward to serving it.

She hoped Layken would make it back before dark with what he needed. Another delay wouldn't be welcome.

And now, with Uncle Seymour here to help, he could get the planting done twice as fast.

Perusing the canned food that now lined the cabinet, she pulled out a jar of peaches. Those would make the perfect dessert.

Leaving Springfield, Layken turned toward home with a sense of accomplishment and hope. A fifty-pound bag of peanuts and a farmer's almanac were a good start.

He contemplated the developments from the past few days. He'd gone from being completely alone in the world to having a partner—a wife, although he struggled to think of Sara Beth in that way. She'd already proved her willingness to work and her worth.

And now, with Seymour's arrival, that made a group of three to work toward a common goal.

Maybe the gods were smiling on him, or perhaps his ancestors were pulling strings to help out. Whatever the reason, he'd take it.

While he didn't like to dwell on it, the war had been brutal. He'd done what he had to. But like many of the other men who'd served and returned home, he put it aside and refused to give it a thought.

Nothing could be gained by reliving the horrors.

Everything could be gained by doing good and working hard.

When he'd returned to the family homestead, he had one goal and determination in mind—to make a go of it, preserve it, if for no other reason than to honor the blood, sweat, and tears that had created it.

He'd never given much thought to future generations. Being an only child, it would end with him unless he had children.

But he refused to think ahead.

Life would unfold as it should.

He walked into the house to the tantalizing smells of a home-cooked meal. His stomach growled in response.

"I'm home." He strode into the kitchen to find Sara Beth and Uncle Seymour sitting at the table with an odd array of strange-looking cards.

Sara Beth jumped up. "And?"

"And I have seeds." He pointed to the table. "What's this?"

"I was doing a tarot card reading." She cleared her throat nervously. "Hope you don't object."

He took off his hat and scratched his head. "How could I object to something I know nothing about?"

Seymour stood. "Sara Beth's good at reading the cards, like her mother was." He pointed to his vacant chair. "Have a seat, and she'll show you."

Layken peered at the cards with strange symbols but ignored the invitation to sit. "I'll take your word for it."

"The reading was positive." Sara Beth scooped up the cards. "They show a favorable outcome to my question about planting."

"Reckon that's a good thing." Layken hung his hat on a nail. "Something's smelling mighty tasty." He had no idea what Sara Beth was talking about but didn't see any harm in the cards. Who was he to judge what he didn't understand?

"Someday, I'll tell you about my mama and her gifts. When you're ready. She taught me a lot." Sara Beth got out plates. "We were passing the time 'til you got home. Didn't want to have supper without you."

"Appreciate that." He turned to Seymour. "I hope you found the room to your liking."

"Yessir. It'll do me fine." He shifted from one foot to the other as if trying to find his place.

Sara Beth set the chicken and dumplings in the middle of the table. "Uncle Seymour carried up all the canned food from the basement, and we discarded what was ruined."

"I can see he's going to be a big help around here." Layken dipped a spoon into the steaming pot. He met the old man's gaze and pointed to a chair. "Please. Sit. This is your home now, Seymour. Don't want you to feel like you have to wait for permission to do anything. Do you understand?"

"Yessir." The old man sat down. "It's just that I'm not used to being treated as an equal."

"Well, here you are. The same way Sara Beth is. This is my place, but it's yours too." He took a bite and sighed. "This is delicious, Sara Beth. My mom sometimes made this on Sundays, and it was always a treat."

She joined the men at the table. "I'm glad you like it. And we have a peach cobbler for dessert."

Layken raised his eyebrows and chuckled. "You're spoiling us, now."

"Good." She smiled.

He liked the way her dark eyes lit up when she smiled from the inside out. And he'd rarely seen it. Maybe she'd relax more and let herself know some sort of happiness in time.

And maybe he would too. For now, happiness would take a back seat to the struggle to keep the land. Or perhaps the two were innately joined.

The little ragtag group sat at the old table that had been the gathering place for generations, with a common goal of survival, and shared a meal to nourish their bodies while the companionship fed their souls.

Tomorrow, he would put seeds in the ground.

And with a little bit of luck, they would grow.

CHAPTER 12

Layken was up before the sun the next morning. An excitement that he hadn't experienced in a long time flowed through him.

He hurriedly dressed and made a beeline for the kitchen, where he was shocked to see a light shining.

Sara Beth turned away from the stove and flashed a quick smile. "Figured you'd need a bite to eat before you head out."

"Thank you. Hadn't planned on eating, but a few more minutes won't make any difference." He stared at her long and hard as she turned back to the stove. He hadn't expected her to be up this early and cooking breakfast. He pulled out a chair, then paused. "Want I should go get Seymour?"

The back screen door squeaked as it opened. "No need." Seymour stepped inside.

The corners of Layken's mouth turned up into a wide grin. "Guess I'm not the only one ready to go to work today." He motioned to an empty chair. "Hungry?"

Sara Beth placed plates of eggs and biscuits in front of the two men, then poured steaming cups of coffee.

"Thank you, young lady." Seymour took a sip of coffee. "You set a mighty fine plate. Yes, ma'am. You sure do."

"It's nothing." Sara Beth fed Cuddles, grabbed her plate, and sat at the table. "Gonna get some vegetables planted this morning."

"About that, Sara Beth." Uncle Seymour laid his fork on the table. "I know I promised to help you, but I have a feeling Layken needs my help getting the peanuts in the ground."

Layken nodded. "Was hoping to hear that. It'll take me an hour or so to get everything ready. You can help Sara Beth 'til then if that suits both of you."

"Of course." Sara Beth leaned forward. "Whatever is the best use of our time. Uncle Seymour, how did you sleep last night?"

"Just fine, little girl. Say, when you empty the coffee grounds out of the pot, save them, and we'll mix a little in with the seeds and dirt." Seymour smeared butter on his biscuit. "Save all the eggshells, too. When they're ground up, they help add nutrients to the soil."

"Sounds like you know a lot about growing things." Layken broke a flaky biscuit in half.

"Been growin' things most of my life. Learned a trick or two along the way."

"You don't know how much I appreciate you showing up when you did. Got an idea about how to water everything once we get the seeds in the ground."

"I took a walk down to Sinking Creek last night before it got good and dark. Was surprised to find water still flowing, considerin' how dry it's been." Seymour finished his last bite. "Might work to haul water up from there."

"That's what I was thinking, too. What if I punch some small holes in the bottom of a fifty-five-gallon drum, load it on the back of the plow, then drive slow down the rows? At least that's the idea I have."

Seymour scratched at the stubble on his chin. "Never tried it, but don't see why that wouldn't work. Course, we'd have to figure out how to get it from the creek to the field without losing it all."

"Thought about that, too. Maybe attach a false bottom that we can slide out to let the water flow. That would be a way to control it."

"I do believe that would do the trick." Seymour nodded.

Layken frowned. "I haven't figured out how to get the water siphoned into the barrel."

"Gravity. Have to make it work in your favor." Seymour stood, wiping his mouth, and picked up his plate. "A right fit breakfast, little girl."

"Glad to do it, Uncle Seymour. Just drop the plate in the sink, and I'll wash them all up in the heat of the day."

Layken joined Seymour laying his plate in the deep kitchen sink. He gulped the last sip of his coffee. "Gonna go get the tractor fueled up. I'll holler at you when I'm ready."

Seymour gave a slight nod. "Soon as we can, we oughta make a trip to the Mason farm and pick up a load of cow manure. That'll go a long way toward helping the peanuts grow."

"We'll do that for sure." Layken reached for his hat hanging on a nail by the door and hurried out.

The trio had much to do before the sun rose high in the sky.

He'd looked at the calendar in the Farmer's Almanac last night. Today was a new moon—the perfect time for putting seeds in the ground.

With Seymour's help, he hoped to have them all planted by dark.

Inside the cool dimness of the barn, he filled the tractor with fuel, then hoisted the bags of peanuts onto the back of the raised plow.

He figured to park the tractor at the edge of the field, then use wooden wagons to distribute the seeds down the rows.

Glad that his father had been the kind of man to keep everything, he pulled two wagons from the back of the barn. He didn't have to worry about flat tires with metal wheels, but they wouldn't work in mud. Maybe it was a good thing the ground was so dry.

After he turned over a fifty-five-gallon metal drum, he examined the bottom. If he used the lid as a false bottom, he might get water from the creek to the field without losing too much of it.

Hope bloomed along with excitement. He would save the family farm come hell or high water. And the good Lord had best be listening.

If the peanuts grew, he'd have a crop to harvest before the first frost.

Laughter drifted across the backyard, and he turned to see Sara Beth attempting to gather eggs from a setting hen. He watched for a minute, enjoying the mixture of laughter and a squawking hen.

Finally, Uncle Seymour stepped into the chicken coop and lifted the hen while she grabbed the eggs.

Again, Sara Beth's valiant attempt to adapt to farm life brought admiration. He was sure it wasn't easy, having always lived in town.

The affection between the old man and girl touched him, and a powerful urge to protect them both washed over him. Shunned by the town folks, they fit in fine on his farm.

And he was more than grateful to have them.

He focused back on the task at hand.

The more they could get done, the better.

Painfully aware of the ticking clock, he worked faster.

Several hours later, Sara Beth stood, brushed her sweaty hair out of her face, and stretched the kinks out of her back. Although her knees were raw from kneeling in the dirt, she had most of her garden seeds in the ground—only one more row to go.

She envied men who got to wear pants to protect their knees. She'd seen pictures in magazines of women dressed in stylish pants. And yet, in these parts, it was considered taboo for women to wear them. Her father would never have allowed it in his house.

But she no longer lived under his thumb.

It was time she looked for a sewing machine. All farm women had them, didn't they? Luckily, she'd learned to sew at a young age and had become adept at creating patterns and putting them together.

She needed sturdy, durable pants.

But that would have to wait for another day.

Checking on Cuddles, she found him sleeping under the back porch. He'd found a cool spot.

Shading her eyes against the sun, she walked to the side of the house where she could see the men in the field.

Surely they'd stop for lunch.

She watched for a few minutes as they worked together, each man pulling a wagon and dropping seeds into the ground.

At the least, she could put together a light meal for them.

Inside, she washed the dirt off her hands, noting two blisters forming. Thankful they'd added basic medical supplies to their shopping list, she'd put salve on them later.

Humming to herself, she marveled at how quickly she'd relaxed in Layken Martin's home. If she was honest, he made it easy.

Searching the pantry, she was glad she'd splurged on a can of Spam. While it was more expensive, it would come in handy today.

It took no time to fry up thin pieces of the Spam and pair them with the leftover biscuits.

She sliced two apples, loaded the food on a tray with cold tea in mason jars, and headed to the field.

Balancing the tray, she stumbled over tree roots and uneven ground. One jar of tea toppled over the side. Thank goodness she'd put lids on them. She picked it up dusted it off, and trudged onward.

The looks on the men's faces made it all worthwhile.

At the heart of things, she wanted to please Layken.

More than anything, she needed to show her worth, that she was capable despite their rocky, forced beginning.

She waved. "Hungry?"

Layken strode toward her and took the tray. "I'll say. More thirsty than hungry. You didn't have to do all of this."

"Figured you could use a break, and everyone needs to eat."

Uncle Seymour lumbered up beside her. "You are a smart woman, Sara Beth. You know the way to a man's heart."

She gave Layken a shy glance.

Did she want to work her way into his heart?

Layken pointed toward the tree line. "A little shade and refreshment will go a long way toward making this day better."

She followed him, Seymour ambling along next to her.

He pulled a rag from his back pocket and mopped his brow. "How's your gardening coming?"

"Good. Got a few more rows to go." She spread her palms upward. "Getting a few blisters."

The old man laughed. "Goes with the territory. They'll soon turn to callouses."

She grimaced. "Not very ladylike."

"Maybe not, but satisfying."

"You're right. It's been years since I've felt valued or needed."

"Don't ever underestimate yourself. You've got a lot to offer. I always knew it."

They reached the tree line and the welcome shade.

Layken set the tray on the ground and leaned against a tree trunk. Stretching his lanky legs out in front of him, he took a sandwich from the tray and passed it to Sara Beth.

"No. These are for you men. I'll eat when I get back to the house."

He passed it to Seymour, then bit into one. "Glad you're making progress with the vegetable seeds."

"I may wait 'til evening to finish." She drew circles in the dirt with her fingertip. "Say, did your mother have a sewing machine?"

Layken nodded, opened the mason jar, and took a long swig of tea. "I'm sure it's in one of the closets. I remember how excited she was when Dad bought her an electric one. Before that, she had a treadle machine."

"If you don't mind, I'd like to use it."

He set the cold jar down and locked his gaze with hers.

It was everything she could do not to look away from the intense stare.

"I told you to use anything you want. You don't have to ask my permission."

"Sorry. I'm not used to that kind of freedom."

Uncle Seymour chuckled. "Girlie, looks like we both have lots to learn and get used to."

"It's a big change, for sure." She wished she could read Layken's mind. His handsome face remained void of expression.

What was she looking for from him?

Affection?

Of course not. They'd only known each other for five days.

Appreciation?

She'd seen that in his eyes more than once.

And beyond any shadow of a doubt, she had his protection and trusted him to keep her safe.

This whole scenario reminded her of how she used to play as a little girl, pretending to have a husband, a house, and someone to love.

It would be unwise to delude herself.

Yes, she had a house to manage.

And yes, she had a husband, in name only.

But someone to care about her?

She had Uncle Seymour.

And she was happier than she'd been in years. That had to count for something.

CHAPTER 13

Sara Beth gathered up the empty tray and jars and strode back toward the house as the men went back to work, dropping peanuts in the ground.

As she rounded the corner of the house, the back screen door slammed shut, and she caught sight of a slight figure sprinting across the open space toward the trees.

"Hey," she yelled. "Stop!"

She dropped the tray on the back porch step and dashed after the intruder. "Stop, please. I want to help you."

The only answer she got was the snapping of limbs and rustling of the underbrush.

When she reached the tree line, she bent over, held her side, and gulped in air.

Finally, she straightened and tucked a stray hair behind her ear. "Whoever you are, I know you're out there, and I know you need food. Come back tonight after the lights are out. There'll be food on the back step for you."

She had no clue if the person had heard her, but she squared her shoulders and hurried back to the house with purpose.

Before working anymore in the garden, she would put together a meatloaf and soak some red beans.

It broke her heart to think of someone all alone in the woods and starving. And from the glimpse she caught of the intruder, it almost looked like a young child.

She stopped mid-stride. But what if they aren't alone? What if it's a family or a group of people? It didn't matter. She'd do what she could.

Times had been hard on everyone with rations and no jobs to be found, especially in tiny towns like Everton and rural areas.

Remembering what Uncle Seymour had told her about the Gypsies, she vowed she would turn no one away.

She wished they'd show their face.

Cuddles hopped out from under the porch, and she scooped him up in her arms and hurried inside.

Layken glanced up at Sara Beth's shouting, as did Uncle Seymour. A strong temptation to stop planting and investigate rippled through him.

But a few minutes later, she walked back toward the house with long determined strides.

"What do you reckon?" Uncle Seymour leaned on a hoe handle.

"Don't know. Looks like whatever it was has passed. Maybe running off a raccoon or something. I'm sure she'll tell us."

Seymour covered another peanut with dry dirt. "Even though she was raised in town, she's pretty resourceful. She had to be to live with Homer Williams, especially after her mama died."

Layken worked alongside the older man. "Does Sara Beth look like her mother?"

"Oh, yessir. She has her mama's dark eyes, big heart, and sweet spirit." He pulled off a chaw of tobacco and stuck it in his jaw. "Esmerelda was a beauty. She was pretty desperate when she agreed to marry Homer Williams. She needed the stability."

The men fell silent.

There was a lot Uncle Seymour wasn't saying, and Layken tried to read between the lines. It wasn't hard to imagine a young beautiful Gypsy girl looking for a home, for roots.

He gazed across the land. He simply couldn't relate to not having any family or home. That kind of security meant everything to him, and he'd fight the devil himself to keep it.

They kept working as the sun made its way across the sky. Once it got too dark to see, they hooked the wagons behind the tractor and secured everything inside the barn.

Delicious smells drifted through the kitchen screen door.

"One thing for sure. Sara Beth is going to keep us well-fed." Layken paused at the outside hydrant and doused water over his dusty face and hands, then took a long drink using his hands for a cup.

"That's a fact." Uncle Seymour followed suit.

With water dripping down the back of his sweaty, dirt-caked shirt, Layken opened the door and held it for the older man.

"Something sure does smell good in here."

Sara Beth came running from the living room, poking straight pins into her apron, carrying Cuddles under one arm. "Dinner's ready. Did you finish?"

"Got close. We can easily finish in the morning, barring no unforeseen issues." Layken pulled out a chair and dropped into it. "Looks like you might've found my mom's sewing machine."

"I did. And with a little cleaning and oiling, it's running like a top." She set Cuddles on the kitchen floor.

Uncle Seymour remained standing and put an arm around Sara Beth's slight shoulders. "I sure do appreciate the good eatin'."

She flicked her wrist. "Pshaw. It's nothing. Sit." She pointed to the table. "I'll have everything out in no time."

While she brought food to the table, Layken leaned back in the chair and closed his eyes. He was accustomed to being outside, but the sun had been extra hot today, and even with a hat and long sleeves, his skin had blistered. He looked forward to a bath and the bed, especially with a full stomach.

He opened his eyes when Sara Beth set a plate in front of him. "Say, what was all the yelling about after you brought us food this afternoon?"

"Someone ran out the back door as soon as I rounded the corner of the house. I gave chase but couldn't catch them." She furrowed her brow. "I swear it looked like a kid. And the rest of the Spam I'd saved for my lunch was gone along with a couple of biscuits."

Uncle Seymour rubbed his bristly chin. "Might explain some of the empty jars in the cellar."

Layken stopped mid-bite. "What empty jars?"

"When I was bringing them up for Sara Beth yesterday, I noticed quite a few empty and discarded. I'd say someone was helping themselves down there."

"And now that we live here, they're scared and starving." Sara Beth sat and filled her plate. "I can't stand to think of anyone being hungry. I intend to set food out on the step tonight before we go to bed if that's okay."

A flicker of worry passed through Layken. After all, they lived in precarious times, and desperate people did desperate things. "We don't want to invite trouble."

Sara Beth raised her chin. "No trouble. Just offering a little food. Maybe whoever it is will come out in the open and not be so afraid."

"Times sure have been hard on folks. No telling. It may be a whole group squatted in the woods." Layken took a bite of meatloaf and groaned. "This is so good."

"Glad you like it." Sara Beth took a bite and chewed slowly, then swallowed. "I had that thought too. But somehow, I get the feeling it's someone alone."

Uncle Seymour took a sip from his water glass. "You got your mama's intuition, little girl. Go with your gut."

Layken looked from one to the other. While the war had closed off a big part of his heart, the open hearts and minds of his two companions touched him. Maybe there was some hope of regaining a fragment of what he'd lost. No doubt that would make his folks happy.

"I don't want to overstep my bounds." Sara Beth nibbled her food. "I mean about putting some food out on the step tonight."

"It's fine. You don't even have to ask. We can share what we have."

"That was always my mama's philosophy, much to Homer Williams' dismay. She'd feed anyone who knocked on our back door, and with the railroad close by, we got lots of hoboes coming through."

"I remember that and how mad Homer would get. He'd stomp around and rant about having to feed everybody in the country." Seymour laughed. "Your mama didn't pay him no mind."

The laughter around his kitchen table did wonders to soothe his tired body. Layken soaked it up while he ate the meal his wife had prepared.

A man could get used to this.

Exhaustion settled in by the time dishes were cleared from the table, and he stumbled toward a cool bath.

He didn't waste any time stripping off his dirty clothes, and soon the cool water and fragrant soap rejuvenated him. He slipped into a clean pair of khakis and a T-shirt and went to find Seymour.

He'd not hear to the old man bathing in the creek or under the outside hydrant.

The strains of a haunting melody drifted through the open front door, followed by a mournful harmonica.

He stepped out onto the porch.

Sara Beth sat on the porch swing, Cuddles at her side. On her lap, she held an odd-looking small wooden box with an array of metal keys on which she tapped out the melody.

Uncle Seymour sat on an overturned box, blowing on a harp.

Layken stood for a long minute in wonder. He'd never thought to ask Sara Beth if she played an instrument. And that reminded him about her fascination with the radio when she'd first stepped foot in his house.

As soon as he got the crop planted and watered in, he vowed to check it out and see if it still worked.

They stopped playing, and Layken clapped. "I had no idea you both played music."

"Me and this old harp have been friends many a year." Uncle Seymour tapped it against his pants leg.

"What is that you're playing, Sara Beth?"

She cast a shy glance in his direction. "A thumb piano. My mother taught me to play."

"Well, I'll be. Never saw one of those before. It sounded awful pretty. Will you do another?"

Uncle Seymour raised the harmonica to his mouth and blew what sounded exactly like a train whistle.

Then, Sara Beth joined in as they played a Jimmie Rodgers tune.

Layken leaned against the wall and tapped his foot. He knew every word to the song and sang along to the chorus. He had a smooth baritone voice that blended perfectly with the music.

The song ended, and Sara Beth shot him a wide grin. "You sing good."

"Why, thank you, ma'am." He bowed at the waist. "Seymour, I came out to tell you that you're welcome to take a bath in the house. I won't hear of you trying to wash off in a sink or the creek."

Seymour raised his hand to object, but Layken cut him off.

"No argument. The bathroom is yours. And I'm turning in for the night. It was nice hearing music in this house again." He opened the front screen door, then paused. "Sara Beth, be sure to lock up the back door after you put food out tonight. Don't want anyone creeping around in the house while we sleep."

"Sure thing." She stood and tucked the thumb piano under her arm, then reached for Cuddles.

Seymour slipped his harmonica into his pocket and groaned as he stood. "I'll wash off a bit and head on out to bed. We got a lot done today."

"Thanks to having another pair of hands." Layken stepped inside and held the door open for the other two.

"Goodnight." Sara Beth headed to the kitchen.

"Night, Sara Beth. Thank you for everything. I appreciate all your hard work, not to mention the delicious meals you're spoiling us with."

"It's nice…" She hesitated for a split second, her dark eyes meeting his. She quickly glanced away. "You're welcome."

He doubted she'd ever heard a word of thanks from Homer Williams. While he couldn't change what the arrogant man had done, he could damned well make sure she knew her value here.

She was as much a part of this tenuous situation as he and her contributions already made a tremendous difference.

"What were you about to say, Sara Beth? You can talk freely here."

"Just that it's nice to feel valued." She stroked Cuddles' fur. "I'm not used to having a say." She gave a slight smile. "It's going to take a bit to get used to it."

He fought the urge to touch her shoulder. "Take all the time you need. And never doubt your value."

"And thank you for not griping me out for wanting to feed whoever is stealing food."

His shoulders tensed, and he fought off worry. Maybe Sara Beth's offering would help ease the poor person's hungry belly. And who was he to deny that?

And maybe eventually, they'd find out more about him or her.

Layken locked the front door. It wasn't like it would keep anyone out. However, it would make getting in a little more challenging. His dad used to say *Locks were invented to keep honest folks honest.*

He reckoned that might be true.

Nevertheless, he secured the door before turning out the light. As he strode down the hallway to his room, he noted with some satisfaction that water was running in the bathroom.

It had been a productive day. Because of Seymour's help, the planting was going twice as fast.

With a grateful heart, he stripped down to his underwear and lay on the familiar bed. The springs squeaked under his weight, and he found it comforting.

No, he couldn't imagine not having roots.

A deep satisfied sigh escaped his throat, and he gave in to exhaustion.

Soft refrains from Sara Beth's thumb piano and Uncle Seymour's harp lingered in his mind.

A gentle breeze wafted through the open windows, cooling his burning skin.

Every muscle ached.

The water stopped running in the bathroom, and doors opened, then closed. Muffled conversation drifted through the hallway.

Slowly, the house was coming back to life.

The land was coming alive as well.

And maybe, in the process, so were he, Sara Beth, and Seymour.

With that thought and a peaceful heart, he closed his eyes.

CHAPTER 14

Sara Beth arose the following day before the sun. Her heart pounded in anticipation as she dressed and hurried to see if someone had accepted her food offering.

She couldn't see much in the early pre-dawn darkness, but the lid was open on the pan she'd set out, and it was empty. Lying next to it was a small bunch of wildflowers made up of yellow coneflower, purple aster, and pale pink barbaras buttons.

A joyous warmth spread through her as she scooped them up and inhaled their sweetness.

She set Cuddles on the ground to do his business and hurried back inside for a jar and water. Before she started breakfast, she set the flower bouquet in the center of the round oak table and stood back to admire them.

A rustling from outside the door and a high-pitched squeal she recognized as coming from Cuddles sent her running in a panic.

The large wings of an owl fluttered in the air as it went airborne. With her heart thumping against her ribcage, she grabbed Cuddles and dashed back inside.

An examination in the dim kitchen light revealed small tears in his posterior. Two seconds later, the tiny bunny would have been the owl's breakfast.

Tears dropped onto her cheeks. "Oh, sweet Cuddles, I'm so sorry. I shouldn't have left you out there."

She rinsed off the blood with shaking hands.

"Is something wrong?"

Layken's deep voice startled her, and she jumped, then whirled around. "An owl almost made off with Cuddles." She held up the rabbit. "Look. He's injured."

Layken took Cuddles from her, gently ran his fingers around the wounds, and wiped away the blood. "Looks like they're not super deep, thank goodness. You should clean the wounds and put some salve on them. Might want to keep him inside for a few days 'til they scab over."

"I feel so awful. I only left him for a minute." She rubbed the back of her hand over her eyes and sniffled. "I got distracted by the flowers."

"Flowers?" Layken raised his eyebrows.

She pointed toward the table. "The food was gone, and these were beside the pan."

"Well, ain't that somethin'? I'd say it's a very nice way to say thank you." He took two steps closer to the table. "Smell good too. I'll get the medicine for Cuddles. He'll be okay."

"Thank you," she whispered. When Layken placed Cuddles back in her arms, she wrapped a kitchen towel around him and made a sling from her apron. "I'll get breakfast going."

"Coffee first, please," he threw over his shoulder with a broad smile as he strode down the hallway.

She put the coffee on to boil, cracked eggs, and got out flour for griddle cakes. Cuddles shivered against her, no doubt reliving the terror of the attack.

There were so many dangers living in the country that she'd never considered in town. She would have to be more vigilant.

Despite the close call for Cuddles, she couldn't quell the excitement that someone had accepted her food and left a token of appreciation. It had been the right thing to do.

The fragrant A&P coffee permeated the kitchen as it boiled in the pot. Sara Beth reached for a cast iron griddle from the hook above the stove.

By the time she had cakes sizzling, Layken had returned with salve for Cuddles. "Sorry, it took a while. Couldn't find it right off." He handed the jar to Sara Beth.

Uncle Seymour came through the door.

She passed the spatula to him. "Can you turn these cakes while I doctor Cuddles?"

"What happened to the bunny?" The old man took the spatula but held her gaze.

Layken poured coffee and took a seat at the table.

While applying the salve, she explained, then pointed to the flowers. "Our hungry guest left those, and that's what distracted me."

Uncle Seymour let out a whistle. "I'll be damned." He reached for the rabbit. "Let me hold him while you finish breakfast."

She treasured the care both men expressed for her pet. In a few minutes, she had stacks of griddle cakes in front of them, along with butter and sorghum syrup.

Layken groaned as he put the first bite in his mouth. "I swear, Sara Beth, I don't know your secret, but these taste like heaven."

Seymour nodded in agreement, with his mouth full.

"Thank you both. It's my mother's recipe." She joined them at the table with Cuddles nestled on her lap. "Want I should prepare lunch again today?"

"No need to cart it out to us. We'll take a break when the sun's hot and come to the house. I won't lie. I got a little overheated yesterday." Layken slurped his coffee. "I'm pretty sure we can get the rest of the peanuts in the ground by midday, don't you think, Seymour?"

"Sure do."

"Then this afternoon, we'll try to get some water on them."

Seymour leaned back in his chair and wiped his mouth. "You got well water here, right?"

Layken nodded.

"How deep?"

"Don't rightly know. My grandfather dug it a long time ago, but it's never run dry. My dad said it's fed by an underground spring."

"Ever tried pumping into a holding tank?"

Sara Beth ate her breakfast and listened to the conversation, an idea forming. "I remember the one you built for us, Uncle Seymour."

He winked. "Then you know what I have in mind."

She laughed. "Maybe. At least it gives me an idea. I spotted an old livestock watering trough in the barn. What if I drag it over near the garden and fill it? It would make watering my seeds a little easier."

Layken flashed what she interpreted as an appreciative smile. "I like the way you think. Tell you what. Me and Seymour will bring it over and get it started filling before we head to the field."

"I hate for you to take the time away from your work. I'm sure I can manage." More than anything, she didn't want to be a bother.

"It'll take us no more than five minutes. It's a good idea."

She couldn't hide the joy his compliment brought her. When was the last time she truly had any value? A long time.

Layken pushed back his chair. "Let's get going, Seymour. The sun'll be up soon. Thank you for another delicious meal, Sara Beth."

"You can leave your plates," she said as she stood. "I'll have 'em cleaned up in no time."

Uncle Seymour put a thick arm around her shoulders. "It's good to be here, little girl."

She gave him a peck on his weathered cheek. "Sure is, Uncle Seymour."

Once they left, she quickly washed the dishes, keeping Cuddles secured in the makeshift sling.

Before heading out the door, she took the time to feed the little bunny.

The sun peeked over the horizon as the screen door slammed behind her. Water already trickled into the trough near the garden area, as Layken and Uncle Seymour left on the tractor.

She put her hands on her hips and swiveled in a full circle, scanning the area. She couldn't shake the feeling someone was watching her.

No time to dawdle. She made a beeline for the chicken coop after stopping to scoop up a bucket of grain for them. Thank goodness Uncle Seymour had shown her the feeding trick to get the hens off their nests so she could gather the eggs without having to fight them.

Once she had the eggs safely in the house, she gathered the coffee grounds and crushed eggshells she'd saved for the past two days and hurried to her garden plot.

With the hoe in hand, she finished making furrows, then dropped the remaining seeds approximately two inches apart, sprinkled a few coffee grounds mixed with the eggshells, then raked the dry dirt lightly over them.

She couldn't wait for new green sprouts to poke their heads through the soil, to see the fruits of her labor. She'd tend them with care.

By the time she reached the end of the rows, the morning sun was beating down on her back, and the trough was full of water.

"Now, where would I find a watering can?" she asked the slight breeze that dried the sweat on her brow. Surely Mrs. Martin had one somewhere?

She ducked inside for a cool drink, then decided to apply more salve to Cuddles and leave him on her bed while she worked. He'd be safe there.

When she stepped back outside, she gasped. A rusty watering can sat next to the trough as if it had willed itself to appear there.

Again, she scanned the area, looking for any sign of a person—nothing. They obviously posed no threat. She loved that the mysterious visitor seemed to want to help.

The barn cat strolled out, stretched, then lay down in the sun. The chugging of the tractor drifted across the way.

There was no way she could have imagined this new life when her father thrust it upon her. Now the dreadful feelings she'd first experienced seemed like light years ago.

Layken had stayed true to his promise. He'd been nothing but kind and appreciative. And it made her want to work harder to earn her keep.

She dipped the can into the trough and carried the first drops of water to the parched soil. It took ten trips to water a single row, but it was almost as if the earth gave her a smile in return for her efforts.

Her heart swelled with happiness.

Even the land appreciated her.

CHAPTER 15

Layken squinted against the sun and pulled his hat down lower. Only a few more rows to go, and all the seeds would be planted.

A comfortable silence rested between the two men while they worked. Uncle Seymour's idea about a holding tank for water storage had Layken's mind working overtime. He mentally sketched the blueprint for the structure and decided on the perfect location.

If only he could work faster. Now he knew how competitors must feel when they begin a race against the clock.

Everything for the future of this farm, his life, and Sara Beth's hinged on the success of this first partial crop. Come spring, he'd get more seeds in the ground as soon as the danger of frost passed.

They reached the end of the last rows with the boiling sun high overhead.

He stretched the kinks out of his back, mopped his brow with a handkerchief, and then slapped Seymour on the back. "We did it—step one, that is."

Sweat glistened on Seymour's face, and his broad smile showed yellowed teeth. "That's where everything starts."

"Let's get to the house for something cool to drink and a bite to eat, and then we can start working on the water situation."

Seymour jumped up on the back of the tractor as Layken started the engine and nosed it toward the barn. The agility of the seventy-year-old continually surprised him.

Repeating what they did yesterday, they stopped outside the house to wash up.

Layken smiled as the fragrance of damp soil in Sara Beth's garden reached his nostrils. She'd been busy, too.

The contrast between the blistering temperature outside and the semi-coolness inside the house brought prickles to the surface of his skin.

Sara Beth looked up from the sink. "I was hoping you might be in soon. The sun is extra brutal today." She motioned toward the icebox. "Got cold tea inside. Help yourselves."

Layken fetched glasses from the cupboard and handed one to Seymour. "I see you found Mom's old watering can."

"Funny thing." She glanced up at him. "I came in to doctor Cuddles and get a drink of water. When I went back out, it was sitting next to the trough. It was like it magically willed itself to be there. Spooked me a little."

Seymour poured tea in first Layken's glass, then his own. "Watering cans can't walk, little girl."

"I know. I think our new friend put it there. Whoever it is wants to help."

"Seems like that might be the case. It's still a little odd that they stay hidden and slink around like some wild animal." Layken sighed when the cool liquid hit the back of his throat.

Sara Beth pulled a tray of meatloaf sandwiches out of the icebox and set them in the middle of the table. "Maybe so. But I don't feel threatened. And it saved me from having to look for a bucket to water my seeds."

"Just be careful," Layken muffled through a mouthful.

"Layken, do you have any lengths of rubber hose?" Seymour asked.

"Only pieces. Mostly what I've found were rotted and brittle."

"Gonna need a pretty decent length to siphon water from the creek."

Sara Beth pulled out a chair and sat between the men. "Why don't you use the water from the well?"

"Not sure that would be a good idea. We need that supply for the house. Wouldn't do to run the well dry."

Sara Beth nodded. "I hate to sound ignorant, but how does water get from the well into the house?"

"Used to have to pump it by hand." Layken washed down a bite with a swallow of tea. "But when they ran electricity out here, Dad bought an electric pump. So far, it's never given any problems."

"Never gave much thought about how it all works." She grinned. "I swear the ground smiled at me when I sprinkled it…like it was saying thank you."

"I've always felt like this place was alive. It's crazy, I know."

She placed a hand on his arm for a brief second. "Not crazy."

He almost involuntarily jerked at her touch. He'd been painfully aware and careful not to touch Sara Beth, but he had to admit her hand was soothing on his sweaty arm. That tiny gesture meant she was relaxing more around him.

No doubt, Seymour's presence had helped.

Once he'd eaten his fill and put his plate in the sink, Layken moved into the living room for paper and pencil. He found it somewhat odd that they'd not spent one evening in that room since Sara Beth arrived. Of course, it was much cooler out on the porch. And they'd each been exhausted at day's end.

Saturday was coming up. He made a mental note to try the radio. Perhaps they could tune in to the Grand Ol' Opry. He'd bet Sara Beth and Seymour would enjoy it, too.

He dropped into his father's favorite chair and balanced the paper on his knee while drawing the blueprint for the water tank as he'd visualized it in his head. It needed to be set between the corner of the house and the water well.

Bits and pieces of conversation drifted in from the kitchen. He paused for a long minute and absorbed the sound. Perhaps being alone was highly overrated.

After he finished his drawing, he called to Sara Beth. "Want I should take a look at Cuddles before we go back out?"

She appeared in the doorway between the living room and kitchen, wiping her hands on her apron. "I'd appreciate it. I'll go get him."

He nodded and strode into the kitchen as Seymour turned from the sink. He held out the drawing. "Here's what I have in mind. Think you can help me build this?"

Seymour squinted at the paper. "Looks doable. I can help."

"Good."

Sara Beth stepped in, holding Cuddles. "He was sleeping. Poor baby is still scared to death."

"Almost getting eaten by an owl for breakfast will do that to you." Layken opened his arms, and she transferred the rabbit to him.

Uncle Seymour peered over his shoulder. "The little fella sure did have a fright."

Layken examined the wounds, petted Cuddles, and handed him back to Sara Beth. "Keep putting the salve on him. Looks like he's already stopped bleeding. That's good."

She carefully tucked the bunny under her arm and stroked his long ears. "Do you think I should cover the wounds to keep dirt out?"

"I think that would be the perfect thing to do." With his hat settled firmly on his head, Layken held open the back door. "Ready, Seymour?"

"Ready."

"Don't know when we'll be back to the house, Sara Beth. Gonna try our best to get water on the peanuts."

"I'm going to work on my sewing for a while. See you tonight."

Layken held her soft gaze for a long moment. He let those words seep into his thirsty soul. When was the last time anyone said they'd be waiting for him? Years.

He broke eye contact and clapped Seymour on the shoulder. "Let's go water."

It took the men a while to locate a piece of hose that was still functional and long enough to reach.

Layken loaded up the barrel and started the tractor. For a brief second, he glimpsed a flash of clothing through the trees at the back of the property. But when he blinked and looked again, nothing was there.

Must be his imagination. And yet, as Sara Beth said, the watering can had mysteriously appeared next to the trough. That was no feat of magic. Someone was watching, and it appeared they had good intentions.

Once they reached the creek, Layken scouted for a place where he could get the tractor close enough to be of any help. When the drum was full of water, it would weigh over five hundred pounds. Even two grown men would struggle to lift it.

The uneven and rocky ground didn't offer much to work with, but Seymour pointed toward a horseshoe-like area where the land gently sloped.

Layken nodded and nosed the tractor into the small spot between two giant oaks, careful not to damage them.

Seymour jumped down, unwound the hose, and put one end into the water. He sucked on the other end. His eyes widened, and he bent over, coughing.

"No tellin' what's inside that hose, Seymour. Let's run a little water through it from both ends."

"Lordy. That was rough." The older man gasped for air and spat on the ground.

Layken slipped off his boots, waded knee-deep into the creek, and submerged the hose. Seymour joined him as they raised first one end, then the other until no more dirt ran out.

"I think that's got it." Layken sloshed back onto the bank. "Hold your end in the water, and I'll try to get it primed, then angle it into the barrel."

Seymour nodded, staying in the creek.

Layken sucked on the end of the hose until a tiny trickle of water hit his mouth. He spit it out and sucked again.

After several tries, water started running through the hose.

He let out a whoop, jumped onto the back of the tractor, and pushed the hose down into the barrel.

While waiting for the drum to fill, he gazed down the creek. A turtle sunned on a log across the way, and the water rippled as a school of fish swam nearby. It had been way too long since he'd sat on the bank and dropped a line. A mess of fresh fish sure would be good.

"Say, do you like to fish?"

A huge grin accompanied the man's answer. "Do birds fly? I love to fish. Been years since I wet a hook. Mr. Williams kept me plenty busy."

"Once we get the watering done, let's see if we can't catch us a mess of catfish. They don't serve fried catfish in the Philippines or in France."

"No, sir. I reckon they don't."

A fish leaped out of the water near where the old man stood.

Seymour took off his hat and slapped at the water. "I see you, boy. I see you."

Layken laughed. "Looks like they're taunting us."

"They know we ain't got a line or a worm, but at least we know they're in here."

"Yep. Caught many of 'em when I was a boy." He jerked around at the sound of snapping twigs. "Who's there? You hear that, Seymour?"

"I heard it. Might be an animal."

"Guess I'm a little jumpy. Someone's out there and on my land."

Seymour turned in the direction of the sound.

They grew quiet but alert.

A fat opossum shuffled from the brush.

"There's the culprit." Layken raised the hose. "We're full. Now, to get it back to the field without losing all of it."

Water dripped from the bottom.

Seymour made his way back to the bank and dropped the hose. "Reckon we can leave it here. We'll be back for more."

"That's for sure. Many times. Think you can drive the tractor? I'd feel better trying to steady the barrel."

Both men took a minute to put on their shoes. "Been a long time, but I can drive it." Seymour climbed onto the seat. "I'll take it slow."

Layken jumped onto the metal bar and spread his legs for more stability. He gripped the edges of the barrel while Seymour slowly let off the clutch and inched forward.

Going forward was excruciatingly slow, but necessary. Only a tiny amount of the water had leaked out by the time they reached the field.

Seymour stopped the tractor. "Now what?"

"Help me get the false bottom pulled out a little, then drive down the rows real slow like."

Both men groaned and grunted as they tried to tip the barrel far enough to slide the makeshift bottom forward to let the water out.

Sweat poured down both their backs.

"Okay. Ease it forward."

Seymour climbed back on the hard seat and let off the clutch.

The barrel rocked precariously, and Layken used his full-body strength to keep it in place. Every muscle screamed in protest.

On the third trip from the creek to the field, Seymour hit a hidden hole. Before Layken could react, he flew off the tractor and hit the hard ground. The barrel full of water landed directly on his chest.

Pain ripped through him, and he let out a primal yelp. He bit his lip until blood escaped in his mouth, and fought for air, pushing against the barrel as water poured out over him.

Seymour jerked the tractor to a stop and jumped down, his eyes wide. "Oh, hell."

He put a booted foot against the barrel and gave it a mighty shove. The drum rolled off a few feet and stopped, spilling the remaining water onto the parched soil.

"Are you all right?" Seymour sputtered, leaning over him, breathing hard.

"Help me up." Layken wheezed.

He took Seymour's offered hand and fought to find footing.

Despite the effort, Layken's knees buckled.

He went down into a suffocating blackness.

CHAPTER 16

Sara Beth came running at the urgency in Uncle Seymour's voice. "Sara Beth, open the door. I need your help. Hurry."

She gasped, and a hand flew to her mouth when she spied an unconscious Layken thrown across the old man's back. "What? Oh, my!" She opened the screen door and pointed to the couch. "There. What happened?"

Out of breath, Uncle Seymour bent over, his hands trembling and resting on his knees once he dropped Layken onto the couch. "Full barrel fell on him. Knocked him clean out. Landed square in the middle of his chest."

She hurried to the kitchen, calling out over her shoulder, "Can you take off his boots while I get some cold water?"

"Sure."

The thud of the boots hitting the wooden floor matched the thud of her heart.

She quickly returned with a bowl of water and pulled the nearest chair next to the couch, then applied a cool compress to Layken's forehead, anxiously watching for signs of returning consciousness. His pale face and the area around his mouth turning blue left no doubt as to the severity of his injuries. The way he wheezed with each breath worried her.

How Uncle Seymour managed to bring him up to the house by himself, she'd never know. For an old man, he was stronger than he looked.

And now, he'd hightailed it on the tractor down to the Grovers' place to get help. Each painful minute ticked by while she waited. Panic seized her at the thought of Layken dying.

He simply couldn't, and that was that. He'd shown her kindness like no other man besides Uncle Seymour ever had.

She dipped the cloth into a bowl of cool water, wrung it out with shaky hands, then laid it back on Layken's forehead.

"Please hurry," she whispered. Where were they?

Finally, the distant hum of a motor reached her ears, and within minutes, the tractor and a car stopped in front of the house.

Sara Beth darted to the door to see Mrs. Grover maneuver herself from behind the wheel of the car.

"Oh, thank God you're here. Please hurry."

Uncle Seymour jumped off the tractor, then reached out to steady Mrs. Grover as she climbed the steps.

The woman slapped his hand away. "I don't need no help. I ain't crippled."

"My apologies, ma'am. No offense."

Sara Beth held the door. "Thank you for coming, Mrs. Grover."

"My Henry's gone to town to fetch Doc Baker." The woman stopped at the sight of Layken stretched out on the couch, wheezing loudly with each breath. "Oh, my Lord. This is not good. He's really hurt."

"Yes, ma'am, he is." Sara Beth wrung her hands. "I've been putting a cold compress on his forehead, but he's not waking up. I'm terrified."

Uncle Seymour put an arm around her shoulders, and she leaned into him, stifling a sob.

Mrs. Grover dropped into the chair Sara Beth had vacated and peered over her glasses at Layken. "I'd bet a nickel a rib's punctured a lung."

Sara Beth gasped. "Is he going to die?"

"Oh no, he won't die. He'll be laid up for a bit, though. No doubt about it." She re-wet the cloth and laid it on Layken's forehead, then glanced up at Sara Beth and Seymour. "Nothing we can do but wait for the doctor. I wouldn't want to make it worse."

"Me either, but I feel so helpless. Surely, there's something that might help."

Mrs. Grover raised her eyebrows. "We can pray. You do know what that is, don't you?"

"Of course." Sara Beth shuddered at the implication. She was a Christian, despite her aversion to the hypocrisy of the church. Why did folks always want to believe the worst about a person?

Just because she read cards didn't mean she wasn't a believer. To her, it was all part of the same. But others simply didn't see it that way.

Oh, how she wished for the comfort and steadiness of her mother's hand.

Mrs. Grover stood and fanned her face with her handkerchief. "I could sure use something cold to drink while we're waiting."

"I'm so sorry. Forgive my manners. A glass of tea?"

"That would be nice."

Sara Beth rushed into the kitchen and returned with two cold glasses in less than a minute. She handed one to Uncle Seymour, who stood in the far corner of the living room, hat in hand, and the other to Mrs. Grover.

She didn't care if the rude woman noticed she served Uncle Seymour first.

Mrs. Grover's Adam's apple bobbed up and down as she drank. How was it even possible to see it beneath the ample folds of skin? Sara Beth tried not to stare.

Layken stirred on the couch and groaned. Sara Beth hurried to his side. "Layken. Layken. Can you hear me?"

His eyelids fluttered for a brief second, then stilled. Each breath grew shallower and more labored. Her heart ached for him.

She glanced at Uncle Seymour, and he gave her a half-hearted smile. "Don't worry. The doc will be here soon."

"I sure do hope so, because Layken seems to be getting worse." She propped a throw pillow under his head. "I wish he'd wake up."

Leaning slightly forward, Mrs. Grover set her glass on the floor. "I remember one time my Henry got hurt. I would've lost my mind if it hadn't been for Layken's sainted folks. Try to think about him getting well."

Murmuring her thanks, Sara Beth repositioned the wet cloth on her husband's head.

Funny how she never thought of him as her husband. But if he died, she'd be a widow and automatic heir to this farm—along with the debt. She swallowed hard.

After an eternity of silence that stretched between them except for Layken's labored breathing, the crunch of tires on the driveway announced the doctor's arrival.

Sara Beth jumped to her feet and flew to the door. "Hurry, Doctor. Please hurry."

The graying doctor with stooped shoulders eased his slight frame out of the car, then reached for his black bag. "Where is the patient?" He stepped onto the porch.

She pointed to the couch, then followed the doctor inside.

Mrs. Grover moved aside. "Thank God you're here, Doc. He's in a bad way."

Doctor Baker nodded, pulled out his stethoscope, and then leaned over the patient. After listening for a minute, he pressed around in different areas on the chest, which elicited loud groans from Layken. "He's got a couple of broken ribs for sure, and one of the ribs has punctured a lung. That's a more critical situation. I can hear air escaping."

"What can you do?" Sara Beth twisted the hem of her apron in her hands.

"I can bind him, but he needs oxygen treatment for a couple of days to let that lung rest and heal."

"How do we get that?" She hated showing her ignorance, but other than her mother's brief illness, Sara Beth had never seen an injured or sick person.

"It will take some time, but I can either transport him to the hospital over in Greenfield or contact them and have them bring out an oxygen bottle or two."

Layken stirred, and his eyes fluttered open. "How'd I get here?" He attempted to move and let out an agonizing yelp. "What happened?"

Sara Beth instinctively laid a hand on his shoulder. "You've been hurt. Don't you remember falling from the tractor?"

He nodded slightly.

The doctor took over. "I'm Dr. Baker. Don't try to move. You'll only make it worse. Son, you've got some broken ribs, and you've punctured a lung. I need to get you to the hospital."

Layken raised a shaky hand to his forehead. "No. No." He tried once more to sit, only to give up the struggle. "Gotta finish watering."

Uncle Seymour stepped forward, crushing his hat in his hands. "Don't you worry none, Mister Layken. I'll get the rest of the field watered. I feel downright awful about what happened. Didn't see that hole."

Sara Beth squared her shoulders and joined him. "It's not your fault, Uncle Seymour." She looked directly at Layken. "I'll help. You have to do what the doctor says. We'll get it done even if it takes a few days."

"Ain't got a few days," Layken muttered.

"Son, you have no choice." Dr. Baker touched his shoulder. "I'll do what I can, but it won't be enough unless you do your part. And that includes strict bed rest and oxygen therapy to help that lung heal, either here or in the hospital."

"No. I can't."

The doctor dropped the stethoscope into his bag. "As I said, you have no choice. Now, I want to give you a shot to help with the pain, but I'd like for you to tell me what you want to do. You can either go to the hospital or stay here, and I can have oxygen delivered."

The frustration showed in Layken's eyes. "This is awful. Don't want a hospital or a shot. You don't understand. I have to work."

"Look. I get it, sir. Really, I do. But I am the doctor. I know what will help you heal quicker so you can get back to work. You need to let me do my job."

"Fine. I'd rather stay here. No hospital."

Even though she'd only known him briefly, Sara Beth recognized his stubborn jaw set and determination in his eyes. "It's okay, Doctor. If you can get the oxygen delivered, Uncle Seymour and I will see that he stays in bed if we have to tie him down."

Layken grumbled under his breath and winced when he shifted on the couch.

Mrs. Grover cleared her throat. "I can bring food if that will help out."

Tears sprang into her eyes as Sara Beth glanced at the woman. Despite her rude demeanor, the woman obviously had a generous heart. "Thank you, Mrs. Grover. That would be a big help."

"Then I'll be on my way and come back in a couple of hours." She lumbered toward the door.

Sara Beth followed her and gave her a brief hug. "Again, thank you for coming and for, well…everything."

Mrs. Grover waved her away. "It's nothin'. What else are neighbors for? I'll pray for him."

When Sara Beth turned back to Layken, she took a deep breath and, at that moment, gained control of her thoughts, emotions, and situation. "Uncle Seymour, can you help the doctor get Layken to his bed?"

"Of course."

Layken raised his hand in protest. "No. Rather stay here on the couch."

She put her hands on her hips. "Are you sure? Your bed would be more private."

"I'm sure."

"Then fine. I'll fetch bed clothes and covers. But you have to promise you'll obey the doctor's orders. I would think your bed would be more comfortable."

"Don't need comfort. I have to see what's going on—stay involved."

She met his pleading steel-gray eyes. "I understand."

When she returned a few minutes later, the doctor and Uncle Seymour had removed Layken's clothes. He was down to his underwear.

She averted her eyes and handed a pair of frayed cotton pajama bottoms to Uncle Seymour. Then she turned her back and gritted her teeth as Layken cried out in pain. Tears sprang unbidden in her eyes, and she blinked them away.

"Okay, Sara Beth. You can turn around now," Uncle Seymour said quietly.

"I'll bind those ribs," Dr. Baker said. "Then I'm going to give you a shot to help with the pain."

Layken's painful cries, grunts, and groans echoed across the room as the doctor wrapped a tight bandage around his chest.

Finally, he lay back and let out a groan.

The doctor administered the shot, then took his leave, promising to return tomorrow. Someone would be out with oxygen before the day was over.

Sara Beth spread a thin sheet over Layken and placed a timid hand on his brow. "Just rest. Try not to worry. I'll help Uncle Seymour. We'll get water on the peanuts or die trying."

She didn't pull away when he reached for her hand. "Thank you. Please, don't die. Be careful."

"Just a figure of speech. Want I should get Cuddles to keep you company?"

Uncle Seymour chuckled. "Already ahead of you." He handed the rabbit to her.

The makeshift bandage around the bunny's rump contrasted with the bandage around Layken's chest. A slight smile formed despite the traumas the day had brought.

The bottom line was they were all still alive, and both patients would heal in time.

"Now, you two behave." She kissed the bunny's soft head, then tucked him in at Layken's side. "No more injuries."

"No more injuries." Layken's eyes drifted shut.

She stood stock-still, gazing at the small bunny and injured man.

They had to recover. There was no other alternative.

And in the meantime, she'd do whatever it took to keep Layken's efforts from being in vain, even if it meant carrying water by hand to the newly planted seeds.

A strong sense of purpose arose deep inside. She squared her shoulders, clutching her fists at her sides.

She would not let her father win.

CHAPTER 17

Once the sedative took effect and Layken fell asleep, Sara Beth tip-toed into the kitchen with Uncle Seymour following. She leaned against the counter and wiped a shaky hand across her eyes. "How are we going to do this, Uncle Seymour?"

"I'm not sure, baby girl. Not sure."

"We've got to get the seeds watered, but we also can't leave Layken alone. What if he needs something?"

"You have to stay here with him. Let me worry about watering."

"But you can't do it by yourself."

The old man chuckled. "I've found in life that a man can purty much do anything he has to. I'll figure it out."

"I want to help."

"The best help you can give is to take care of Mister Layken, and that's a fact." He rubbed the gray stubble on his chin. "We need him back on his feet as soon as possible. You heard what the doctor said."

She nodded. "I did, and I also know it's going to be hard to keep him down."

They both jumped when someone knocked on the front door.

Sara Beth hurried back into the living room with Uncle Seymour close behind.

Two strangers stood on the front porch. When Sara Beth stepped forward, they jerked their hats off. "You Sara Beth Martin?"

She pushed the screen door open. "I am. What can I do for you?"

A small, wiry man stuck out a calloused hand. "I'm Henry Grover. My wife said you'uns had a bit of bad luck today."

"Oh my goodness, yes." She shook his hand.

"I'm John Blackhorn." The taller man stepped forward. "I live on the other side of Henry. Heard about the accident. We came to help."

Sara Beth stifled a gasp. Did people really do that? She'd never seen it happen in town. Maybe things worked differently in the country.

Henry Grover cleared his throat and glanced at Seymour. "Gladys said you needed to get water on the seeds. It's way too late in the year to plant, but I understand your circumstances aren't normal."

"Please come in." Sara Beth held the door wide, but the men remained rooted to the porch. She pointed to Uncle Seymour. "This is our friend, Seymour King. He's been helping Layken with the planting."

Uncle Seymour stepped up to the door and stuck out his hand. "Sure do appreciate the offer. Was trying to haul water from the creek when things went sideways."

"We can work 'til dark. Gladys said she'd be bringin' up supper."

Sara Beth struggled to speak, blinking away unbidden tears. "You have no idea how much we appreciate your kindness." She glanced at Uncle Seymour to see his rheumy eyes misting.

"Let me show you what we was doin'. Maybe you fellas will have a better idea." Uncle Seymour nodded to Sara Beth, then pointed toward the tractor.

Sara Beth stood on the front porch listening to the men converse about how to get the most water to the field in the shortest amount of time. While she couldn't make out everything they said, it became apparent that they had a plan. Seymour cranked up the tractor, and the two men hopped on either side. She watched until they disappeared, still in shock over the show of kindness from strangers.

Her heart and spirits lifted, and she went back inside to check on her patient.

Satisfied he was sleeping comfortably, as was Cuddles, she moved to the sewing machine, determined to finish making the pants she desperately needed for farm work.

While Layken recovered, she would have to help Uncle Seymour with the daily chores. So, the pants were a necessity. Plus, doing a familiar task was the best way she knew to calm her nerves and help her focus.

An hour later, the sound of a truck approaching got her to her feet.

Once it pulled to a stop, a man in a white uniform got out and then unloaded a large tank. "Got an oxygen delivery for Layken Martin."

She opened the door. "Come on in." She pointed to the sleeping Layken. "It's for him."

"Thank you, ma'am." He set the heavy tank on the floor next to the couch. "Know how to use it?"

She shook her head. "Never saw one before."

"It's pretty simple." The man opened a small box and pulled out a clear mask with plastic tubing. "This mask goes over his nose and mouth. The tube attaches to this valve." He pointed to a brass valve sticking out on the top of the tank. "Once you've attached it, turn this handle to start the oxygen flow."

Layken stirred, opened his eyes, and slurred, "Sara Beth."

"Yes. I'm here." She moved closer. "This man brought your oxygen and was showing me how to use it. It's going to help your lung heal quicker."

"Need to use the bathroom."

Sara Beth panicked. Oh, dear. She hadn't thought of that.

"Hang on," the delivery man said. "I've got something in the truck that'll help."

She couldn't imagine what he would get, but he was only gone for a minute, then came bounding back inside carrying a clear plastic jug with a lid. "Here. It's a hospital urinal."

Sara Beth cleared her throat. "I think I better step into the other room." She picked up Cuddles.

"Hey, where you goin' with my partner?" Layken forced a grin.

"Not far. Tend to business, and I'll bring him back." She smiled at the delivery man. "And we can finish with the rest of your instructions afterward."

"You bet."

She hurried into her bedroom and took a deep breath. This nursing job was going to be more challenging than she thought. She wished he'd have agreed to go to his bedroom. That would make it more private.

"Stubborn man." She stroked Cuddles' head. "Might as well change your bandage while we wait."

The rabbit twitched his ears and nose and squirmed. "Oh, right. You need to potty, too."

She chewed her fingernails as she tried to figure out how to get past Layken and out the back door without intruding on his privacy.

Finally, she grabbed a magazine she'd been reading, held it to the side of her face where it blocked her vision, and sprinted across the living room.

"Whew!" She set Cuddles down outside the back door and waited for him to finish his business.

She scanned the area, looking for any sign of Uncle Seymour and his two helpers. The chugging of the tractor engine drifted across the way, and soon, it came into sight with the two wagons hooked onto the back of it. Each wagon held a smaller barrel with hoses hung over the side.

Uncle Seymour waved to her.

It looked as if they'd figured out a less dangerous watering method.

Once Cuddles finished, she went back into the kitchen. Thank goodness she'd left the salve sitting on the cabinet. A clean dishtowel would serve as a makeshift bandage for her rabbit.

Bits and pieces of conversation drifted in from the living room. Layken's words were mostly slurred, still under the effects of the pain shot.

She finished applying a new dressing to Cuddles. Pausing at the doorway separating the living room from the kitchen, she asked timidly, "Is it okay to come in?"

"Almost," the man in white said.

She really should ask his name.

A couple of minutes passed before he called out. "All clear."

With Cuddles under her arm, she eased back into the room, keeping her eyes off the plastic jug. She'd empty it once their visitor left.

"I've got another delivery to make, so let me finish showing you how to use this." The man pointed to the tank.

Sara Beth put Cuddles on the sofa with Layken.

She paid close attention while he placed the mask on Layken's face and tightened the straps around his head. He then handed the tubing to Sara Beth. "You attach it."

She fitted the tubing onto the nozzle until it was fully connected. "Okay. Now what?"

"See that black mark here on the tank?"

She nodded.

"Turn the lever to that mark. No farther."

Following his instructions, a hiss of air flowed through the tubing to the mask. "Like that?"

"It's that simple. This tank will last until I come back tomorrow to switch it out."

Layken mumbled something indecipherable behind the mask. No doubt he was protesting. Well, too bad.

"Thank you." Sara Beth offered her hand. "And what's your name? I need something to call you besides the man in white."

"Ned. Ned Sanders, Mrs. Martin. I'll see you tomorrow." He waved and headed out the door. "Oh yeah, one more thing. Don't smoke around this tank. It could blow up."

"Thanks, Ned, and no problem. We don't smoke." She waved.

Layken motioned to her.

"Yes?"

He lifted the mask slightly. "This is god-awful."

She grinned. "I suppose it is, but you'll have to live with it 'til the doctor says different. You want to heal faster, don't you?"

He nodded.

"Me too. Can I get you anything?"

"Water."

"Sure thing."

She decided on a mason jar with a lid, filled it, and brought it back. Then she scooted the coffee table close to the couch and set the jar on it.

He slid the mask up, reached for the jar, and took a sip. "That's good."

"You hurting anywhere?"

"Everywhere and nowhere. It doesn't hurt to move my head. Everything else is iffy. Feels like I've been in the sauce."

His eyes closed as he lowered the mask and sank back against the pillow.

She found the soft hiss of the oxygen oddly soothing.

After she tucked Cuddles in next to him, satisfied they'd drifted off to sleep, she emptied the urinal and returned it to a place he could easily reach.

She put the final stitches in her pants and took them to the bedroom to try them on.

As she stared at her reflection in the mirror, an older, more mature version of herself gazed back. Had she really only been here for a matter of days?

So much had happened. She'd taken on greater responsibility than she'd ever imagined possible.

But more than anything else, she had earned respect, been given purpose, and gained value.

Turning in a full circle, she noted with satisfaction that the newly sewn pants and cotton blouse accentuated her curves. The reflection of a woman capable of solving problems stared back at her.

Sucking in a deep breath, she went to check on her patient.

She'd never seen him without a shirt. A long scar ran along his left shoulder, and she fought the urge to touch it.

He'd suffered before. She'd read horror stories about what war could do to men.

She knew so little about her husband.

Maybe one day, he'd share his deepest, darkest secrets with her.

It shocked her to realize how much she'd like that.

But would she be able to return that kind of openness?

CHAPTER 18

With no concept of time or knowing how long he'd been asleep, Layken forced his eyes open and blinked several times until his vision cleared. His head pounded, and undoubtedly, his mouth was stuffed with cotton. He shoved the aggravating oxygen mask off his face.

A dim light shone from a nearby lamp, and voices drifted through the open screen door.

He raised his head and spied the jar of water Sara Beth had left. Searing pain shot through his chest as he tried to sit. Dammit! He desperately needed water. He ran a dry tongue over his parched lips, then half-rolled to where he could reach the water. Even tepid, it brought relief.

The entire scenario came flashing back.

He was falling. Something extremely heavy crushed his chest, and water spilled everywhere. Oh yes. He remembered. They were trying to water the peanuts.

Agony washed over him. He'd ruined everything. The peanuts wouldn't grow without water. Precious money wasted. He could visualize Homer Williams' triumphant sneer when he came to take the land.

He had to get busy.

Forcing back a yelp, he swung his legs over and pushed up into a sitting position. The room spun, and he tried to draw in a deep breath, only to find it impossible. Then, with every ounce of energy he had, he got to his feet.

He stood spraddle-legged and focused on the screen door until nausea and dizziness abated. Glancing down at his feet, he wondered for a brief second where he might find his boots.

Instead of searching, he shuffled toward the voices.

"Sara Beth. Seymour." He pushed the door open.

Sara Beth jumped from the porch swing with Cuddles under her arm. "Layken Martin. What do you think you are doing?"

"Lookin' for my boots. Gotta get busy."

She reached him in two strides, Uncle Seymour a short step behind. "You'll do no such thing. Besides…" She swung her right arm wide. "It's dark. You can't work in the dark."

Uncle Seymour offered an arm for support. "It's all taken care of, Mister Layken. Come on back inside, and we'll tell you everything."

Layken hated to accept the old man's help, but his strength was waning quicker than he'd thought possible, and he leaned on Seymour's strong arm. "What's happened? What have I missed? How long have I been out?"

He couldn't stifle the groan that escaped when he sank back onto the couch.

Sara Beth set Cuddles on the end of the couch and fluffed Layken's pillow. "You don't remember what happened?"

"I remember. Don't like it none."

"I understand, but lay back down, please. You've got to give yourself at least a couple of days to rest. Are you hungry?"

"Hadn't thought about it. Suppose I could eat something." He leaned against the back of the couch but remained sitting and waved the oxygen mask away when she attempted to put it back on. "Fill me in, Seymour."

"Two men came—neighbors. They helped me haul water up 'til dark. Then Mrs. Grover brought supper and fed us."

Layken ran a hand through his thick brown hair, leaving ends sticking up in all directions. "Neighbors, you say? Did you get all of it watered?"

"Not all, but pert near. I can easy finish by myself in the morning."

"But that's not the end. They'll have to be watered often if they are to grow." He groaned when he tried to sit up straighter.

Sara Beth strode from the kitchen carrying a tray. "We know. And I'll help Uncle Seymour with it until you're back on your feet." She set the tray on his lap. "Mrs. Grover made a pot roast with all the trimmings."

Layken fought against the lump that threatened to block his throat. Not only had neighbors stopped their lives to step up and help, but Sara Beth and Seymour offered to do whatever it took to keep it all going.

He cleared his throat. "I don't know what to say."

Sara Beth dropped into a nearby chair while Uncle Seymour leaned against the wall.

"Nothin' to say." The old man stuck his hands in his overall pockets. "We're all in this together."

"Besides," Sara Beth added, "Our future depends on your success as much as yours."

Layken took a bite of the tender roast and savored the spices and juices that reminded him of Sunday suppers from long ago. "I'm indebted to you both and the neighbors." More than he could put into words.

"It's what decent people do when there's trouble." Sara Beth leaned forward and smoothed a wrinkle out of her new pants. "My guess is we'll have the chance to help them out at some point." She met his steady gaze. "And, of course, we will."

He nodded. "I look forward to that day." He pointed to the oxygen. "I'll keep that on through the night, but I'm not staying tied to this couch for days on end. That's not who I am. I've been hurt worse than this before."

He caught the glance between Sara Beth and Seymour.

"What?"

Sara Beth grinned. "I told Uncle Seymour it would be a big job keeping you down."

"You can't blame me. Everything hinges on this first crop. If it fails…" He swallowed hard and broke apart a piece of homemade bread, then dipped it into the roast juice. "That woman may be cantankerous, but she sure knows how to cook."

Seymour chuckled. "And she baked a chocolate cake."

"She even brought some fresh carrots from her garden for Cuddles." Sara Beth reached for the rabbit and stroked his head.

"I'll be damned. I guess under that harsh exterior, she has a heart, after all." He took another bite. "How did you haul the water, Seymour?"

"We got the two wagons, loaded them with smaller barrels, and tied the wagons behind the tractor. Hauled it that way. Lots safer, and we got a lot done with three of us."

Layken nodded. "We'll stick with that method. Ain't takin' no more chances."

"I'm awful sorry about what happened, sir." Seymour rubbed his chin. "Shoulda' watched where I was goin' better."

"Not your fault. We were foolhardy to try and balance a heavy load with nothing to secure it."

Uncle Seymour shuffled his feet. "Still."

"Still nothing." Sara Beth shook her finger at her friend. "Nobody's to blame. Accidents happen."

Layken settled his gaze on her soft face. "You been doctoring me?"

She blushed and looked away. "Just keeping an eye on you."

"You're wearing pants." And he couldn't help noticing how they accented her curves that had been hidden behind her dresses.

Her blush deepened. "I needed pants for work. Made 'em on your mom's sewing machine."

Layken admired her initiative. She continued to surprise him, not only with how she'd jumped in with both feet to learn about farm work, but also with her easy attitude about it all. "Good idea. Always wondered how women could work in dresses."

"Me too. My father would have a hissy fit if he saw me wearing pants."

"That's something you'll never have to worry about. He ain't welcome here." He took another bite of the roast. How long would it take for her to overcome the oppression Homer Williams had imposed? Damn the man!

"I know." She leaned back. "Need anything else?"

"Some new ribs would be nice."

He liked the way her eyes crinkled at the corners when she smiled. "I meant more food."

"Maybe a piece of that chocolate cake Seymour bragged about."

"Let me get it, Sara Beth." Seymour pushed away from the wall.

Layken passed his empty plate to Sara Beth, and her small hand lightly brushed his. "You didn't have to make the kind of effort you have since you've been here. I want you to know I see and appreciate it."

She took the plate, passed it to Seymour as he walked to the kitchen, and glanced away. "What else am I going to do? I want to help. Always did. Never got much chance to be more than a maid."

"I hope you know you are much more than that here." A sudden desire to make her feel valued washed over him. "You've gone above and beyond to learn things, and you're a hard worker. That means a lot."

Sara Beth cleared her throat as her face turned a deep shade of red. "Thanks for noticing." She pointed to the radio. "Think we might try it?"

"Sure. Plug it in first, then flip on the power button. It takes a few minutes for the tubes to warm up."

When she jumped up from the chair and bounded toward the radio, her refreshing, childlike enthusiasm was like a soothing balm to his soul. Somewhere deep in the recesses of his mind, he vaguely remembered that feeling, but it had long been dead and buried.

She followed his instructions, and soon, the tubes hummed as they warmed, followed by static. "Now what?"

"Turn the dial and see if you can tune anything in."

The static grew louder as she turned the dial.

Uncle Seymour returned with a slice of rich chocolate cake for Layken and one for himself. The old man grinned. "Couldn't let you eat alone."

"I like the way you think."

The radio squawked, and Sara Beth squealed as a man's voice came in loud and clear. "Howdy, folks. You're listening to WLS 870 from the great city of Chicago on your AM dial. This is your ol' friend, Bill, the late-night rambler, and I've got a treat coming up for you. But first, a word from the biggest retail store in the world."

An ad for Sears & Roebuck played.

Sara Beth turned to Layken. "This is so exciting. Shall I leave it here and see what the treat is?"

"It's your choice." Layken took a mouthful of the cake and rolled his eyes as the rich, moist chocolate hit his tongue.

Sara Beth settled onto the floor in front of the radio.

Seymour pulled up a chair and devoured his piece of cake. "Can't rightly say as I've ever listened to a radio before. Mr. Williams wouldn't allow it."

"Said it was a devil box." Sara Beth pulled her knees up under her chin.

"I can assure you both it's nothing more than entertainment."

The advertisement ended, and a Perry Como song played. Sara Beth swayed to the music while Uncle Seymour sat glued to one spot.

They listened as the late-night rambler played one song after another. The rapture on Sara Beth's face and the wonderment in Seymour's eyes said it all.

It struck him how far removed from the real world this little spot in Missouri was. Yet, in many ways, he saw it as a blessing.

During his time in the military, he'd seen more of the world's ugliness than he cared to and hoped never to see again.

After a time, the signal faded, and even though Sara Beth turned the dial in every direction, only static came through the speaker. Finally, she turned it off. "That was amazing. So many instruments and beautiful voices."

"It's here anytime you want it." Layken swung his legs onto the couch with a stifled groan and gingerly lay on the pillow. "There's something I'd like to ask of you, Sara Beth."

She turned her doe eyes toward him. "Of course. Whatever you need."

"It's an imposition, but could I ask you to get your cards out and see what they say about this new turn of events?" Surprise registered in her widened gaze. "I mean, with the accident and all."

"I'm shocked that you'd ask. You sure?"

He nodded. "Seymour believes you have a gift. That's good enough for me."

Seymour gathered the empty plates. "She does have the gift, sir. I've seen it in action more than once." He took the dishes into the kitchen.

"Leave the dishes in the sink, Uncle Seymour. I'll tend to them. Gotta put out some roast for our little hungry friend before I go to bed, anyway." Sara Beth tucked Cuddles in next to Layken and he draped an arm around the bunny.

He loved her big heart and willingness to share with the less fortunate. If he was looking for a wife, which he wasn't, he'd look for someone exactly like Sara Beth.

She hurried down the hallway and returned with the cards wrapped in a brightly colored silk cloth.

After clearing off the coffee table, Sara Beth sat cross-legged on the floor, and then shuffled the worn cards. "I'll do a five-card pull. That's common when a specific question involves the immediate future." Her eyes took on a soft glow as she touched the cards.

"Whatever you think. I'm daring to hope for a positive outcome to all of this." Layken readjusted his legs.

Once she shuffled, she separated the cards into three stacks. "I need you to pick up the cards and make sure your question is firmly set in your mind."

Following her instructions, he concentrated hard, then picked up each stack and put them on top of each other. "Like this?"

She nodded.

The first card she laid face-up was The Tower. "This card represents something that's already happened. In this case, I'd say it's your accident."

Layken peered curiously at the card depicting a burning and falling tower with people running away in all directions. "Sure looks like something bad."

She laid out the following three cards. "These cards represent a solution to the problem. See, there is the Ten of Wands, Seven of Wands, and the Four of Swords."

"What does that mean?"

Without glancing up, she touched each card. "The Ten of Wands represents a heavy burden and hard work. The Seven of Wands is about facing challenges with perseverance, and the Four of Swords indicates rest, relaxation, and recuperation."

Layken contemplated the images on the cards. Sara Beth's explanations made sense and certainly fit the situation, although he hated the thought of having to rest and recuperate. "What else?"

She turned over the last card. "This is the outcome card. It shows how everything will work out. The Magician is in the Major Arcana of the tarot, which means it is a more overarching theme than the present time. It affects your overall life, and it's a great outcome."

"How so?"

"The Magician holds all the resources and power to create anything he wants." She glanced up. "That's you."

"Don't feel much like a magician right now. Feel more like a fool."

"That's because you've got to give your body time to heal." She tapped the Four of Swords card. "Then you can work your magic."

Uncle Seymour returned from the kitchen, wiping his hands on his pants. He peered at the cards. "Well, what do you think, Mister Layken? Does she know what she's doing or what?"

Layken formed a lazy grin, followed by a yawn. "She most certainly does." He touched each card. "Thank you for giving me hope."

"You're welcome." Sara Beth stood and scooped up the cards. "And now it's time for rest. And you're wearing that oxygen mask, like it or not."

"Fine. But first, a sip of water. That stuff dries my mouth out something fierce." She passed him the jar of water, and he took a sip. Then he lay still while she slipped the oxygen mask on his face. The gentle touch of her fingers against his face brought soothing comfort.

He'd always found it difficult to accept help from anyone, but at this point, what choice did he have?

Maybe there was still hope.

Hope to make some magic.

Hope to build a future.

And even after such a short time of being together, he could no longer visualize a future without Sara Beth and Seymour.

They'd become his family.

CHAPTER 19

Sara Beth arose early the following day before the sun came up. Her mind focused on Layken, she was eager to see how he made it through the first night.

She hurriedly dressed in her new pants and tiptoed into the living room.

Layken lay sprawled half on the couch, the oxygen mask askew on his face, blowing onto his closed eyes. She covered her mouth to stifle a giggle.

The urinal was full. Before daring to wake him, she rushed to the bathroom to empty it.

As soon as she returned, she gently slipped the oxygen mask off and turned the handle to the off position.

Cuddles had retreated to a nearby rug sometime in the night and lay curled up, his tiny face tucked under one leg. A pang of guilt ran through her. It was the first night she'd spent without the bunny. But Layken had seemed to need him more.

She studied Layken's odd angle. Should she try to put him back on the couch? Maybe it would be better to wait for Seymour. Despite her pleas for him to sleep in the house last night, the old man had refused, saying he'd be more comfortable in his quarters.

Deciding to leave Layken as he was for now, she picked up Cuddles and went into the kitchen to start a pot of coffee boiling.

A loud groan sent her flying back into the living room.

Layken struggled to sit up and slipped farther off the couch onto the floor.

"Wait. Let me help you." She put Cuddles down and slid under his armpits.

"I'm too heavy. Don't want to hurt you. I can do it. Give me a minute."

"You are as stubborn as a Missouri mule." But she backed away.

Once seated on the couch, he raked a hand through his hair. "Is it morning?"

"Almost. Coffee's boiling."

"Thank heavens."

"Rough night?"

"Might say so. But today, I'm going to get up and move around. I cannot stay here while the rest of you do all the work."

"That wasn't what the doctor said," she admonished. "But I understand."

He let out a loud groan, pushed to standing, and wobbled for a second until he gained his footing. "I need a good washing and some clean clothes." With each step an effort, he shuffled down the hallway to the bathroom.

A part of her longed to help him, but the practical part of her screamed no. He'd manage. He was certainly no weakling.

Satisfied he would be okay on his own, she picked up Cuddles and unlocked the back door.

Even in the dim early morning light, she could see that her food offering was gone. She sniffed the air. It smelled of wet dirt, as if it had come a rain. Only it hadn't. Or had it rained, and she missed it?

She set Cuddles down to tend to his business and took a few steps toward her garden while keeping a sharp eye on the bunny.

There was no mistaking. It had recently been watered, while the ground around it was dry.

Gazing across the yard to the trees, she wished the hungry stranger would show himself so she could give a proper thank you.

As soon as possible, she would make it a point to search the forest and see if she could find any signs of a campsite. It had to be somewhere nearby.

Cuddles hopped over to her, and she picked him up as Uncle Seymour emerged from the barn, the cat rubbing around his legs.

"Looks like you've made a friend, Uncle Seymour." She then pointed to the garden. "Did you water last night?"

Uncle Seymour hitched up his suspenders. "Darned cat has taken to sleeping on the foot of my bed. Guess it ain't as wild as we thought. I didn't do anything last night but sleep. Was plumb tuckered out."

"Someone watered during the night, and I suspect our elusive hungry visitor."

"I'll be. Ain't that somethin'?" Uncle Seymour shooed the cat away and joined her. "It's surely been watered in the last little while. How's Mister Layken?"

"He's awake and in the bathroom. A more stubborn man I've never met."

Uncle Seymour chuckled. "Reckon he's got a lot on his mind. He know about this?" He pointed to the wet soil.

"Haven't had a chance to tell him yet. I came out to let Cuddles go to the bathroom. Coffee's boiling."

"Then let's get this day started."

She cast another hopeful glance over her shoulder before picking up the empty dish from the back porch and opening the screen door.

"I'll feed the chickens and gather the eggs for you this morning," Uncle Seymour said. "Then I'll be on in."

"Thank you." She paused, holding the door half open. "Between you and our hungry stranger, I'm going to get spoiled."

"That wouldn't be a bad thing, little girl." Uncle Seymour dipped a scoop into the feed bin and stepped into the chicken coop.

Sara Beth hurried into the kitchen and, after setting Cuddles down with a carrot to munch on, reached for the flour and eggs.

She couldn't get past the nagging thought of the mysterious visitor. Whoever it was obviously wanted to be helpful.

Maybe they were like the wild cat in the barn, just needing someone to show kindness. A grin formed as she thought about the cat jumping onto Uncle Seymour's bed.

By the time the old man joined her, she had breakfast well underway. She took the basket of eggs from him. "Would you mind checking on Layken for me? I wouldn't want to catch him in a compromising situation."

He chuckled. "I'll check on him." He made his way down the hall with stooped shoulders and a slight limp. Sara Beth couldn't help but wonder if he'd overdone it yesterday. He certainly wasn't getting any younger, and it had been a long hard day.

When Seymour returned, Layken was with him, holding a yellow metal tin in one hand.

She spared Layken a glance, pulled out a chair for him, and then poured coffee. "You're lookin' a little pale."

"That small amount of effort tired me, but I'll be damned if I'm going to lay around the house all day while you and Seymour work." He accepted the steaming cup and rattled the tin. "Found some Bayer aspirin in the medicine cabinet."

"That should help with the pain." Sara Beth held the coffeepot in her hand. "Someone watered the garden for me during the night."

Layken raised his eyebrows. "You don't say."

"It has to be our hungry visitor. I have to wonder if he watches the house and knows about the troubles we had yesterday."

"Whatever the case, they obviously want to repay you for your kindness." Layken held a protective arm over his ribs.

"He has to be somewhere nearby. I want to search the area for a campsite." She stirred gravy. "But not until you're up and around good. I can help Uncle Seymour finish watering the peanuts today."

"No need in that. I can drive the tractor."

Uncle Seymour cleared his throat and lifted his eyebrows.

Sara Beth put her hands on her hips. "You're going to overdo it and set back your healing, Layken Martin. I'm perfectly capable of helping."

"I know you are, and I appreciate it, but there's no reason I can't sit on the tractor seat as well as I can sit on the couch."

"What will I tell Ned when he comes with a new oxygen bottle?"

"He can leave it. I promise I'll use it during the night. And I'm taking my bed back, so have him put the bottle back there."

"You sure?"

"Look. I promise, if I get to hurting too bad or tire out, I'll come to the house." He glanced at Seymour. "Trust me, both of you. I've been hurt worse than this before."

"Hmph." Sara Beth turned to the stove, mumbling, "Stubborn man."

Uncle Seymour raised his cup. "I'll keep a close eye on him, Sara Beth."

"Fine. Then, once I'm finished with my chores, I'm going to look for our elusive visitor and pick some berries for a pie." She wiped her hands on her apron.

Layken nodded. "Be careful. Copperheads like to hide under berry bushes this time of year to stay cool."

Sara Beth started laughing. "Aren't we a fine lot? Each of us worrying about the other. I'll be watchful."

"And if you find that campsite, don't take any risks." Uncle Seymour chuckled, leaned back in his chair, and hooked his thumbs in his suspenders. "Wouldn't want anything to happen to our chief cook."

"Me either. Maybe I'll consult the cards before I go. If there's any warning, I won't."

"Good idea." Layken ran a finger around the rim of his coffee cup. "That reading you did last night gave me hope."

"The cards never lie." She refilled both coffee cups.

Uncle Seymour nodded. "Never do."

"I keep thinking about that magician card. I want to be like that, create some magic here, on this old place."

Sara Beth set plates on the table and caught his gaze. "You will, Layken. The way I see it, Uncle Seymour and myself are part of your resources."

"And, I couldn't have chosen any two better people."

Conversation lagged as they ate their breakfast.

By the time they finished, the sun had peeked over the horizon.

Sara Beth cleared away the dishes while the two men headed out to the barn. She couldn't help but notice how Layken rolled his shoulders forward slightly. She guessed it was to help take pressure off the aching ribs.

While she'd never had an injury like it, she could well imagine how painful it must be.

Once her chores inside the house were done, she retrieved her tarot cards and pulled three. None of them gave any warning. The Three of Cups, Three of Pentacles, and Three of Wands indicated friendship, teamwork, and progress. And she had a particular affinity with the number three.

Satisfied, she grabbed a pail, secured Cuddles in a sling with her apron, and headed toward the woods as the sun fully rose.

Alert for any sounds, she stepped lightly to avoid disturbing any of the wildlife. A young buck raised his head for an instant, then returned to peacefully grazing. A family of raccoons scuttled through the underbrush, and the metallic chirp from a cardinal split the air while rustling tree leaves as it flew. She took a deep breath and paused to absorb the wild, untamed beauty.

It was easy to see why Layken was willing to fight so hard to save this place.

A few yards ahead, she spotted a group of brambles laden with reddish-green gooseberries. Careful to avoid the prickly thorns on the bush, she plucked the fruit. Each berry landed with a slight thump in the bottom of the pail.

She liked the idea of combining gooseberries and blackberries for her pie. Or maybe she'd make it into a cobbler. Once she had a third of the bucket filled, she moved onward toward the creek.

Careful to take note of her path, she moved deeper into the dense woods.

After a few minutes of traipsing through the underbrush, her nose twitched. Smoke! She scanned the area for the source.

Her heart sped up at the thought of finding their elusive visitor.

A tiny wisp of smoke rose from a stand of trees a hundred feet to her left. She slowed her steps, taking care not to snap a twig or shuffle a leaf.

With the tiny campfire almost in sight, she ducked behind a large oak and peeked around.

Bent over the small fire, a young boy who couldn't be a day over ten or twelve, of slight build with a mop of unruly black curls, stirred the coals.

She crouched and waited. Surely, the rest of the camping party would show.

A movement in the tree above the boy caught her eye, and she sucked in a surprised gasp. A crudely built treehouse perched among the branches. It would be easy to miss unless one was explicitly looking upward.

What to do?

The last thing she wanted was to frighten the young boy. She couldn't imagine him living out here all alone.

After watching for a few minutes, she took a deep breath and made her move. Standing slowly, she called out. "Hello."

The boy jumped to his feet and shimmied up the tree like a monkey.

"Sorry. I didn't mean to scare you." She stared up, only to see frightened, wide brown eyes peeking through the leaves.

She took Cuddles from the makeshift sling and stroked his head. "This is my pet rabbit, Cuddles. Won't you come down and meet him?"

The boy stirred but didn't respond.

"Look. I know you're the one who watered my garden last night. I want to thank you properly."

Still no response.

"I hope you've been enjoying the food I left for you. Do you have a name?" She drew closer to the tree. "Please come down and talk to me."

The boy stirred again.

"My name is Sara Beth. What's yours?"

"Tab," came a muffled reply.

She smiled up at him. "Tab. That's a nice name. It would make me happy if you'd come down so we could visit. I promise I'm not here to hurt you. I'll let you hold Cuddles."

She sat cross-legged by the small fire with Cuddles on her lap and waited.

Patience came easy. Perhaps it had been ingrained in her from the years of living with her overbearing father.

At any rate, it paid off now.

The rustling of leaves told her Tab was coming down.

CHAPTER 20

Sara Beth sat still, barely breathing, as Tab cautiously made his way down the tree trunk, sending a cascade of leaves below. A million questions flew through her mind.

How old was he? Why was he living in the woods alone? Where was his family?

Instinct told her to ease into the asking.

If she gave him half a reason, he'd bolt like a wild animal.

While she waited, she took in the makeshift camp. A faded pair of pants and a shirt hung on a tree limb. Mismatched pieces of wood and tin that made up the disjointed tree house told her he'd scavenged for what he needed to build it.

No doubt he'd found some of these things on Layken's abandoned farm. She wondered for a minute why he hadn't squatted in the farmhouse. But maybe he hadn't been here all that long. Or maybe he had a deep fear of being closed in. She'd bet on the latter.

She petted Cuddles and hummed an ancient tune.

Tab reached the ground, pushed back his mop of curls, and dug the toe of his worn shoe into the dirt.

"Here." She held out Cuddles. "Sit with me."

The boy took the bunny in his arms and dropped to the ground on his knees.

"You know you should be careful building campfires. It's so terribly dry." She kept her voice soft and gaze unfocused on his face.

"I know. I'm not stupid." Tab huffed and settled back on his haunches.

"Of course, you're not. Were you going to cook something?"

He pointed toward a rusty pot. "Caught a fish."

"I see. Thank you for watering my garden."

"You needed help." He rubbed the bunny's velvet ears and eyed the bandaged area. "What happened to your rabbit?"

"An owl almost had him for breakfast. And you're right. I did need help. I truly appreciate it." She motioned toward the pail on the ground next to her. "I'm picking berries to make a cobbler. So far, all I've found is gooseberries." While she knew where the blackberries grew, she wanted to engage the boy's help.

Tab licked his cracked lips. "I know where a bunch of blackberries are."

She smiled and leaned forward. "Oh good! Will you show me?"

He jerked a nod and wiped his nose with a dirty hand.

From the scratches on his arms, he'd been fighting with the under-brush. A couple of larger wounds were scabbed over, and Sara Beth wanted more than anything to clean him up and doctor him. Instead of suggesting it, she focused on the small fire. "Would you like for me to cook your fish?"

"Nah. I can do it later."

The boy sized her up, no doubt trying to decide if he could trust her. She flashed a wide smile, wishing she could hug the hurt out of him. "You're pretty self-sufficient, aren't you?"

"Yep." He raised his chin and squared his skinny shoulders. "What happened to the man?"

That question confirmed her suspicions that he'd been watching. "You mean the man who owns the farm where I live? His name is Layken. He fell off the tractor. A big barrel of water fell on top of him and broke some ribs. But he'll be okay."

"That must've hurt."

"Most definitely. You out here all by yourself?"

The wary glance warned her to slow down with the questions.

"What if I am?"

"No reason. Can't help wondering why a boy would be living in the woods alone. You don't have to tell me." Pride showed in his dark eyes. A boy having to be a man.

He continued to stroke the rabbit's soft fur with his dirty hands. "I like your bunny."

"He's been my best friend for a long time."

The boy sniffled. "Don't have any friends."

"Yes, you do. I could be your friend, and Cuddles loves everyone."

Tab pushed to his feet, his mouth set in a thin line. "I can show you the blackberries."

"We better put out this fire first. Wouldn't want the woods to go up in flames."

Sara Beth stood, and together, they kicked loose dirt onto the fire.

She shook her head when he handed Cuddles back to her. "You hold him."

As he made his way through the thick underbrush toward Sinking Creek, she followed, careful to avoid thorny bushes and brambles.

A few yards ahead, he stopped and pointed. "Don't touch that. It's poison ivy."

Once more, she realized how little she knew about country life. "I'm glad you showed me. I've never noticed it before."

Tab took on a superior air. "There's poison oak around here, too. I know 'em all."

"What about snakes?"

"I'm not afraid. They mostly run away."

"Just the same, I wouldn't want to run across one." Sara Beth casually returned to her questions. "How long have you been living out here?"

"A while." He looked off into the distance and chewed his cracked bottom lip.

"I think it would get mighty cold in the winter."

He hesitated, as if trying to decide how much to say. "I can manage."

"Tab, stop. I need to rest a minute." She didn't, but wanted a chance to continue the conversation.

He turned toward her. "You okay, lady?"

Pretending to be winded, she put her hands on her knees, the pail hanging loosely on her arm. "My name's Sara Beth, not lady. I need a minute to catch my breath. We almost there?"

He pointed ahead. "Up ahead."

"Where are your folks? Are they out here with you?"

He screwed up his face. "Don't know where they are."

"Forgive me for asking so many questions, but I've never seen a boy as young as you living out in the woods. How old are you?"

"Twelve. Almost grown." He stood straight, as if to add to his height.

"It's none of my business. I'm sure you have your reasons for living out here."

"Yep, I do." He hooked a thumb over his shoulder. "Ready to go?"

"Sure." She straightened.

The blackberry patch was one of the largest she'd ever seen. The boy had obviously explored his surroundings thoroughly. That told her he'd been in the woods for a while. She couldn't help but wonder about his parents. Were they dead? Abusive? She couldn't imagine a mother abandoning her child for any reason.

For now, she'd have to wait for more answers. If she pressed too hard, he'd clam up.

Once she gained his trust, maybe he'd tell her everything.

He helped her pick blackberries, then pointed the way they'd come. "That'll get you home."

"You're not going with me?"

After he handed Cuddles to her, he shook his head. "Got things to do."

"Okay. Will you come around later? There will be food waiting for you."

He nodded.

"And thank you again for helping me water my garden. You're welcome anytime."

His reply was a muffled, "Goodbye, lady," as he stomped away.

She stood rooted to the spot until he disappeared. Well, at least now she knew where to find him. That is, if he didn't abandon his camp and move somewhere else.

Making her way back through the underbrush, she trudged toward home. She had lots to tell Layken and Uncle Seymour.

She hoped Layken wasn't pushing and overdoing it. And she needed to be at the house when Ned arrived with the fresh oxygen bottle.

Layken stifled an anguished groan each time the tractor went over the slightest bump. Dammit to hell! Why did this have to happen at a time when he needed all of his physical strength?

He thought about the full urinal that had been magically emptied when he'd awakened this morning. It embarrassed him that Sara Beth had to tend to it.

Well, from here on, he'd make sure he could take care of himself no matter how much it hurt. She didn't deserve to have to wait on him hand and foot. And yet, she'd willingly done so with no hesitation. The more he learned about his partner, the more he admired her.

He hadn't been lying when he told her and Seymour he'd been hurt worse than this. His shoulder still ached sometimes, where bullet fragments remained. The military doctor had tried to dig them all out but gave up. That had been early in his military career, shortly after they'd sent him to the front lines.

Remembering the tears on his mother's cheeks and the concern in his father's eyes when he was sent home to recover, he regretted the worry he'd caused.

That was on top of everything else they already had to stress over. His father was fighting a losing battle with the crops even way back then.

Maybe all of this hard work now was in vain. Maybe he was destined to lose the land.

But the cards had indicated success. They'd also strongly suggested some recuperation time.

Once they got the full planting of peanuts watered, he'd go to the house. But he refused to sit idle while Seymour and Sara Beth worked. That wasn't in his makeup.

He remembered the buckets of paint remnants Seymour hauled in his wagon when he'd arrived. If nothing else, he could paint. God knows there was plenty that needed a fresh coat.

Seymour yelled up at him as he siphoned creek water into the barrel. "This one oughtta finish it."

Layken nodded with relief.

But this was only day one.

They'd have to haul water at least every other day. The size of the task overwhelmed him. He cast a hopeful glance up at the clear blue sky. They needed rain in a bad way.

But chances of that were slim in July.

Still, a man could hope.

When they finished with the last load of water, the sun had risen high, scorching the earth and everything it touched. Sweat dripped down his back, soaking his shirt and the bandage still wrapped tightly around his ribs.

How long could he fight the elements?

When would he catch a break?

The image of the Magician card came to mind. Sara Beth had said he had all the resources he needed to make some magic.

Maybe so, or maybe not.

Either way, he was determined to give it his best shot.

He wondered for a brief minute if Sara Beth had any luck in finding the helpful stranger.

Another set of hands would certainly be welcomed.

But where would he house another person?

The farmhouse only had two bedrooms. His folks had never seen the need for more.

Remembering a roll of screen wire he'd seen in the barn, the idea of screening in the front porch might provide a solution.

He let out a sigh, his injured ribs protesting loudly at the effort.

So much work to be done.

At Seymour's indication that they were finished, he turned the tractor toward the barn.

A cool drink of water, relief from the sun, and rest prompted him to shift the machine into high gear.

And he was anxious for a report from Sara Beth.

CHAPTER 21

Layken struggled to find the energy and strength to climb down from the tractor as the midday sun beat down on his back. Favoring his right side, he limped toward the house while Seymour unhooked the wagons and parked the tractor next to the barn. What would he do without the old man's help?

He came to a dead stop inside the kitchen, gasping in shock. "What the hell happened? Are you okay?" Sara Beth sat at the kitchen table, her face and right arm covered with angry red welts and blisters. Layken's heart sank.

She met his gaze, a tear leaking from the corner of her right eye. "I think I must've gotten into poison ivy or oak while I was out picking berries."

"I'd say it's a tad bit more than just thinking. What have you put on it?" He shuffled closer.

Sara Beth raised her hand. "Don't come any closer. Don't want to spread it to you."

She swiped at the escaping tear. "I haven't put anything on it yet. Don't know what to do."

The screen door squeaked as Seymour stepped inside. "Good Lord, child."

"Sara Beth got into poison ivy." Layken took a step closer despite her protests. "My mom used to make a paste from baking soda and something else, but I can't remember what. She would also put cold compresses on it to help stop the stinging and itch."

"It hurts awful bad," she managed through swollen lips. "I'm sorry to add to your troubles."

"No apology necessary, Sara Beth, so don't even go there." Layken shifted to take all the weight off his right side. He needed to console her, to let her know he wasn't upset with her.

Seymour moved to the sink. "Let's get a cool rag on it. I've got Calamine lotion out in my stuff. That'll help a lot, but Mister Layken's right about the baking soda."

Layken took the rag and moved closer to Sara Beth. He wiped it gently across her face, sweeping away her tears. "Here. You're probably better at this than me."

Her eyes spoke her thanks when she took the rag from him. "I'll mix up some baking soda and water."

"Be right back with the lotion." Uncle Seymour patted her shoulder. "We'll get you fixed up in no time. I've gotten into that nasty stuff more than once."

As the back screen door slammed, a loud, insistent knock came at the front door.

Sara Beth gasped. "Oh, that must be Ned with the oxygen delivery. I look awful."

"Don't worry. I'll go." Layken shuffled toward the living room, wanting nothing more than to drop onto the couch and stay. Yet, his heart ached for Sara Beth and her misery.

Instead of Ned, Mrs. Grover stood on the porch. "Glad to see you up and around, young man."

"Thank you. I'm glad I can be up and moving. Won't you come in?" He opened the screen door.

"Can't stay long. I wanted to get my dish and leave this pot of beans for you'uns."

"I can't thank you and your husband enough for all your help yesterday. Please, if I can do anything for you, anything at all, let me know. I'll be healed up before you know it."

"Neighbors are supposed to help each other. It's an unwritten rule of farm living."

He nodded. "Say, do you know how to treat poison ivy?"

"Of course. Don't tell me you got into that mess on top of everything else?"

"No, ma'am. Not me. It's Sara Beth." He motioned toward the kitchen. "She's in there."

Mrs. Grover passed a covered bowl to Layken and bustled toward the kitchen. "Sara Beth," she called out. "It's me, Mrs. Grover."

Layken followed her, setting the dish on the stove as Sara Beth turned around from the sink.

"Sorry. I'm not much fit for company, ma'am."

"I didn't come to keep you company, young lady, but oh, my! You sure got yourself in a fix." She squinted and stepped closer. "What are you doing to help?"

"Uncle Seymour went to get Calamine lotion and told me to make a baking soda solution to put on it."

"That'll sure help. And if you have any oatmeal, I'd recommend an oatmeal bath. And you'll need to wash your clothes as soon as you take them off. The oil can linger on any surface and keep spreading."

Sara Beth nodded. "I didn't think of that. How long will it take to go away?"

"It should be better in a week or so. Mainly, you need to be careful not to scratch and spread it." She placed her hands on her ample hips. "You young folks are gettin' some big lessons in being more careful."

"I suppose we are." Sara Beth moved the wet cloth across her face and arm.

"Well, I've got to be moseying on. Try to stay out of trouble." The older woman motioned toward the dish on the stove. "I need my pot roast pan back."

"Of course." Sara Beth grabbed the pan from the cabinet. "It's clean. We sure did enjoy it."

Layken leaned against the doorframe, taking all the weight off his right side. "And that chocolate cake melted in my mouth. Your help is more than appreciated."

Mrs. Grover picked up the empty pan. "Like I said, that's what neighbors are for. Take care of yourselves, if you can."

"We'll do our best. And truly, we thank you for everything."

Mrs. Grover shook her finger at Layken. "And you should still be in the bed, young man. You're looking a little green around the gills."

"I promise I'll rest. I had to finish watering the peanuts."

"I'll see myself out." Mrs. Grover mumbled all the way to the front door.

"She's right about getting out of those clothes and washing them right away. Don't want the oil to spread." Layken scrubbed a hand across his chin. "I know my mom had a washtub somewhere around here. And oatmeal was the other thing I was trying to remember."

Uncle Seymour hurried into the kitchen, holding a bottle of pink liquid. "Took a minute, but I found it." He pressed it into Sara Beth's hand. "Apply this after you've washed good."

"I hate to ask, but could you possibly look around and see if you can find a wash tub, Uncle Seymour?"

"Don't have to look. I spotted the whole setup in the root cellar the other day. And there's a wringer, too. I'll fetch everything while you get yourself cleaned up. I can help wash the clothes or hang 'em on the line for you."

Tears dripped off her cheeks, landing on her blouse. "What would I do without you? I would hug you, but, well, you know why. Can't take a chance on spreading this stuff. Would you look after things while I bathe?" She gave a pointed glance toward Layken, then took the bottle from him, grabbed the baking soda, and hurried down the hall.

"Of course. Just tend to yourself, little girl."

Sara Beth stopped and spun around on her heel. "Oh, and I found the boy today."

Layken's heart hammered. "The boy?"

"Yes. A boy. I'll tell you everything after I get bathed."

Layken sank into a kitchen chair. "Don't know how much more we can handle right now."

Seymour ran a hand through his white hair. "It'll get better. Always does. Want I should fix you a bowl of beans?"

"I'll settle for a drink of water. Then I'm going to lay down for a bit. If Ned comes, can you let him in?"

Seymour nodded. "Sure thing."

"You go ahead and eat. I'll get something later." Bracing one hand on the table, he pushed up. A sharp shooting pain almost took him to his knees. He stood stock still until a wave of nausea passed, then, with a glass of water in hand, stumbled toward the bedroom.

As he passed the bathroom, he could hear water running in the tub. He hoped Sara Beth would find some relief. "What next?" he mumbled.

Right now, he could use some of that so-called magic from the tarot card.

And what did Sara Beth have to tell him about finding the boy?

At the least, he was someone who seemed determined to help.

He would welcome that, no doubt about it.

But for now, he had to give his body some rest.

He'd pushed as far as he could go.

CHAPTER 22

Seymour stood vigilant in the kitchen doorway until Layken cleared the end of the hallway and disappeared into his room. The bed springs creaked from his weight, accompanied by a loud groan as he dropped down onto it.

He scrubbed a hand across his bristly chin. Damned if things hadn't taken a turn for the worse.

Not that he regretted his decision to join Sara Beth on the farm. No, sir. In fact, he felt a little guilty for lying to Sara Beth and Layken about the widow Jones firing him. The truth was, he'd quit. He couldn't tolerate Homer Williams and his pompous ways or the hateful widow for one more minute.

Besides, he'd made a solemn promise to Sara Beth's mother to always watch after her. And it was a promise he'd keep as long as he drew a breath.

While tangled thoughts meandered through his mind, he dished up a bowl of beans and carried it out to the front porch, where he rested on an overturned crate.

He stared across the field they'd finished watering, noting how the soil changed from a dusty brown to a rich dark color where water had soaked it.

Thunder rumbled in the distance, and he peered up at the sky. A nice, slow rain would offer a welcome reprieve. Clouds gathered off to the east, but it meant little. He'd seen plenty of thunderstorms that didn't produce a drop.

Still, a man could hope.

He sniffed the air, hoping for the scent of moisture—nothing but dust.

His mind drifted back to a hot, humid summer day many years ago. He could smell the Mississippi mud and feel it squish between his toes as he worked his way down the endless rows of tall cotton. Lack of rain was never a problem in the rich bottomland.

Sharecroppers were the poorest of the poor, with the landowners taking the lion's share of every harvest to line their own pockets.

Backbreaking work from morning 'til night was all Seymour had known from the time he was big enough to drag a cotton sack behind him.

That was until the Gypsy caravan stopped, seeking a place to camp for a few days.

The lilting voices singing around the campfires, their strange musical instruments, and colorful dresses intrigued him. The wagons had been camped near their shanty for two days. He'd hidden behind one of the largest wagons on the third night to afford him a better view.

Even though his father had admonished him to stay out of white folks' business, when a swarthy man drunk on red wine jerked a beautiful young lady to her feet and dragged her away from the camp, he couldn't stand by.

He'd struggled with what to do for a good twenty minutes or more, remembering a lynching he'd witnessed not too long back when a neighbor had interfered. But her cries for help finally spurred him into action.

He did what any decent man would do.

The stickiness of the blood on his hands, the gurgling that came from the dying man's throat, the smell of fear, and Esmerelda tugging her torn clothes closer. Her heart-wrenching sobs shot a fresh chill up Seymour's spine at the remembrance. He ground his teeth. He'd do it again if faced with the same.

Then, Esmerelda helped him bury the man in a shallow grave. The next day, she offered him a way out of the miserable life of sharecropping.

And he took it.

Seymour sighed and rested his aching back against the side of the house. He ate the last bite of the beans and set the bowl on the porch.

They shared secrets, he and Esmerelda.

And one of those secrets involved Sara Beth.

But it was a secret he'd take with him to the grave. No good could come from letting it out.

It filled his heart with contentment that Sara Beth was happier than he'd seen her since Esmerelda died.

Layken Martin was a good man. That much was obvious. Whether he'd ever be a husband to Sara Beth remained to be seen, but at least he treated her with respect. For now, that was good enough.

Wheels crunched the dirt as a vehicle approached the house. Seymour got to his feet.

A car stopped near the porch, and the doctor stepped out, waving to Seymour. "How's the patient today?"

"He's been up and around all morning, sir. Just laid down to rest."

The doctor shook his head as he stepped onto the porch. "I see he paid no attention to my advice."

"It's hard for a man to lay up when there is work to be done."

"I suppose it is."

Seymour held the door open for the doctor and followed him inside. "Want I should go get him?"

"No. Point me in his direction. No need for him to get up."

"Down that way." Seymour pointed down the hallway. "Last door at the end."

"Thank you."

The doctor strode down the hall carrying his black bag, and Seymour struggled with whether to follow him.

After a few minutes, he retrieved his empty bowl from the porch and washed it before making his way down into the root cellar.

Both wash tubs were full of cobwebs, which he swept out with his hands. He then hauled each up the steps before returning to get the wringer apparatus.

When he glanced around the back area, he spotted the frame leaning against the side of the house.

Soon, he had both tubs set in the frame and began the process of attaching the wringer. It had been a while since it had been used, and the cogs resisted his attempt to turn them.

He hadn't thought to ask Sara Beth if she'd seen any washing powder around. If not, he'd used bar soap more than once to wash clothes.

As he finished tightening the wringer to the side of a tub, soft footsteps behind him turned him around. "You found them." Sara Beth had a bundle of clothes under one arm and Cuddles under the other.

"Yes, I did, child. Feel any better?" She looked a slight bit better than she had before the bath.

"A little. The lotion is soothing. You don't reckon Cuddles can get this do you?"

"No. His fur protects him." He hooked a thumb toward the hallway. "The doctor's here."

"I thought I heard voices."

Seymour took the bundle of clothes from her. "Have you seen any washing powder around anywhere?"

She nodded. "I found a partial box in the kitchen cabinet. I'll get it. Wonder if the doctor has any other remedies to help heal this rash faster?"

"Why don't you go see?" Seymour laid a large hand on her small shoulder. "It couldn't hurt."

"Okay, but wait for me. I want to help you. I'm sure Layken has some clothes to add to the washing. And how about you?"

"Got a few."

"I'll go see the doctor, then meet you back here with Layken's laundry."

Seymour turned on the water faucet. He jerked around at a rustling sound.

"Who's there? I say, who's there? Come on out, now. I won't hurt you none."

He squinted against the sun.

A head of black tousled hair and two wide, dark eyes peeked around the corner of the house.

"Come on out, boy. I sure could use a hand here." Seymour turned his attention back to the water. If he didn't make eye contact, maybe the boy would come on out.

Two small hands took the hose from him.

Seymour didn't attempt to hide a wide smile.

CHAPTER 23

Sara Beth placed Cuddles on her bed, then paused outside Layken's bedroom door, knowing how much he hated lying down in the middle of a workday. And she certainly didn't want to catch him in a compromising situation.

After a long moment, she knocked softly. "May I come in?"

"Of course," Layken replied with a grunt.

She stepped into the room to see the doctor leaning over a half-dressed Layken, listening to his lungs.

When the doctor raised, he slipped the stethoscope around his neck. "I do believe the wheezing is a bit less than yesterday, which tells me the oxygen is doing its job. I want to keep you on it for two more days."

"I'll agree to use it at night." Layken drew the sheet up to his chin. "But I am not going to lay around all day with that damn mask on my face."

The doctor laughed. "I didn't expect that you would." When he turned to Sara Beth, he drew in a sharp breath. "Oh, my!"

She tried to force a smile through swollen lips. "Poison ivy, sir. I was wondering if you might have any suggestions."

The doctor squinted and moved closer. "This happen today?"

She nodded. "A few hours ago. I was picking berries."

"I've got a fairly new drug I can give you that shows good promise for helping with things like this. But it will make you drowsy, so don't take it and expect to be alert. No operating any machinery. It's called an antihistamine. It will help heal the rash quicker."

"If it will help, I'll take it. But maybe I should wait 'til closer to evening."

"Tell you what. I'll leave four tablets with you. It should help with the recovery." He peered over his glasses. "Do you have any ointment?"

"Calamine. And I took a baking soda bath."

The doctor nodded. "Both are good. I'd recommend you do that at least twice a day until the seeping stops."

Layken raised a hand. "Sara Beth, would you mind getting my bill-fold from the dresser so we can pay the doctor?"

"Sure." She looked around the neat bedroom and spotted a brown leather wallet lying on top of a tall chest of drawers. "How much, doctor?"

"I hate to take your money. Really, I do, but maybe enough to cover the cost of the medicine and gas." He dropped his stethoscope into the black bag and snapped it shut. "I'd say ten dollars should be fair."

"You sure that's enough?" Layken shifted on the bed.

"I'm sure. Two more nights on the oxygen, and you should breathe easier, Mr. Martin. Ned will be here directly. I'll make sure he knows to leave two bottles."

Sara Beth opened the worn leather wallet, counted the bills, and placed them in the doctor's hand. "Thank you so much."

"No problem. I hope I don't have to see you again anytime soon." He chuckled. "Not that you ain't fine folks, I sure hate for you to have more troubles."

"We feel the same." Sara Beth glanced at Layken to see him nodding in agreement.

"If you come with me out to the car, I'll give you those antihista-mines." The doctor stepped toward the doorway.

She turned to Layken. "I'll be right back. I have something to tell you."

Layken nodded and adjusted the pillow behind his head with a groan.

Sara Beth hurried after the doctor. "Sir, are you sure Layken is going to be okay? He's so pale."

"The oxygen will help with that, too. Give him a few days, and he'll be much better. I'm encouraged by what I heard today." The doctor rummaged through a box of supplies in the backseat until he found the right bottle. "Here you go. Now, most definitely do not take more than one at a time, or else you'll be asleep for hours."

"I can't afford to do that." She chuckled. "I'll take one after I finish the chores for the day. Thank you." She dropped the bottle into her dress pocket.

Once the doctor started the car and put it in reverse, she turned back toward the house and went straight to Layken's bedroom, hesitating for a long minute in the doorway. It was the one place in the house that was entirely his, and she wasn't sure she'd ever get comfortable with going into it freely.

She knocked softly before sticking her head around the door facing.

"Come on in." Layken patted the bed. "Sit. Talk to me."

Sitting gingerly on the edge of the bed, she glanced down at her hands twisted together on her lap. No matter how often Layken reassured her that this was her home to do as she pleased, she couldn't fully embrace it. She kept waiting for a shoe to drop, for something to ruin the comfortableness developing between them.

"Well?"

"I found the boy who's been stealing food. He admitted to watering the garden for me."

"Where did you find him?"

"He's built himself a tree house in the woods, close to the creek. It looks like he's been out there for a while."

"His family?"

"Said he didn't know where they are." She met his steady gaze. "I didn't push too hard because he's as skittish as that wild cat out in the barn, which, by the way, is turning out not to be so wild after all. The cat has adopted Uncle Seymour."

Layken chuckled. "I'll have to rib Seymour about being a cat tamer. How old is this boy?"

"Said he is twelve." A sob caught in her throat at the weight of those words. "Layken, he's been living out there all alone for God knows how long. It breaks my heart."

"Must've had a damn good reason for taking off by himself like that." He scrubbed a hand across his eyes. "One thing I can't tolerate in life is someone abusing children, old people, or animals."

"I feel the same. I wanted to find out more, but after he helped me pick blackberries, he took off. He has some scratches on his arms that could use washing and doctoring, but I don't know if I'd ever get him up here to take a proper bath."

"If anyone can help him feel at ease, it's you. He tell you his name?" The softness of his voice did not belie the honesty of his words.

She nodded. "Tab was all he told me. Didn't offer up a last name. And, even if I could convince him to stay with us, where would we put him? There isn't another bedroom. Besides, I have a strong feeling he's scared to death of being closed in."

"Been thinking about screening in the front porch. That might be a possibility."

While Layken's easy acceptance of another mouth to feed didn't surprise her, that he'd be willing to make accommodations for the boy touched her. "You'd do that?"

"Of course. The boy don't need to be living in the woods alone, especially come winter."

"I don't know how I can convince him to trust us."

"Easy. Be your kind and gentle self. That speaks more than words ever can." Layken's eyes began to droop.

"Thank you for the kind words, Layken," she whispered. "I'll let you rest for a while. I want to gather your laundry. Uncle Seymour is going to help me with it."

He pointed toward a basket in the corner. "Over there, but I can do my own laundry. You don't have to."

"I know, but I want to." She stood and straightened the bedcovers. "I'll check on you in a little bit."

He reached for her hand. "You're a good woman, Sara Beth."

While she wanted to pull away, she had to admit his slight show of affection awakened something deep inside. So, she let him grip her hand that didn't have blisters, squeezed his in return, then dropped it.

"Get some rest." She gathered the basket and lingered in the hallway for a long moment, listening to the sound of his ragged breathing.

Was she developing feelings for this man who was her husband in name? How could she not respond to kind words and compliments?

Yet, from the beginning, he'd made it plain that they were only partners until he paid back his debt.

After that, he'd cut her loose and each go on with their lives.

She'd best not get her hopes up for anything more, but for some strange reason, Sara Beth could no longer picture a future without Layken.

She hurried through the house and pulled up short at the kitchen door.

Tab stood next to Uncle Seymour, helping him methodically wash clothes in one tub, rinse them in the other tub, then run them through the manual wringer.

Hesitation to interrupt made her linger before opening the door. She pasted on a smile as bright as her swollen face would allow.

The boy jerked when the screen door slammed behind her.

"Tab! You came." She was glad to see his dirty hands in the soapy water.

He grinned sheepishly and blew the hair out of his eyes. "The old man asked for help."

Seymour winked. "I did for a fact, and this young'un pitched right in."

The boy scrunched up his face. "You got in poison ivy, didn't you?"

"Afraid so. I think I had already touched it before you warned me about it. But I've got some medicine, and I'll be fine in a few days." She set Layken's laundry basket down. "Want me to take over?"

"Nah. I can do it."

Seymour backed away from the rinse tub. "If you want to take over rinsing, I'll hang 'em on the line. We'll be done in no time."

It felt right to stand beside the lonely boy and work in silence. She didn't press for conversation. He'd open up if and when he was ready.

For now, she'd employ Layken's idea of showing kindness with no strings attached.

After a while, Tab's stomach growled, and he shifted uncomfortably.

"You need to eat. And we've got beans. Let's take a break and get some food." She wrung out her blouse and rolled it through the wringer. "I'm hungry, too."

She passed the garment to Uncle Seymour, who pinned it on the clothesline stretched across the yard.

He tousled the boy's hair. "They're good too. I already had some."

"Guess I could eat." Tab kicked at the dirt with the toe of his worn shoe, water dripping from his arms.

"Good. Then come on in, and I'll dish it up. Bet you could use some cold tea, too."

He licked his dry lips. "Can't go inside."

"Why not, Tab? It's only me and Uncle Seymour. You know we aren't going to hurt you."

"Where's the man?"

"He's resting in his bedroom. There's nothing to be afraid of."

The boy finished washing the last garment in the tub. "Can't."

"Can't or won't?" Sara Beth struggled not to wrap her arms around him and hug him so tight he couldn't breathe.

"Both."

"What if I get Cuddles?"

His eyes brightened. "Could I hold him again?"

"Yep."

He eyed the back door as if it were a serpent's mouth that would swallow him whole. "Why can't we eat out here?"

"We can. But it's much cooler in the house. Please. Come in, just for me. I need to get out of the heat."

Still, he hesitated. "Maybe I should get going."

She fought to keep the alarm out of her voice. "No, Tab. Please. Eat, and then you can go."

Uncle Seymour pinned the last garment on the line and laid a large hand on Tab's frail shoulder. "I promise you, son, there's not a thing to be afraid of. Mister Layken is the kindest man I've met. He took me in without hesitation when I had nowhere else to go. Besides, Sara Beth said he's sleeping. You won't even see him."

"You sure?"

"I'm sure."

"And so am I." Sara Beth took a step toward the door. "I'll get Cuddles." She flashed Uncle Seymour a grateful look.

Getting the boy to go inside the house was huge. She was sure he wasn't ready, but maybe with a bit of persistence, he'd see they wouldn't hurt him. "Don't be too long. Wouldn't want the beans to get cold."

Tab sniffled and swiped at his nose with his shirtsleeve.

"It's all right, boy. You can trust us." Uncle Seymour pointed toward the door.

Sara Beth held her breath. Would Tab come inside, or would he bolt? It had a fifty-fifty chance of going either way.

CHAPTER 24

Sara Beth chose not to look backward as she stepped through the kitchen door. Instead, she walked straight to her bedroom and gathered Cuddles from the bed.

A glance at the angle of the sun slanting through the window told her it was well into the afternoon.

The day already felt as if it had been three instead of only one.

But if Tab came inside to eat with them, it would be a small miracle. She took a minute to peek in on Layken, relieved to find him resting. A bit of color had returned to his face.

When she reached the kitchen, Tab stood nervously inside the door with one hand still on the screen.

"Oh, good. I'm so glad you came in. I know you've been in here before, so don't be shy."

Tab blushed, dark red splotches covering his face. He looked down at his feet, where he purposely covered the hole in the toe of his left shoe with his right foot. He mumbled, "Didn't mean to steal. Was just hungry."

Sara Beth smiled. "I know. We don't begrudge that." She pointed to the table. "Sit. It'll take me a couple of minutes to warm the beans."

Seymour pulled out a chair. "How about something cool to drink?"

"Tea?" The boy's eyes widened.

"Yes, son, tea."

How he gulped it down the minute Uncle Seymour placed the glass in his hand assured Sara Beth he had enjoyed nothing that good in a long time. "There's plenty." She lit a burner, then held Cuddles out to the boy. "Will you hold him?"

"Sure." Tab sprang up like he had a wire attached. He stroked the bunny's head. "I like your rabbit."

"I'm glad you do." Sara Beth stirred the pot while Tab sat on the edge of his chair, one leg bouncing as his eyes darted around the room, almost as if he expected someone or something to jump out and grab him.

Uncle Seymour cleared his throat. "Sara Beth has had that bunny for a long time. Ever since her mama died."

Wide-eyed, Tab stared at her. "Your mama died?"

"Yes. Five years ago."

A pained look marred his dirty face. "I'm sorry."

Sara Beth glanced at Uncle Seymour, who raised his eyebrows. "Is your mama still alive, Tab?" She kept her voice soft and even, choking back her sorrow.

He squirmed in the chair. "Don't know."

"We don't mean to pry." She dished the beans into bowls and set them on the table. "Eat up."

Tab held the bunny with one arm and shoveled spoonfuls of beans with the other, barely taking time to chew.

A growing boy needed food. His slight build made it apparent he hadn't gotten nearly enough for a while, if ever. She wondered if he'd cooked the fish she'd interrupted earlier.

Sara Beth wished she knew his story. So many scenarios flashed through her mind, but until Tab was ready to talk, there was no way to know if any of them were right.

A loud groan came from Layken's bedroom.

Tab's face turned ashen, and he froze for half a second. He shoved Cuddles toward Sara Beth, dropping his spoon on the floor and spilling bean juice on the table. In a flash, he dashed out the back door. Something metallic bounced off the wooden floor.

After she set Cuddles on the floor, she picked up a mangled locket and stood. "Oh no! This must have dropped out of his pocket. Should I go after him?"

Seymour frowned and rubbed the back of his neck. "Don't think so. We made good progress today, but it's not something we can force. Let me see what he dropped."

Unshed tears stung her eyes as she handed Seymour the locket and peered over his shoulder. "I need to find a way to help him. Poor kid. I can't even imagine what happened to cause him to be so afraid and so alone."

"Well, I'll be." Seymour pried the locket open with his thumbnail to reveal a faded picture of a woman with a soft smile and tired lines around her eyes.

Sara Beth gasped. "That must be his mother. And looks like the locket has seen better days."

"I'd say it found the heel of a boot at some point in time. And I agree with you. I'd bet a nickel this is his mother." He closed it and handed it to Sara Beth. "You keep it. He will want it back."

Layken shuffled into the kitchen, his hair sticking up and shirt untucked, one hand protectively covering the injured ribs. He took in the almost empty third bowl on the table and paused. "What did I miss?"

Sara Beth reached for the bowl and wiped away the spilled juice. "We got Tab to come in the house to eat."

"That's good, isn't it?" Layken leaned against the door frame.

"He's terrified of you." She held out the locket. "And this fell out of his pocket when he ran out."

"Why is he afraid of me?" Layken took the locket and turned it over in his hand.

"We have no idea. He calls you the man. When he heard you, he took off like lightning." She still stood in the middle of the floor, holding Cuddles. "I think I should go after him, but Uncle Seymour says to let him go."

"Seymour is right. If the boy is as skittish as you say, he's like a wild animal. He has to come to you." Layken passed the locket back to her. "He'll come back around after this."

"I feel bad for him. And he was so hungry." Her shoulders sagged as she pocketed the shattered locket.

Layken's eyes softened. "You've got a good heart, Sara Beth." He closed the space between them, laid a hand softly on her shoulder, then leaned in and brushed a kiss across her forehead where the poison ivy had missed.

She sniffed and swiped at her eyes, letting her hand linger where Layken had placed his lips. "Don't know if that's a blessing or a curse sometimes." Her heart tripped over a beat. Layken had shown affection twice in the same day. What did it mean?

Uncle Seymour pushed back from the table. "It's a blessing, little girl. Don't ever think different. I'm done eating. Gonna go drain the washtubs."

Layken eased into the chair Tab had vacated. "When you finish, come back. Got an idea in mind."

Uncle Seymour nodded and reached for his hat as he left. "Won't take me long."

Sara Beth turned to Layken. "Hungry?"

"A little. But you don't have to wait on me."

She handed the rabbit to him, thinking how comfortable she'd gotten with sharing her bunny. "I want to. It's no trouble." She grabbed a clean bowl from the cabinet and filled it. "I was going to make cornbread to go with these, but we got busy doing the laundry."

Layken petted Cuddles and leaned back. "You're a hard worker, Sara Beth."

"Just doing what needs to be done. Tab helped."

"Really? So he's not scared of you or Seymour, only me."

"I have a feeling a man has hurt him terribly, but until he's ready to talk, it's only speculation."

"I suppose that's true." He took a bite of beans and stared past Sara Beth. "There's so much I want to do to this place. I've got dreams of making the house bigger and planting bigger crops. I intend to do so much more." He pointed to his side. "But then this…"

So Layken had dreams. It was the first time he'd shared anything remotely close to his thoughts and wishes other than the burning need to save the farm. "Your injury will heal. You're already on the mend." She cleared her throat, not trusting her voice. "What other dreams do you have? A family, maybe?"

Layken stopped eating and stared at her, then dropped his gaze to his hands resting on the table. "Time will tell. What about you, Sara Beth? You know once I pay the bank note, you are free to go live your life however you see fit."

She kicked herself for asking. The wall visibly closed in, and he shut down and turned it back around on her. She lowered her eyes. "As you say, time will tell. I apologize for prying."

"No apology necessary."

Uncle Seymour opened the door and stepped inside. "You wanted to talk to me, sir?"

At the same moment, someone knocked on the door.

Sara Beth stood. "I figure that's Ned. I'll go let him in while you two talk."

While she wondered what Layken wanted to talk to Seymour about, it was none of her business. If it involved her, they'd tell her.

Surprise registered on Ned's face when she greeted him.

"Yes. I know. It looks worse than it is. Poison ivy." She held the screen door open while he wheeled in an oxygen bottle.

"Ouch. Sorry."

"Thanks. The doctor said you were to leave two bottles today, and once Layken uses them both, he should be finished with it."

"Yes. That's what he said. So, I'll take the empty one and leave two. Show me where you want me to put them."

She led the way down the hall. Would she ever feel comfortable walking into Layken's bedroom? The rumpled bed and discarded boots lying haphazardly on the floor were telltale signs that Layken wasn't at his best. It was the closest she'd seen to a mess since she'd been there.

It stunned her to realize she'd only been Layken's wife for a few days. So much had happened in such a short time. Finding Tab ranked right up at the top of that list. She would go find him as soon as she could. Somehow, she had to let him know he was safe around them and return his locket.

Poor kid.

While waiting for Ned to situate the oxygen bottles, she straightened the rumpled bed and put Layken's boots within easy reach. She mentally kicked herself for asking Layken if he wanted a family. To be honest, the question hadn't referred to herself but what might come after their contract ended. Or who might come after he set her free, as he'd promised?

The possibility of another woman taking her place as his wife left an unsettled feeling in her gut.

Her musing ended when Ned wheeled the second bottle into the room.

He positioned it next to the first one and dropped it. "When you need to switch bottles, you only have to change out the tubing. It's long enough to reach."

Sara Beth nodded. "Thanks, Ned. You've been so kind."

"Just doing my job, miss."

He wheeled the dolly into the hallway with Sara Beth following.

"I'll be back in a couple of days to pick up the empties. Take care."

"You too." She let the door close softly behind her. "Have a good rest of your day."

Ned tipped his hat and loaded the bottle into the back of his truck. "Always."

Sara Beth waved and stepped back inside.

A movement in her peripheral vision caught her attention. She whirled in time to see Tab dart behind a nearby tree.

She stood for a long moment, then sighed and walked toward the kitchen. No doubt the boy was curious.

That might work to her advantage.

And when he discovered the locket was missing, he would surely seek her out.

Layken sat at the table long after Uncle Seymour had gone. With the roll of wire in the barn, it wouldn't take much to screen in the front porch. And from the looks of things, if Sara Beth had anything to do with it, the boy would soon be staying with them. Besides, the farmhouse used to have a sleeping porch. For a moment, he wondered what had made his father decide to change it.

He contemplated his current situation. He'd gone from being completely alone to having a wife and a handyman helper in a matter of days.

And he'd be lying if he said he didn't enjoy having both of them there. But he'd better pull back some. He'd shown affection toward Sara Beth twice in the same day. He wouldn't want to give her a wrong idea or influence any future decisions she might make about her life.

She'd proven herself to be a worthy partner in a short time. A part of him hoped against hope that she might stay.

His mother's favorite saying about the future rolled through his head—*no need to cross that bridge until it's built.*

He sighed. She was a wise woman. She would have liked Sara Beth's simple and honest approach to life.

With Seymour's help, they'd watered the peanuts for a day. And they'd repeat that again tomorrow and the next many days following.

A good rain would surely be welcomed.

After taking the last bite of food, he got to his feet, unable to stifle a groan as pain shot through his midsection. Looking out the kitchen window while washing his bowl, gave him a good view of the laundry hanging on the line. Something about the familiarity of it brought a comforting feeling.

He wished he had a nickel for every time he'd helped his mother hang their washing out to dry.

A large black crow landed on the clothesline pole and stared at him before letting out a string of caws.

The hair raised on the back of his neck. While he wasn't a superstitious man, it seemed the crow had a message for him.

What was coming?

CHAPTER 25

Several days passed as Layken and Sara Beth progressed in their recoveries. Between the baking soda baths, Calamine lotion, and medicine the doctor had left, Sara Beth was pretty much back to her usual self.

She'd sought out the boy and returned the mangled locket, but got nothing more out of him than a mumbled thank you. Despite all her efforts, she'd been unable to convince him to come back inside the house again, so she continued to put food out daily.

They'd settled into what resembled some sort of routine. Layken and Seymour watered the peanuts every other day while Tab continued to show up to water Sara Beth's garden during the night. Tiny green shoots were springing up through the soil, making the labor worthwhile.

In between times, the three joined in painting the weathered wood on the outside of the house. Sara Beth had discovered bolts of colorful material in the back of a closet and busied herself sewing new curtains for the living room windows.

The old place was taking on a new life. How Layken wished his folks could see it.

Two days ago, he and Seymour had gone into town for more paint and returned with a small herd of goats, including a mama goat that was giving milk. Their bleats blended perfectly into the atmosphere of the farm, and Layken smiled each time Sara Beth petted them or sat cross-legged on the ground to let them nuzzle her. She had a quiet and gentle way with people and animals.

With the front porch now screened-in, Layken had moved a narrow cot out to spend his nights outdoors. The air was cooler, and the sounds of nature soothed him into restful sleep.

The newly painted porch swing made the perfect place to sit and contemplate with a southerly evening breeze.

His favorite times were when they listened to the radio, or Seymour and Sara Beth played their musical instruments, like tonight.

A perfect ending to a day of hard work.

Layken resisted the urge to turn around at a rustle of leaves near the edge of the porch. He caught Sara Beth's gaze, and she nodded. Tab had joined them in the only way the poor kid could allow himself.

If only there was a way to help him understand, he would never hurt him. He'd watched for any opportunity, but so far, it hadn't come.

"Sara Beth, would you please play and sing that Judy Garland song about the rainbow? It's one of my favorites." Layken rested on a straight-backed chair he'd brought from the kitchen.

She plucked the melody on the thumb piano, and Seymour interjected soulful harmonica notes.

As she played and sang, the rustling grew closer until Layken could see the boy's shadow crouched at the edge of the porch.

Her lilting voice drifted across the open space—soothing and hypnotic.

Soft, almost undetectable sobs came from the shadows. Layken's heart twisted as if in a vise. Life wasn't fair.

Sara Beth stopped singing and swiped at a stray tear. "Tab, we know you're there, son. Please come on up and join us. No one here is ever going to hurt you. I give you my word."

Seymour got to his feet and moved to the new screen door he'd only recently helped hang. He pushed it open without a word and motioned.

Tab slinked onto the bottom porch step and hung his head as if ashamed.

Sara Beth laid her thumb piano down on the porch swing and picked up Cuddles, who rested next to her. She thrust the bunny toward him. "Here. Hold Cuddles for me. Please."

Seymour moved back to an overturned wooden crate he perched on.

Tab reached for the rabbit, casting a wary glance toward Layken.

"Layken will not hurt you. He wants to help if you'll give him a chance."

"She's telling the truth." Layken leaned forward, placing his elbows on his knees. "I want to help you. But you've got to trust me."

The boy moved to the top step, his back against the screen door, holding it open. He apparently needed a clear exit in case he had to run. Ignoring Layken, he petted Cuddles. "You sing pretty, lady."

Sara Beth smiled. "I'm not lady, remember? I'm Sara Beth."

Tab nodded, but offered no reply. "Will you sing some more?"

"Of course." She picked up the thumb piano and sat back on the porch swing. "Anything you want to hear?"

Tab screwed up his face. "Know a song about angels singing?"

"There are lots of songs like that. You'll have to tell me more. Did your mother used to sing it?"

"I remember one my mother used to sing. Maybe it's the same one." Layken straightened, letting out a soft groan, the ribs still tender.

He watched the kid for any sign of terror flashing across his face, but all Layken noted was wistfulness. No doubt the boy missed his mother.

"How did it go?" Sara Beth asked.

Layken hummed a few bars, then sang, "We meet, and the angels sing. The angels sing the sweetest song I ever heard."

Tab sucked in an audible breath.

"Is that it?" Sara Beth angled toward the boy.

He nodded.

"I don't know the words." She pointed to Layken. "But you sing it, and we'll play."

"All I remember is the chorus." Layken ran a hand through his hair. "It's a Benny Goodman song from the thirties. I used to hear it a lot when I was in France."

Uncle Seymour blew a few notes on his harmonica. "Let's do the chorus, then. It's a pretty song."

For a moment, Tab seemed to forget his fears, and Layken sang the words he knew.

Time stood still for the little group on the front porch of the ancestral farmhouse, separated from the world, yet bound together by an invisible thread of fate.

The boy stayed for a couple more songs, then set Cuddles down and left without saying goodbye.

"I'd like to call that progress." Layken stood and moved to the end of the porch, where he watched Tab moving away in the shadows. A heaviness squeezed his heart.

Sara Beth joined him. "He's been through something awful. I'm glad we could offer a little happiness for a minute."

"The world's full of hurt and sadness. We each have to find whatever bit of peace we can." Without giving it any thought, he slipped an arm loosely around Sara Beth's slender waist.

Seymour stood and stretched. "Speaking of peace, I'm calling it a night. See you kiddos in the morning."

Extracting herself from Layken's arm, she stood on tiptoes and placed a kiss on the old man's weathered cheek. "Goodnight, Uncle Seymour."

Layken waited until Seymour left before turning to Sara Beth. "I need to share something with you."

She picked up Cuddles, and a frown creased her brow. "Okay. What?"

"It might be nothing, but I saw a crow perched on the clothesline pole a few days ago, and he seemed to be trying to tell me something. I hadn't said anything before because I thought it was my imagination. But the feeling still lingers. I want you to know. It could mean trouble."

"What kind of trouble, Layken?"

He scrubbed the back of his neck and paced the length of the porch. "I wish I knew. Maybe you should get your cards and see what they can tell us. All I know is something's coming, and it's not good. I don't know if it's Homer Williams or something else entirely."

"Take Cuddles. I'll get the cards." She handed him the bunny and stepped inside.

He didn't want to alarm her, but the gnawing, uneasy feeling wouldn't let go.

Within two minutes, she returned with the cards and scooted the wooden crate in front of the porch swing. She shuffled the worn cards, then handed the deck to Layken. "You know what to do."

He cut the cards into three stacks, then moved them on top of each other.

Sara Beth turned over the first card. "The King of Swords. I'd say that represents you. The aspects of this card are mental clarity, authority, power, and truth."

"Okay. Guess that fits, although sometimes I doubt the mental clarity."

"You sell yourself short." She flipped over the next card. "Another sword card. The Seven of Swords shows deception, betrayal, trickery, and theft. Not sure how that applies unless it's the warning you're looking for."

"Could be, but certainly not from anyone here."

The third card landed upside down. "The Ten of Wands upside down represents a heavy burden, feeling like you have to do it all, and advises delegation. Does any of that answer your question?"

"Not really. Guess I'll have to wait for the hammer to fall to figure out how to deal with it. And it could be nothing more than a bird sitting on a pole."

"I believe all animals can be messengers from the spirit world. They give us warnings, carry messages from loved ones, and help us move forward. I often see cardinals, and when I do, I know it's my mother letting me know she's nearby."

He blew out a sigh, trying to dispel the heaviness that lingered in his gut. "I feel the same. Guess there's no sense in worrying about something that hasn't happened. Or at least that's what my mom would tell me."

Sara Beth gathered up the cards. "Your mother was wise. I'm turning in. I hope you have a good night."

He laid a hand on her arm. "There's something else I want to say."

She raised her eyebrows. "Go ahead." Her soft voice reinforced his courage.

"I'm starting to have feelings for you. More than as a partner and friend. I am truly beginning to care for you."

"Go on." Her doe eyes widened.

"Well, that's all. You are a wonderful person, Sara Beth, and your father did a good thing when he made us marry, even though we didn't know it. I hope that maybe someday you'll come to care for me."

She leaned forward and touched his cheek, leaving a spreading warmth. "I do care for you, Layken. You're a good man. And for the record, I'm glad my father forced us together."

Layken grinned. "We make a pretty good team, don't we?"

"Yes, we do. I like being part of your team." She pulled at a loose thread on her dress.

He scrubbed the back of his neck. "Well, then, goodnight, Sara Beth."

"Goodnight, Layken."

He sat unmoving long after she went inside, wishing he could kiss her.

Wondering what her soft lips would feel like.

Awakening desires he'd long ago buried.

CHAPTER 26

In the wee hours of the morning, footsteps crunching the dried grass awakened Layken. He raised up on his cot and wiped the sleep from his eyes. The darkness told him it was mighty early for visitors.

But the smell of coffee boiling meant Sara Beth had beat him up again. He slipped into his pants and boots, then shirt. Still buttoning it, he called out. "Who's there?" He flipped on the porch light.

A tall, thin man with oil-slicked dark hair and close-set beady eyes stepped up to the door. "Hey, mister. Heard you were looking to hire a hand."

Layken raked a hand through his hair and tucked in his shirt. "Sorry. You heard wrong. Ain't got money to hire anyone."

The man lazily rolled, then lit a cigarette and lounged against the doorframe. "You sure? The man that told me seemed pretty confident."

Layken took two strides toward the door, the hairs raising on his arms. "Told you. I ain't hiring. So, you can mosey along."

At that moment, Sara Beth stuck her head out. "Layken? I heard voices."

The stranger blew out a stream of smoke. "Well, now, ain't you a purty thing?"

Layken stepped in front of Sara Beth, his voice hard as granite. "That's my wife, mister, and I suggest you turn around and leave. Now."

The intruder craned his neck to see around him, then raised both hands. "No offense." He turned to go down the steps, then stopped and whirled. "Say, you ain't seen a boy anywhere around these parts?"

"A boy?" His pulse quickened, every warning signal firing beneath his skin.

"Yeah. About twelve, skinny little runt with a head of curly black hair."

Layken cleared his throat to hide Sara Beth's gasp. "Nope. Ain't seen any kid. Why are you asking? You his pa or something?"

The stranger released a wad of spit on the ground and ignored the question. "Damn kid ran away a while back. His mama's fit to be tied. Won't even give me the time of day. Thought I'd try this part of the county. Stole something that belongs to me."

"Well, there's no kid here. So, again, I'm asking you politely to get off my property."

"I'm going. But if you're lyin' about that kid, you'll regret it."

Layken clenched his jaw and squinted, taking a step closer to the intruder. "You threatening me, mister?"

"No. Just statin' a fact."

"Like I said, you best get gone before I do something you'll regret."

The stranger threw back his head and laughed, revealing tobacco-stained crooked teeth. "See you around."

"I hope not." Layken fought the urge to wipe the smug look off the man's face. He stood, legs spread wide in a fighting stance, until the intruder disappeared down the lane that led to the county road. Taking slow, calming breaths, he turned to face Sara Beth. "Guess we know who Tab's hiding from. Can't say as I blame him. That man is as low-down and dirty as they come. I hope he's not his pa."

Sara Beth moved closer. "He gave me chills. Poor Tab. No telling what all that man has done to him." She twisted the hem of her apron between her fingers. "I hope the boy didn't see him. If he did, he's sure to pick up and move on somewhere else."

"That wouldn't be good. At least we can keep an eye on him where he is."

She raised her eyes darkened with anguish and met his gaze. "Oh, this is awful. What's to stop the man from coming back?"

Layken hooked a thumb toward the living room. "Time to get Dad's rifle cleaned. I won't stand for anyone threatening any of us in my own home."

"I hate violence." Her voice quivered.

"I'm not fond of it. Had enough of it overseas to last me a lifetime. But I won't let anyone hurt you, Seymour, or the boy." He meant it with every fiber of his being.

He barely heard Sara Beth's soft whisper. "Thank you."

"Let's get this day started. Did you notice the clouds? I'm feeling mighty hopeful for rain. Not gonna let that bastard ruin it."

She rewarded him with a shaky smile. "That would be a wonderful blessing. Coffee's ready."

She whirled and strode toward the kitchen, leaving the gentle fragrance of sweet wildflowers behind.

Sara Beth pasted on a smile that she didn't quite feel. She agreed with Layken that she wouldn't let the man ruin the day. But the urgency of finding the boy and getting some answers gnawed at her insides. And what if the man hid and watched them? If he did, he'd be sure to see Tab coming and going. Nothing could untangle the knot in her gut.

A rumble of distant thunder accompanied Seymour when he came through the kitchen door. "I smell rain." He set a basket of freshly gathered eggs and a bucket of goat's milk on the counter.

"We should be so lucky." Layken filled a steaming cup and passed it to Seymour before filling his own. "Seen too many summer storms that didn't produce a drop."

Seymour nodded. "Seen a few myself. I saw a man leaving when I left the barn."

Sara Beth fought against the sinking feeling of doom while listening to Layken's explanation.

Seymour let out a low whistle. "You think the boy really stole something from him?"

Layken sipped his coffee. "My bet is that maybe the boy knows too much. That man is pure trouble. I could smell it and feel it. And I hate he saw Sara Beth. I'd rather him think I lived here alone."

"Well, we can't let him find the boy. That's a given." Sara Beth put scrambled eggs in front of the men. As soon as breakfast was over, she would go find Tab.

A loud crack of thunder shook the house, and she jumped. Dark clouds boiled in the sky, blocking the barely rising sun.

Layken stood, strode to the back door, and peered out. "Sure would be nice if it'd come a gully-washer."

Sara Beth joined him, staring up. A jagged flash of lightning raced through the clouds, followed by a deafening clap of thunder. "Oh, the poor goats. They'll be terrified. And so will Tab."

"We can get the goats rounded up and put them in the pen 'til this passes. Maybe Tab will show up for some breakfast."

She wrung her hands as another bolt flashed, and the house shook. Even though she couldn't see it, she stared in the direction of Tab's treehouse, hoping against hope the boy would appear.

"Let's go, Seymour, before it gets any closer. That lightnin' is striking a little too close for comfort." He turned to Sara Beth. "Stay inside and watch for the boy." He reached for his hat, and Seymour followed him out.

She worried for their safety but was thankful the goats would at least have shelter under the lean-to. She hurried to the bedroom to get Cuddles. He'd be terrified, too.

In less than a minute, she resumed her vigil by the back door. The wind picked up and rattled the windows. Layken and Seymour struggled against it as they attempted to get the goats to follow them. With a goat under each arm, Layken deposited them in the pen, then went back for more. Seymour followed suit.

Two seconds later, a blinding, jagged flash tore across the darkened sky. The earth rumbled as it made contact. No doubt, it hit something.

With her heart in her throat, she could only imagine Tab's fear.

This was no ordinary storm.

In the distance, a violent wind whipped up loose dirt and sent it sailing in a whirling vortex.

She chewed her bottom lip, never leaving her post, hoping Layken and Uncle Seymour could make it back to the house.

Now she understood why all the farmhouses had root cellars. Not only did they need one to store food but also to provide a safe place to ride out a tornado. But she didn't want to go down there alone.

A small tendril of smoke rose over the tops of the trees.

She clutched Cuddles close and said a prayer that the boy was okay. It took all of her willpower not to go after him.

Large drops of rain pelted the earth, raising bits of dust when they hit. A few landed on the screen door, leaving droplets of moisture on her cheeks.

Then he came into view.

Tab clutched a burlap sack close to his chest while running, tears streaming down his face, his screams being ripped away by the wind.

The long scratches on Tab's arms spoke to his frantic thrashing through the underbrush.

Her heart beat in triple time.

She prayed hard that the stranger wasn't lurking in the shadows, waiting.

The boy stumbled over his own feet and almost went down.

"Come on, Tab," she whispered. "You're almost here."

CHAPTER 27

As soon as he got close, Sara Beth threw the door wide open. Tab dashed in, his small chest heaving, snot running from his nose, his hair plastered in ringlets against his head. He dropped his bag and threw his arms around Sara Beth's waist.

She patted his back and smoothed his hair. "It's okay, Tab."

Between gasps and sobs, he blurted, "My tree…got my tree. Almost got me."

"Are you hurt?"

He raised his head, stark fear reflected in his eyes. "Scared. So scared."

"Well, you did the right thing to come here." She pointed to the table. "Sit down and take a deep breath. I'll get you something to drink. Then we need to clean up those cuts. I've got some salve to put on them."

The forlorn, defeated look he gave her shattered her heart. No child should have to bear such a heavy burden alone.

A gust of wind rattled the window over the kitchen sink, and Tab gripped the table's edge with white knuckles.

"We're safe in here. I promise." She handed him a glass of water, and he gulped it down, letting it trickle down his chin onto his shirt.

He set the glass on the table. His face ashen, he cast a furtive glance around. "The man?"

"Him and Uncle Seymour went to get the goats into the pen. They'll be back. But don't you be afraid. I give you my word the man, Mister

191

Layken, will not hurt you. In fact, we both have something important to tell you." Sara Beth wet a cloth and wiped his face where tears had streaked through the dirt.

Rain pelted the roof like ricocheting bullets. She cast a worried glance toward the goat pen. Maybe they'd decided to ride out the storm inside the barn. However, she'd feel better with them all under one roof, especially if the storm worsened.

She chewed her bottom lip. Should she take Tab down to the cellar? Something told her he would refuse to go.

Finally, she spotted Layken and Seymour making a run for it, Layken holding his side and Seymour ambling more than running.

The rain had to be stinging their backs and shoulders.

"They're coming."

Tab got to his feet and whimpered.

She grabbed his hand. "Don't you even think about taking off. I won't let you." The strength in her voice surprised her. She couldn't remember ever having to be stern with anyone.

"Okay, lady." Tab trembled next to her, but gripped her hand.

She sighed, feeling his scrawny body tense. "When are you going to call me by my name? I'm Sara Beth."

The two men dashed inside, leaving a trail of muddy footprints. Layken slapped his hat against his leg, then stopped short at the sight of the boy. "Hello."

Sara Beth tugged Tab closer. "Lightning struck Tab's treehouse. Thank goodness he wasn't hurt. Really scared him, though, so he came here."

Seymour hung his soaked hat on a hook. "Good choice, young man."

Layken hooked his hat next to Seymour's. "This storm is something. I'm glad you trusted us enough to come here. It's dangerous out there."

Tab nodded, his gaze glued to the floor.

"Are we safe in the house?" Sara Beth tried to hide her anxiety as she met Layken's calm, smoky blue-gray eyes.

"For now. But we might have to hightail it down into the cellar if it gets any worse."

"No!" Tab took a step backward and tried to squirm his hand out of Sara Beth's.

She hung on. "It's okay. We won't go unless we're in danger. Layken wants to make sure none of us gets hurt."

"Sara Beth, how about you boil us some coffee?" He covered the gap between the door and table and dropped into the chair Tab had vacated. "Please sit down, Tab. There's something we need to tell you."

The gentleness of his voice almost brought tears to Sara Beth's eyes as she turned toward the stove. Her husband had a soft side, and this young waif was bringing it out in a big way. Maybe Layken related to something of himself in the boy.

Seymour put a hand on Tab's shoulder. "I'll sit with you. You trust me, don't you?"

He hesitated. "I guess." A loud crack of thunder caused him to jump. He chewed on a broken fingernail.

"Sit down." Seymour pointed to the table. "You like coffee?"

"Nope. Tastes awful." Tab screwed up his face.

"Not the way Sara Beth makes it." Layken winked at her.

"How about I make you a cup of tea, then?" Sara Beth reached for the kettle.

"That'd be good." Tab sat on the very edge of his chair, gripping the edges.

Rain and small pellets of hail slammed against the north side of the house.

Layken cleared his throat. "You know, this house has stood for almost a hundred years. I don't think no summer thunderstorm will take it down." He glanced at Tab. "My ancestors settled here when there was nothing. They built this place."

Admiration sparked in the boy's eyes. "When I grow up, I'm going to have some land, and I'm gonna plant crops just like you, mister."

While the water boiled, Sara Beth pulled a chair next to Tab and sat down. She handed Cuddles to him. "That's a fine idea, Tab. We all need to have dreams." Stroking the rabbit's long, velvety ears seemed to have a calming effect on the youngster. "How about a snack? You hungry, Tab?"

The boy gave an almost imperceptible nod.

"Sara Beth makes the fluffiest pancakes I've ever had." Layken grinned and stretched his legs out.

While she hated spending time cooking, Layken did have a wonderful idea. What child could resist pancakes with sorghum syrup?

Tab glanced up at her. "Really?"

She smiled. "Really. Want I fix some?"

"My mama used to make me pancakes a long time ago."

Sara Beth cleared her throat and nodded at Layken. "I think you need to tell him."

While she gathered ingredients, Layken leaned forward. "A man came early this morning asking for work. Then, said he was looking for a kid who'd run away. Mentioned the boy's mother."

Tears filled Tab's eyes, and Sara Beth fought to keep from wrapping her arms around him. She moved to the child and kneeled. "But we didn't tell him anything. We said we hadn't seen a boy. He was a bad man, Tab. Tell us about him."

"I...I can't." Tears wet his cheeks.

"Can't or won't?" Layken asked gently.

Sara Beth put a comforting hand on the boy's shoulder. "Look. I understand you're frightened. Something or someone scared you so bad you decided to live alone in the forest. We want to help you. Is your mother in danger?"

"Don't know." Tab sniffled.

"Then why don't you start at the beginning and tell us everything?" Sara Beth stood and moved to the stove, pouring coffee for the men and tea for herself and Tab. She scooted her chair as close to Tab as possible and placed a warm cup in his hand.

Lightning crackled, and the sky darkened.

Tab jolted, spilling the tea.

Layken reached for his cup. "Know how to tell when the storm is moving away, Tab?"

The child shook his head.

"Count the seconds between a flash of lightning and thunder. The longer the time between, the farther away it's moving."

Sara Beth wiped up the spilled tea and draped an arm around Tab's shoulder. "Now, back to our question. Start at the beginning, before you came to live in our forest." He relaxed under her touch.

"It was after my daddy died." He stared at the cup as if seeing a memory. "My mama couldn't find enough food for us to eat, and we didn't have a house anymore. We camped wherever anyone would let us. Mama was always so sad and tired. She'd do laundry or pick beans or clean houses to get food for us kids."

"You have brothers and sisters?" Seymour sipped his coffee.

"One brother and one sister. But I'm the oldest. So, I tried to help."

"I can see that. You are very helpful and don't mind working." Layken's eyes softened.

"What happened then, Tab?" Sara Beth prodded.

"Then Mama met Earl." He took a sip of the warm tea and waited until the roll of thunder passed.

"Earl is the man looking for you?" Layken questioned.

Tab nodded.

"What happened? Why did you run away?"

The boy raised his head in defiance. "At first, he seemed okay, and we had a little more food. But then he got to drinking heavy, and it got worse. He beat on my mama and us kids, mostly me."

Sara Beth gasped. "Oh, Tab. I'm so sorry." She squeezed his shoulder. "But go on."

"I'm not going to be in trouble, am I?" He aimed the question at Layken.

"I can assure you that you are not. Please go on."

"Then he started making me help him."

"Help him do what?" Seymour put his elbows on the table, thunderous emotions flickering across his weathered face.

"Steal." The boy's voice broke, and then he rushed forward as if he couldn't get it out fast enough. "He'd make me climb in through windows and open the door for him. Then he'd steal anything worth a dollar."

"That's horrible." Sara Beth wiped a stray tear from his cheek with her thumb. "What happened next?"

"We moved over to Greenfield. He said there was better pickin's over there. Then he started breaking into stores and talking about robbing banks." He stopped and glanced at Sara Beth, as if seeking her reaction.

"Go on," she whispered.

"One night, I said I wasn't gonna do it anymore, and he couldn't make me. He beat me with an iron rod and locked me in a tiny closet in the kitchen. I could hear him tearin' into Mama and my little brother. All I could do was listen."

Layken's jaw twitched, anger flashing in his eyes. "How did you get away?"

"For two days, he left me in there. My mama would sneak and give me a little food and water when he passed out." He glanced down at Cuddles, who serenely napped on his lap. "I even had to use the bathroom in there. I thought I was going to die." His voice dropped to almost no sound as he relived the painful memory.

"Now I know why you don't want to go down in the cellar." And Sara Beth couldn't blame him.

Seymour scrubbed the back of his neck. "How did you get away?"

"One night, when he was gone from the house, Mama let me out, gave me a change of clothes and some food, and told me to run. So, I did and never looked back."

"How long ago was that?" Sara Beth questioned.

"Don't know for sure. Maybe a few months. Stayed off the roads and in the woods, then found this place."

"I'm glad you did. No child should have to endure that kind of abuse." Layken ran a shaky hand through his hair. "Earl said you stole something that belonged to him."

Again, the child raised his chin. "I took his gun. Then I threw it in the creek so he'd never find it. And I hope he never does. He was gonna rob banks, and he was gonna make me help him." He shivered, even though it wasn't cold in the room.

Layken blew out a long sigh. "Tab, we're going to help you. I have a gun, and I'll shoot the bastard if I have to. But he'll never get his hands on you as long as I'm around. And that's a promise."

Sara Beth fought to steady her voice as she brought Tab in for a hug. "Layken was in the army. He'll know how to take care of Earl if he comes back. What is your last name, Tab?"

"Chesson." He gulped the now lukewarm tea.

"Is your mother married to this man?" She rubbed his small shoulders.

"No. He just moved in and took over."

"I know you must be worried sick about your mother and the other kids. I'll try and figure out what to do to help them, too." Layken glanced at Seymour, who nodded.

"I can't go back there. Earl will kill me."

"Don't worry, son. I would never send you back with that man. But you've got to trust me. Can you do that?"

The boy looked at Sara Beth, who offered a genuine smile.

"I can try."

"That's good enough. Now, how about those fluffy pancakes, Sara Beth?"

She jumped to her feet. "And listen, Tab. The time between lightning and thunder is getting longer, so it's moving on." While she wanted nothing more than to gather him up in a tight hug, she made pancakes instead.

Tab's story had torn her heart in two, and from the looks on Layken and Seymour's faces, they shared the same sentiment.

Her chest swelled with pride for the gentle but strong way Layken had assured the frightened boy.

Layken Martin was a good and kind man.

Thank God her father had forced her to marry him.

But now, where would Tab go? Where would he live?

She couldn't let him walk out and return to the forest. Not now that they knew the entire story.

The boy was in danger.

Safety lay in sticking together.

CHAPTER 28

The storm subsided around midday. Layken and Seymour left to examine the damage and let the goats out of the pen.

Sara Beth persuaded Tab to get into the bathtub and insisted he give himself a good scrubbing, including his tangled hair.

While he bathed, she looked inside the child's bag that held his belongings. She pulled out a halfway-clean set of clothes.

There was no doubt about what her next sewing project would be. The boy needed more than one change of clothes. The ones he had were hardly more than rags.

She could do nothing about the worn shoes with the hole in the toe except to clean them up. Maybe they could buy him a new pair. Or perhaps the church would donate some. But at the same time, they couldn't afford to do anything to draw attention. She'd talk with Layken.

She considered her arrogant father, who had so much. He could buy shoes for the boy and never miss the money. But she'd die before she'd ask for a single penny.

When Tab came out of the bathroom, he looked like a new boy, except for the dirty, ragged clothes. His skin glowed pink from scrubbing. Even some of the scabs had disappeared. He tugged at his overalls and curled his toes under his feet, avoiding Sara Beth's gaze.

"Well, look at you. Aren't you a handsome young man?" She thrust the change of clothes from his bag toward him. "Go back and put these on, and we'll wash the others."

He took the clothes and returned to the bathroom. When he came out, he had the dirty clothes wrapped up in a bundle.

"Much better. But you are in dire need of a haircut."

He shuffled his bare feet and looked down. "Yes, ma'am."

"I'll get the scissors, and we can go outside."

"But what if Earl sees me?" He bit off a piece of a fingernail.

She put her hands on her hips. "Then we won't take that chance. We'll cut it right here in the kitchen."

He nodded and blew an unruly curl out of his face. "Thank you, Miss Sara Beth."

"You finally called me by my name." Her heart swelled as she pulled a straight-back chair out into the middle of the floor and pointed to it. "There you go."

The boy dropped down into it and crossed his feet at the ankles. "My mama used to cut my hair." He looked up, tears pooling in his dark eyes.

"I know you miss her, and she must be heartbroken. But trust Mr. Layken. He'll figure this all out." Sara Beth caught a lock of hair between her fingers and snipped it off. "You're not alone anymore. You have us now."

Their little tribe was growing.

But where would they put Tab?

Maybe he'd take Layken's empty bedroom.

Whatever they decided, she wouldn't let him go back into the forest to live all alone.

Layken and Seymour returned a short time later, leaving their muddy shoes on the back porch.

Layken hung his hat on a hook and blew a low whistle at Tab's clean face and trimmed hair. "Well, you look like a completely different kid."

Even though the boy didn't look like he wanted to run, he still wouldn't meet Layken's gaze. "Thank you, sir," he mumbled.

Sara Beth turned from the sink, where she washed Tab's extra clothes. "How are things? The goats and chickens all okay? Any damage?" Soap and water dripped from her elbows.

"Some minor damage. Mostly things blown around. Nothing we can't fix. The goats are fine. They were a little skittish, but easier to get out of the pen than they were to get in. The cat came out to help." He chuckled.

Seymour grabbed a cup from the cabinet. "That darned cat ain't nearly as wild as he'd like us to believe. Any coffee left, little girl?"

She nodded toward the stove. "Just needs heating up."

Layken pulled out a chair. "Been thinking about someplace safe for you, Tab. You certainly can't go back to your tree house. I don't figure you'll want to be too confined. So we were looking at the loft in the barn. Windows open on each end to let through a breeze, and it gives you a good vantage point. How does that sound?"

Tab glanced at Sara Beth, then dropped his gaze to the floor. "Don't wanna be no trouble, sir. That would be fine."

"Good. We'll need to do a little bit of work, but I think with all of us pitching in, we can have you a decent bedroom in no time."

Sara Beth wrung out the small pants and shirt, then ran the rinse water. "That's a good idea, Layken. And Uncle Seymour will be close by." She flashed a wide smile before turning back to the sink.

"Then it's settled. There's a storage room out there I haven't opened since I've been home. Am hoping to find a bed frame or cot." He accepted a steaming cup of coffee from Seymour. "We got almost a quarter inch of rain. That's gonna do wonders for the peanuts."

"And the garden." Sara Beth swished the clothes in the water.

"And the garden." He took a sip and turned back to the boy. "What can you tell me about where you lived before you ran away?"

An uneasy look spread over the boy's face, and he focused on his hands. "Wasn't much more than a shack." He glanced at Sara Beth's back as she rinsed his clothes. "Over on Maple Street at the end of the block. But please don't go over there, Mister Layken. Earl is mean."

"I promise you I won't bring any trouble to your mother. Mainly, I need to see that they are all okay. Maybe ease her worry about you."

"If you tell her where I am, Earl will beat it out of her." A sob caught in his throat, choking off his words.

Layken's voice hardened. "I won't tell her anything except that you're safe. If I can even find her and Earl's not there." He gripped his coffee cup harder than necessary but kept his voice low and steady, belying the anger that surged through him. "But if they're hurt or in danger, I won't leave 'em there."

"I'm scared," the child whispered, sniffling.

Laying a hand on Tab's shoulder, Layken forced a smile that hid the chill running up his spine. "Nothing to be scared about. You're protected here."

"You don't know Earl." He wrung his hands.

"No. But I've known lots of men like him. He's not so special."

Tab scrunched up his face. "You ever kill a man?"

"Only when forced," Layken fought hard to dispel a memory as the coffee churned in his gut. "When you're fighting in a war, you aren't given a lot of choices."

"Earl used to brag about killing. But I didn't believe him. He'd rather pick on a woman or kid than another man."

"Exactly." The boy's perception and wisdom surprised him. He finished his coffee and stood, tousling the boy's hair. "Let's go get a loft room set up for you."

Sara Beth wrung out the clothes. "I'll be on out after I look through the closet and see what I can find."

Layken set the cup on the counter before following Seymour and the boy. He winked at Sara Beth. "Ain't it funny how things work out?"

She grinned. "Sure is."

Grabbing his hat, he stepped out the door.

As soon as he got the boy settled, he would drive over to Greenfield.

He meant what he'd said. If Tab's mother and siblings weren't safe, he wouldn't leave them. Where he'd put them, he didn't know. But they'd figure it out.

Inside the barn's dim, damp coolness, he examined the remnants of stalls from when the farm used horses to pull the plows. With a bit of lumber, hammer, and nails, he could put together some makeshift rooms if need be.

And, if it came to that, he'd insist on giving Tab's mother his bedroom. He'd continue sleeping on the porch. That would put Seymour and the young'uns in the barn.

He'd have to clear that with the old man. It would be a lot of responsibility.

Tab scrambled up the ladder to the loft and peered over the edge. "This is great up here. Even better than my treehouse."

Layken grinned up at him. "I'm glad. Now, let's see what we can find to fix you a bedroom."

For once, he was thankful that his folks never threw away anything. A weathered door in the back of the barn opened into a good-sized storage room piled high with all sorts of farm implements, tools, and discarded household items.

When he moved a rusted washtub, a snake slithered out.

Before he could react, the barn cat lunged out of nowhere and grabbed the snake. It was over in less than three seconds, and the snake lay dead at his feet. The cat rubbed against Layken's legs, then sat and purred while licking his paws.

"Whoa! Did you see that?" Tab scurried down the ladder, leaving a cloud of dust behind him, and scooped up the cat.

"Careful. Wouldn't want him to scratch you. He's pretty wild."

Uncle Seymour rubbed the cat's head. "About as wild as that rabbit in the house."

"Looks like you're right, Seymour. He's certainly less wild than we first thought." Layken turned back to the storage room. "Hopefully, that snake is the only one in here." He grabbed a nearby hoe, in case there were more.

After digging around, he found an old army cot. It would do for a bed.

He added a chair with a busted bottom that he could repair and a box of his old books from childhood to the pile.

He pulled a book from the box. "Tab, do you know how to read?"

"Sure do. I like to read. Only Earl said that was for sissies." He reached for the book Layken held. "Tom Sawyer. Always wanted to read this one."

"Earl was wrong, and you're welcome to read them all. They kept me entertained when I was a boy." The idea of sharing things from his childhood brought a warmth that spread throughout Layken's chest.

Only a few short days ago, they were each alone. Now, they were all joined together with purpose.

And Tab's arrival added to the purpose.

He'd protect the boy with his life.

Through the wide barn door, he spied a rainbow forming.

It turned into a brilliant hue and doubled.

That had to be a good sign.

Rainbows represented hope.

And sometimes, hope was all a man had to cling to.

CHAPTER 29

Sara Beth pulled a worn quilt from the top shelf in the hall closet, along with a feather pillow. She doubted Tab had anything resembling comfort in his treehouse. That he asked for nothing increased her desire to make things better for him.

Excited to help create a space for this boy who had wriggled his way into her heart, she grabbed a broom on the way out the door.

Layken stood in the wide barn entrance and pointed. "Sara Beth, look up."

She gasped at the double rainbow that stretched across the sky. Her heart thrummed in her chest. If ever there was a good sign, that was it. "That's gorgeous." She handed him her bundle. "And a sign that everything is going to be okay."

"I thought the same thing."

She paused inside the barn, letting her eyes adjust to the dim light. Tab peered over the edge of the loft. "Miss Sara Beth. Come up and see."

His contagious enthusiasm made every effort worthwhile.

Layken took the bundle of bedding from Sara Beth and set it down on a nearby empty shelf and lowered his voice. "I'm thinking that while you help get Tab settled, I'll take a ride over and see if I can locate his mother."

"That's a good idea. Will you take Uncle Seymour with you?" She fought down panic.

He scrubbed the back of his neck. "No. I won't leave you and the boy here alone." He motioned toward Seymour. "He already knows."

She touched his arm. "Please be careful. We don't need any more troubles."

With a tip of his hat, he strode from the barn.

By mid-afternoon, they had the barn loft swept clean. The cot, covered with soft bedding, occupied the space nearest the outside wall, while a small end table held a lantern. The box of books occupied the corner nearest the boy's bed.

Seymour grunted as he climbed down the ladder. "These old bones ain't made for climbing. Gonna go take a look at the chickens while you two finish up here."

Tab tugged on Sara Beth's arm.

She glanced down to see his dark eyes wide and shining. "Yes, Tab."

"This is the nicest place I've had since my pa died." He sniffled and looked away. "And look what I found at the bottom of Mr. Layken's box of books." He held up a baseball.

Sara Beth's throat constricted. She could imagine Layken and his dad tossing the ball around. "That's great. Maybe we can find the bat that goes with it."

A wave of sadness flashed through the boy's eyes. "My dad used to play ball with me."

She drew him in for a tight hug and swallowed a lump. "I'm so sorry. But I bet Mr. Layken will love playing with you. You're not afraid of him anymore, are you?"

Tab shook his head and slipped out of her embrace. "No. He's nice, like you said."

"Sara Beth. Tab. Come out here." Uncle Seymour's voice carried an urgent tone.

Her pulse quickened as she swung one foot onto the ladder. "Coming."

What now? She hoped Cuddles hadn't found a way out of the house and gotten into trouble. She'd left him safely inside.

Uncle Seymour rested on his haunches next to the back porch steps. He pointed. "Looks like we've got a visitor."

"Is it another snake?" Tab squatted beside him.

"Not a snake." The old man held out his hand and whistled. "Come on. Come on out."

Sara Beth peered under the porch. A skinny, wet, and muddy dog hunkered underneath. She held out a hand to let the dog sniff. "Come on out. We're not going to hurt you."

It took some coaxing, but soon the dog crawled from the hiding place. "Oh, you poor thing," Sara Beth crooned. "You've surely seen better days."

Uncle Seymour reached over and patted the dog's muddy head. "Wonder how long it's been there?"

"I don't know, but I think we would have noticed it if it'd been here long. I'd say it took shelter from the storm." She stood, and the dog scurried back under the porch, bumping its head against the wood. "I'm going to get a towel and something to eat. Poor thing looks like it's starving."

Tab leaned over and called to the dog. "Looks like a mama dog to me, Miss Sara Beth. Her belly is pooched out, but her bones are skinny."

Oh, dear. Just what they didn't need, but she couldn't turn the animal away, no matter what. "Okay. See if you can coax her back out. I'll get some food."

As she hurried inside, Tab called to the dog in a singsong voice that made her smile. His fear had dissipated, leaving behind a curious and bright little boy. Her heart broke for his mother. She must be worried sick. Maybe Layken could find her and relieve her stress.

Inside, she grabbed a cold biscuit, then hurried to the bathroom.

Surprised that Tab had hung his used towel on a nail, she grabbed it. The child liked things orderly. That much was apparent.

Softly opening the back screen door so as not to frighten the dog again, she blinked away hot tears at the sight of the muddy dog lying across Tab's lap. No doubt both boy and dog would need cleaning up. But it didn't matter.

Uncle Seymour had moved to sit on the step but slid over to let her out.

With the thin towel draped over one arm, she held her hand with the biscuit toward the dog.

The pup's sad brown eyes blinked and met hers. "Here you go, girl. I know you're hungry."

After sniffing, the dog devoured the food in two gulps.

"She's still hungry." Tab glanced up at her. "Can we give her more?"

"Of course. Here." She handed him the towel. "Wrap this around her. She's shivering. I'll be right back."

What could they spare to feed the dog? She settled on scrambling a couple of eggs. Thank goodness for the chickens.

Over the next hour, they got most of the mud cleaned off the dog. Tab was right. It was a mama dog. A sharp contrast to the protruding bones, the size of her stomach, meant she could give birth any minute.

"I want her to stay in the barn with me." Tab had attached himself to the animal.

"That's a fine idea, Tab." Sara Beth nodded at Uncle Seymour. "Perhaps Uncle Seymour can find her a nice box to sleep in."

"I'll look down in the cellar. She's welcome to stay in the barn with us, young'un. She'll fit right in with the cat."

Sara Beth laughed. "This I have to see."

Tab screwed up his face. "The cat is nice too." He glanced around. "Everyone here is nice."

"I'm glad you're with us."

"Me too. But I'm worried about Mr. Layken."

Fighting to keep her voice steady, she tried to reassure him. "He can take care of himself. He'll be back soon with news about your family."

At least, she hoped so.

The sky turned brilliant hues of red and orange as the sun began its descent. *Where are you, Layken? Please hurry home.*

In the half hour it took to drive to Greenfield, Layken mulled over all the information Tab had shared. He could be walking into a hornet's nest. But the old rifle lying on the seat at least evened the odds.

He considered stopping at the sheriff's office, but decided against it. After all, they could insist he give the boy back. He wouldn't take that chance. Tab trusted him.

Seeing the creeks swollen after such a hot, dry summer was refreshing. A couple of the low-water crossings had water rushing over the narrow road. He angled the old pickup toward the middle and shifted into a lower gear. It wouldn't do to flood the engine.

He wished he'd remembered to ask the boy Earl's last name. But what did it matter? It wasn't Earl he was seeking.

After he reached Greenfield, he stopped at a gas station for a dollar's worth of gas and asked for directions to Maple Street.

He made a left turn onto the narrow street within five minutes and slowed. The houses matched, all needing a coat of paint, hammer, and nails. An occasional rusty bicycle leaned against a sagging porch, along with wash tubs and boiling pots. Signs of the Great Depression lingered on every residence. While the rest of the country might have moved on, for these folks, time stood still.

Hopelessness permeated the air. Thank goodness he lived in the country. There was something about poverty linking folks together in town. Close enough to know everyone's business.

He pulled next to a curb and killed the engine. No, this wasn't the right house, but maybe a talkative neighbor would help him know if it was safe to keep going.

Before he could knock on the wood-framed shotgun house door, a tired woman with a baby on her hip stuck her head out the door. "You lost, mister?"

He jerked his hat off and ran a hand through his hair. "Well, maybe. I'm hoping you can help me. I'm looking for Mrs. Chesson and heard she lives around her somewhere."

The woman stared at him long and hard. "You ain't a bill collector, are you?"

"No, ma'am. I assure you, I'm a friend."

"Hmph. I seriously doubt that. With Earl around, poor Mildred ain't allowed to have any friends."

Layken's eyebrows shot up, and a chill raced down his spine. "I'm sure sorry to hear that. I have some family news."

By now, the woman had stepped out onto the sagging porch. "I sure hope you have news about her boy. She's been worried sick ever since he took off." She shifted the baby to the other hip. "Not that I blame the kid for running away. Hell, I would too."

"Yes, ma'am. Can you point me to her house?"

"What did you say your name was, mister?"

"I didn't." He pointed down the street. "Which house?"

She crooked a thumb. "Last one on the right."

"You wouldn't happen to know if Earl's home, would you?" He didn't want to chance making things worse for Tab's mother.

"If his old jalopy ain't there, then he ain't either."

Layken put his hat on and nodded to the woman. "Thank you for your help. You have a nice day."

"Yeah, like that's gonna happen. What with our men not being able to find work and no food, the days are anything but nice." She turned and stomped into the house.

Back in the pickup, Layken started it and rolled slowly down the block. He didn't see any sign of a vehicle at the house the woman had pointed toward. Maybe he was in luck.

He wanted to carry the rifle with him, but imagined how frightening that would look to Tab's mother. He parked at the end of the street and watched the house for a long minute.

Taking a deep breath, he muttered, "Might as well get it over with." He braced for a confrontation with Earl in case the woman was wrong.

Pulling his hat down low, he walked up the muddy walkway and knocked on the door. Scurrying sounds came from inside, as if they were hiding. Who did they think he was? Maybe the law? Or, as the neighbor had said, a bill collector.

He called out. "Mrs. Chesson. I need to talk to you. It's about your son, Tab."

Light footsteps registered on the wooden floor, and the lock on the door clicked. When it opened, Layken faced a haggard-looking woman not much more than skin and bones. Her eyes sunk back into her head, and she sported a large bruise on one jaw.

She squinted up at him. "You know where Tab is."

"Yes, ma'am. I ain't at liberty to tell you where. He's afraid Earl will beat it out of you, and then he'll come after him. I'm here to set your mind at ease. He is safe. Me and my wife are taking care of him."

She sagged against the door frame. "Oh, thank the heavens. You better get out of here, mister. If Earl catches you, there'll be hell to pay." At the sound of a car engine, she cast a wild-eyed look toward the street.

Layken followed her glance. "Ma'am, I'll go, but I promised Tab if you were in danger, I'd bring you and your other two children with me."

"No." She sucked in a shaky breath. "You don't understand. I have to stay here. Tell Tab I love him and that I'm sorry." With that, she darted back inside and slammed the door. Then she re-opened it a tiny crack. "Thank you."

Layken put a hand against the door. "I meant what I said, ma'am. If you aren't safe here, come with me now. I promise I can protect you."

The door shut against his open palm.

His gut twisted with anger at the monster who called himself a man.

Something told him this wasn't the last time he'd be seeing Mrs. Chesson.

The car chugged closer, a trail of black exhaust smoke following it.

CHAPTER 30

Fighting the urge to sprint, Layken lowered the brim of his hat and sauntered toward his pickup with his hands in his pockets. No matter what, he wouldn't show fear. He balled his fists inside his pockets, imagining connecting them with Earl's smirk.

Once inside the vehicle, he cranked the engine and shifted into first gear.

Since he had parked at the end of the street, he had no choice but to turn around and face the oncoming vehicle. He doubted Earl would even recognize him, but still didn't want to chance it, for Tab's sake.

When he was even with the car, it turned into the driveway next door to the house he'd just left. He blew out a relieved sigh and drove out of the shabby neighborhood.

As he passed a five-and-dime store, he threw on the brakes, overcome with a sudden urge to buy something pretty for Sara Beth.

But what? She asked for nothing.

The familiar scent of lemon furniture polish and the spotless glass cabinets brought back childhood memories of when he'd accompany his mother on expeditions to purchase material for a sewing project. The wood floor creaked under his boots.

A display of colorful hair ribbons caught his eye. While he'd never seen her wear one, it would look pretty in Sara Beth's brown hair. Most of the time, she wore it in a single braid down her back or pulled up into a bun. What would she look like with it rippling down her back, brushed to a silky shine? When things settled down, he needed to take her into town to do something fun. He had a feeling she'd had little of that in her lifetime, especially since her mother died. Maybe they'd show up on a Saturday night to enjoy the live music that always happened on the little rock bandstand in the middle of the street in Everton.

He cleared his throat and reined in his thoughts. A hair ribbon sporting all the colors of the rainbow hung at the top of the rack. After viewing the rainbow in the sky earlier in the day, this was perfect and only twenty-five cents.

Penny candy sat in neat rows next to the checkout counter. He grabbed a paper bag and picked out a few that had been his favorites as a boy. He'd take it to Tab. It would be worth it to see his face light up when he popped a piece of the candy into his mouth.

Under the glass counter, a short row of Marine Band Hohner harmonicas caught his eye. "Ma'am, how much is the cheapest harmonica?"

A matronly lady bustled behind the counter and laid her feather duster next to the cash register. She brought out a bright blue and red box. "This one is four dollars."

He rubbed the back of his neck. That was a lot of money. "And that's the cheapest one?"

She squinted at him, then smiled. "You got a little boy?"

"Sort of. A boy is staying with us, and he don't have much."

She pushed the box across the counter. "Don't tell my boss, but for you, how about three dollars? Would that help?"

"It sure would, ma'am. I'll take it."

Maybe Uncle Seymour could teach Tab to play. Now, that would be something to see.

Whistling, he hurried back to the pickup and pointed it toward home.

Yet the desperate and weary look on Mrs. Chesson's face haunted him. He almost wished she'd agreed to grab the kids and go with him. He'd check on her again soon.

In the meantime, he should start thinking about building another room or two onto the house. In time, they'd need it.

The small sack on the seat wasn't much in size or cost, but it reflected the trueness of his heart and how he'd come to care so much for the people under his charge.

He couldn't wait to see their faces.

The sun was disappearing fast behind the trees when he pulled into the driveway. There was something about lights shining in a window that made a man feel welcome.

As soon as he parked, he took the steps two at a time, careful not to jar his still-tender ribs, and opened the front screen door.

He stopped and sniffed. Did he smell chocolate cake?

"Sara Beth, Seymour, Tab, I'm home."

Sara Beth rounded the corner from the kitchen, wiping her hands on her apron. "Oh, thank goodness. We were getting worried. Tell me everything."

Tab appeared behind her, then Seymour.

"I found your mother, Tab. I talked to her and told her you was safe and that you'd be staying with me and my wife." He looked pointedly at Sara Beth, and she blushed.

Tears pooled in the boy's eyes. "Thank you, Mr. Layken."

Layken removed his hat and tossed it onto a nearby end table. "I'll tell you the truth. She didn't look too good. Had a bruise on one cheek. Tried to convince her to come with me, but she refused."

Tab nodded. "She's afraid, like I was."

"I give you my word. I'll go back and check on her again." He pulled the small sack from behind his back. "Picked up a little something."

Sara Beth gasped when he handed her the hair ribbon. "Oh, it's beautiful, like the rainbow this morning." She stroked the silky length of it. "I'll save it for a special occasion."

He made a mental note to make sure and create a special occasion for her soon.

"And I got this for you, Tab."

The boy shuffled forward, head down. "Ain't nobody ever got me anything. You didn't have to."

"I know I didn't. I wanted to." He pulled out the sack of candy, then the harmonica. "I was thinking maybe Uncle Seymour could teach you to play. Here. Take them."

Again, Tab hesitated, and his face flushed. Then he raised his eyes and met Layken's gaze. It wasn't hard to see a forgotten sparkle hidden deep, trying to burst through all the sadness.

Sara Beth touched Layken's arm. "What a thoughtful thing to get for him."

Tab tore into the candy. "Can I have a piece, Miss Sara Beth?"

She laughed. "Only one, before supper. Wouldn't want to ruin your appetite."

"Lookee, Uncle Seymour. I'll share them."

Seymour tousled the boy's hair. "That's okay, son. You enjoy all of it. I'm way too old for candy."

Tab stared at him. "Really? I hope I don't ever get old." He popped a hard candy in his mouth and sucked on it.

"I hope you don't either." Seymour chuckled, then clapped a hand on his shoulder. "Let's go get the table set for supper. Then, after we eat, maybe I can show you a note on the harmonica."

Sara Beth stood rooted in the same spot as Seymour and Tab hurried to the kitchen.

Layken cleared his throat and folded his arms across his chest. If he didn't, they seemed to have developed a mind of their own and very much wanted to wrap themselves around Sara Beth.

She held the ribbon gently between her thumb and forefinger, then took two steps toward him, stood on tiptoes, and kissed his cheek. "You're a kind and good man, husband."

Before he could stop himself, he unfolded his arms and embraced her. "Maybe my new family brings out the best in me." The sound of his voice was like that of a stranger, low and husky. Perhaps it was due to the lump lodged in his throat.

She murmured against his chest, "Could be."

He tucked a stray hair behind her ear. "Did I smell chocolate cake when I came in?"

Pulling back, she smiled up at him. "Yes, you did. And Tab helped me make it. Wait 'til you see how we fixed up the loft for him."

Her hand nestled snugly in his as they walked toward the kitchen.

She'd called him husband.

And twice today, he'd called her his wife.

Perhaps they were getting used to the idea.

Before he let go, he squeezed her hand and grinned widely.

When she settled her dark eyes on his face, something new shone through them. Something more than gratitude and respect. He wouldn't call it love, but something damned close to it.

He let out a satisfied sigh and joined his makeshift family at the kitchen table that held so many memories of good times for him.

Now, it was time they made new memories to mesh with the old.

The farm was slowly coming back to life.

He soaked up the satisfied looks on the faces around the table.

Tab slipped the harmonica into his pocket, then put his elbows on the table. "Mister Layken, we have a surprise for you, too."

Layken raised his eyebrows. "How about we eat Sara Beth's delicious food first? Then I'll be ready for any kind of surprise." He winked at the boy. "Providing it's a good one."

He caught the glance between Sara Beth and Tab and her almost imperceptible nod.

What had they cooked up while he was gone?

CHAPTER 31

Sara Beth touched the colorful hair ribbon in her apron pocket. How thoughtful of Layken to purchase gifts for her and Tab. She'd seen the shine in the youngster's eyes. Then, the same spark reflected in Uncle Seymour's when he mentioned teaching Tab to play harmonica.

It seemed they were all finding a purpose in living besides simply trying to save Layken's farm. The next thought took her breath away... her farm.

By law, it belonged to them both as husband and wife.

For the first time since the death of her mother, Sara Beth belonged to someone. That made her almost giddy, and a broad smile formed.

The chatter around the table brought her out of her reverie. Tab seemed more like a normal kid should be. No doubt, the news about his mother's condition shook him. Yet what could a child do?

She placed dinner on the table, then joined her little tribe.

With his mouth full, Tab held his fork midway. "This is the best food I've ever had."

Her heart swelled.

Layken took a bite. "I do believe you're right, young man. And I hear there's chocolate cake. Then I want to see your bedroom and what surprise you have waiting for me."

For a split second, Sara Beth hoped Layken wouldn't turn the dog away. But he'd shown he had a big heart.

Tab grinned. "I helped Miss Sara Beth make the cake, and so did Uncle Seymour."

Seymour raised his glass. "Now, don't go giving me too much credit. All I did was gather eggs."

"We are becoming more like one unit working together, and I sure do like that." Layken laid down his fork. "It all started because I was determined to save the farm. But look where it is taking us." He motioned around the table.

Sara Beth's eyes misted. Layken was right. They'd all become intertwined in the process. And the circle kept widening.

A sharp bark from outside the back door jerked Layken to his feet. "What's that?"

Tab jumped up beside him. "It's the surprise, Mr. Layken. Please let us keep her."

Sara Beth put a soft hand on Tab's arm. "Let's introduce Sadie to Layken." She avoided Layken's quizzical stare. "Then we can finish our supper."

Tab hurried to the back door with Layken close behind.

Seymour took another bite and nodded at Sara Beth. "Best let the two of them handle this."

Her stomach clenched. If Layken refused to let Sadie stay, it would devastate Tab. She sat back down, keeping an ear tuned to the two, man and boy.

"See, Mr. Layken. Sadie's so nice and sweet. She's going to have puppies." His words gushed. "And Uncle Seymour found her a box, and I fixed it up nice and warm in the barn. I promise she won't be any trouble. I'll take care of her."

"She sure is a pretty dog. What kind do you reckon she is?"

"Uncle Seymour said she's part spaniel. She's awful skinny and was all muddy when we found her, but Miss Sara Beth fed her, and we got her cleaned up." Tab's next statement went straight to Sara Beth's heart like an arrow. "She's just like me. She's got nobody."

Layken's words came out low and husky, the way they had before, when he'd hugged her. No doubt emotion clogged his throat. "Tab, son, you're not alone anymore. You have the three of us, and now looks like you have a dog. I'd say that makes all of us pretty lucky."

There was no way Sara Beth could resist the urge to twist in her chair so she could see them.

Tab threw his arms around Layken's waist. "Oh, thank you, sir." Then he threw his arms around Sadie. "You get to stay, girl." The dog whimpered, then let out a short bark.

Layken tousled the boy's hair. "Let's go finish our dinner. I'm ready to dig into some chocolate cake."

"Yes, sir." Tab followed him back inside.

Sara Beth reached for Layken's hand as he passed next to her and gave it a squeeze. He winked at her, and she mouthed, "Thank you."

As soon as the meal was over and the dishes cleared away, Tab grabbed Layken's hand and took him to the barn.

The way the boy had settled in since this morning amazed Sara Beth. Once again, she secretly thanked the lightning for striking his tree and forcing him to join them.

Uncle Seymour ambled out to the front porch, and Sara Beth joined him. She held Cuddles and gently rocked the porch swing.

"It sure is a fine night." The old man dropped into a nearby chair.

"That it is, Uncle Seymour. I didn't know if Layken would let the dog stay, but he's proving to have a big heart."

"He's a good man, little girl." He closed his eyes and rocked backward.

"I think tonight's a fine night to listen to the radio. I'll ask Layken when they come back."

Seymour opened his eyes and sucked air between his teeth. "You know you don't have to ask permission. Go turn it on."

"You're right. I don't know if I'll ever get used to that kind of freedom." She stood and handed the rabbit to Seymour.

"You will in time." He nestled the bunny on his lap. "Everything takes time."

He was right, and she knew it in her heart of hearts. Everything worth building would take time, and she liked the progress she and Layken were making on building a relationship, a genuine friendship. And who knew, maybe eventually it would grow into something more.

And if not, it was good, the way it was.

Layken followed Tab up the ladder to his loft, feeling his way in the darkness. When they reached the top, Tab struck a penny match and lit a coal oil lantern. A soft glow reflected a tidy and functional bedroom.

The army cot positioned next to the outer wall had a soft, worn quilt covering it. Layken swallowed past the lump in his throat when he recognized the quilt his mother had often wrapped around him when he was sick. She always said it carried magic. He had no idea where it came from, but suspected a great-grandmother may have made it. How fitting that it would now comfort the boy. Next to the small bed, an overturned crate served as a shelf. Inside, the volumes of books Layken had loved as a boy faced outward, while on top, a ceramic figurine of a dog, with one ear broken off, kept watch. Sara Beth's loving touch lingered everywhere he looked.

He let out a soft whistle, which brought a whimper from Sadie, who had followed them to the barn and waited patiently below.

"This is nice, Tab. But remember to always be careful with the lantern. It could start a fire."

"Yes, sir. I know. I've used one before, and I'm always careful." Tab pulled out the baseball from the box that held the books. "I found this. Did you used to play?"

Layken reached for the ball. "My dad used to play with me, and I played at school. Did you find the bat?"

He scrunched up his face. "No, but we didn't look too hard. Soon as we finished up here was when Uncle Seymour found Sadie."

"I'll look for a bat tomorrow after chores are done. Maybe we can play a little ball."

The glow on the youngster's face was more than a reflection from the lantern. "That'd be swell." As soon as the excitement showed, deep sadness took its place. "I sure do miss my pa."

"I understand, son. I miss my dad, too. But we do the best we can. That's what they'd want."

The boy fisted his hands. "No way my pa would have stood for Earl hurtin' my mama. Wish I was bigger. I'd kill him."

"Now, don't talk that way. I understand the feeling, but trust me, you don't want to kill anyone. That's not an easy thing to live with. I know."

Tab lifted his chin. "Wouldn't bother me a bit to kill that sonofabitch."

"Whoa, now. Don't let Sara Beth hear you using that kind of language."

He dropped his head. "Sorry, sir. I won't. But I mean it."

Layken put a hand on the boy's shoulder and handed the ball back to him. "I understand." He swept one hand around the space. "I think you're gonna be comfortable up here."

"Oh, I will be, sir. It's the nicest place I've had to live in a long time."

"Let's go back to the house. Maybe Uncle Seymour will show you how to blow on the new harmonica."

He waited until the boy extinguished the lantern, needing to know for sure he knew how. Satisfied, he followed him down the ladder, making a mental note to find a flashlight. The matches and coal oil made him a tad bit nervous, even though Tab seemed to know how to handle them safely.

As the two neared the house, music drifted through the night air. Tab stopped and stood still. Sadie sat on her haunches next to him.

"It's okay, Tab. Looks like Sara Beth turned on the radio." He touched the boy's shoulder.

They hurried through the kitchen to the living room, then out to the porch where Sara Beth and Seymour sat.

Tab's wide eyes and slack mouth showed excitement. Finally, he spoke. "How does that work? How does it grab music out of the air?"

Layken chuckled. "It's pretty amazing, isn't it?"

"Sure is, Mr. Layken."

"There's a thing called a transmitter on top of a tall tower at the radio station. The transmitter sends the music through electromagnetic waves, and our radio picks them up."

Sara Beth patted the porch swing. "Sit here with me, Tab."

The boy dropped onto the swing and leaned forward with his elbows on his knees, listening intently.

The deejay's voice came on as the song ended. "Stay tuned, folks, because right after this commercial, we have a brand new single that arrived at the station today, and I'm gonna play it for you. Don't go anywhere."

A commercial played for Red Cross shoes for women. "Keep that youthful swing in your steps, ladies, with fit-tested Red Cross shoes…"

Tab squinched up his face at Sara Beth. "Do you believe that, Miss Sara Beth?"

She laughed softly. "Not really, but it sounds nice, doesn't it?"

"When I get big and have money, I'm gonna buy a pair of those for my mama."

Layken cleared his throat. Life was so unfair. He'd never understand why people like Homer Williams had so much when honest, hard-working folks had so little.

Once more, the gaunt face of Tab's mother haunted him. His gut told him he'd have to do something, but what? He couldn't force the woman to come with him.

The deejay popped back on. "And now, like I promised. You're hearing this little ditty for the first time right here on WLS 870 in Chicago. *Smoke, Smoke, Smoke that Cigarette* from Tex Williams."

The music started, and after a minute, Tab let out a giggle. "That's the silliest song I've ever heard."

Sara Beth tapped her foot. "I have to agree with you, but it's a catchy number."

Layken leaned back and watched them.

Somehow, though he couldn't see it, things were going to turn out all right for Tab's family. Guess he'd have to wait and see how it all unfolded.

But tomorrow, he'd take Sara Beth into Everton and discreetly get some things for the boy.

His gaze wandered to the boy's foot next to Sara Beth's.

From where he sat, they looked close to the same size.

That would work out nicely for getting new shoes for Tab without raising suspicion.

He wouldn't do anything that would jeopardize his little makeshift family.

Her small, dainty foot pushed the swing back and forth. Little by little, he was learning more about his wife. And he liked everything he knew about her.

Once Seymour and Tab went to bed, he'd talk to Sara Beth and share his plan.

He warmed at the anticipation.

Maybe, with any luck, he'd even steal a kiss.

CHAPTER 32

The following day, with the sun high in the sky, Layken finished his chores in record time and escorted Sara Beth to the pickup for the drive into Everton to get some necessities for Tab.

He shot a sideways glance as he turned the key and started the engine. "You look very pretty today, Sara Beth. I think mothering Tab agrees with you."

Her cheeks turned pink, adding to her glow. "He's a sweet boy, and I won't deny he's wiggled his way into my heart. But I'll never replace his mother."

"No, of course not." He nosed the pickup toward the blacktop road. "It's apparent that having him around agrees with you. And you trust him, or you would never have left Cuddles with him today."

She chuckled. "He adores Cuddles. I know he'll take care of him." She clenched her hands together on her lap.

"What is it, Sara Beth? Something's bothering you." He was learning to read the signs when she wasn't at ease.

"I'm afraid Earl might show up again while we're gone."

Layken tugged the brim of his hat lower. "I share the same worry. But I trust Seymour to handle it if he does."

"You're right." She sighed and stared out the window at the passing scenery. "I've never told you this, but I ran to Uncle Seymour right after my father informed me I was to marry you. He made me promise if you

227

ever laid a hand on me, I would find him and tell him. I don't know what he intended, but I do know he'll watch out for Tab."

"It's obvious Seymour adores you and would defend you to the death." Layken chuckled. "Glad I'll never give him a reason." No doubt the old man was more capable than his age might lead one to believe.

They fell silent as Layken pondered Sara Beth's words. It would be no surprise to learn that the widow Jones hadn't fired Seymour at all. He came to look after Sara Beth. That kind of devotion deserved respect.

After a few miles, Sara Beth turned on the seat to face him. "Our plan is to go to the dry goods store, in and out as fast as possible?"

"That's what I thought."

"I have to wonder if the child has ever had new clothes. If I buy a few yards of material, I can make him some shirts and overalls for a lot less than what store-bought ones cost. But he needs underwear, socks, shoes, and maybe one set of clothes?"

"Sounds good. Just wondering how we'll make the purchase without getting any tongues wagging."

She folded and unfolded her hands on her lap. "What if we tell the clerk about a neighbor kid that is in need of some things? Maybe that will be enough cover."

Layken could hope so. He didn't want to raise any unnecessary suspicions. "Mainly, we want to get in and out as quick as we can."

"Hopefully, Mabel is working today." Sara Beth tugged at a loose thread on her blouse. "She never pries or gossips. I know this is taking money away from the farm budget, but it's worthwhile."

"Don't you worry none about the money. We can spare a few dollars to get what we need." Layken drummed the steering wheel. While he did worry about the money, he'd never let on to Sara Beth. "Besides, the peanut crop is looking good. That ought to bring us a bit of a return."

"Thank goodness for the rain and for your healing."

"Your help has been a godsend, Sara Beth. Don't discount that. Not to mention Seymour." No longer having to face the monumental task of saving the farm alone brought a comfort that spread across his chest. "And now, with Tab pitching in, we have a team."

"It's uncanny how life can turn around, isn't it?" She turned back toward the window.

"That it is." They fell silent again as they neared the outskirts of Everton.

Sara Beth whispered, "I hate coming to town. I'm always afraid I'll run into my father or, God forbid, his new wife."

Layken reached across the seat and squeezed her hand. "I'll be right there with you. No one is going to disrespect you. Hold your head high and look 'em in the eye."

Slowing the pickup to a crawl, they passed by the café, where a couple headed inside. The eight-foot-square rock bandstand sat prominently in the intersection of two streets.

A long mournful whistle announced the arrival of the daily Louis-San Francisco Railway train. A bustle of activity always accompanied the arrival and for a short time, the train depot came alive with people and activity as goods were loaded and unloaded from the cars and travelers stepped inside the cool interior of the hotel for a respite.

Layken maneuvered around the bandstand, past the bank and feed store, pulling to a stop in front of Wilson's Dry Goods, and killed the engine. The weathered wood on the exterior of the aging establishment spoke of the need for an upgrade. But it matched the rest of the tiny town. Folks couldn't find much reason to spread on a coat of paint. After all, it didn't change what was inside the store. "Ready?"

Sara Beth nodded and opened the truck door. "Let's go."

"Welcome to Wilson's. Come on in." A lady's singsong voice rang out, along with the bell on the door as they stepped inside.

The familiar smell of lemon oil mixed with coffee and tobacco brought back a rush of memories for Layken. He'd stepped inside the store many times with his mother.

Sara Beth paused beside the counter. "Hello, Mabel. We need to get a few things."

"Well, you kids give me a shout if you need help." She swiped a feather duster across the counter. She pointed to a large red and white box next to the front door. "And lookie at that. We're getting modern here at Wilsons. For a nickel, you can have an ice-cold Coca-Cola."

Layken tipped his hat. "We may have to try one of those before we leave."

Sara Beth stared at the machine, then glanced at Layken. "That's pretty special, Mabel. Can't say that I've ever had a Coca-Cola."

With his hand in the crook of Sara Beth's arm, she led him to the clothing section. "Then it's settled. I'll buy you a coke." He motioned toward the storefront. "Looks like we're in luck with her working today. You've seriously never had a Coke?"

"Seriously, I never have." Sara Beth flashed a smile.

"Then let's gather our purchases and I'll get us one on the way out."

They quickly picked out a blue chambray shirt, a pair of cotton overalls, a package of socks, and one of underwear. Then Sara Beth tried on several pairs of shoes, finally settling on a brown pair of lace-up boots.

"These are a little snug on my foot, so they should fit Tab perfectly." She glanced up. "Then we're all set except for picking out some material."

"I'll take these on up." Layken carried their selection to the counter.

Mabel raised her eyebrows. "Buying for a young'un?"

"Got a neighbor kid that's in dire need of some things, so helping out."

"That's mighty kind of you." Mabel pushed her glasses up on her nose. "Your folks were always generous and helping others, especially during the Depression. Glad to see you carrying that on."

Layken nodded and laid a dollar on the counter. "And I need change for the new coke machine."

She quickly gave him three quarters, a dime and three nickels, and he hurried to the machine. He stared out the front window, tapping his foot. *Hurry, Sara Beth. Let's get the hell outta here.* He couldn't find a reason for the prickles on his skin and the clench of his gut.

Within a few minutes, Sara Beth brought the material she'd chosen, and Mabel cut it. "You're looking well, Sara Beth. We miss you around town."

"We, Mabel?" Sara Beth let out a soft chuckle.

Mabel blustered. "I can only speak for myself. Always liked you."

"I always liked you too, Mabel. You're kind."

Finally, Mabel wrapped their purchases in brown paper tied with twine, and they headed toward the door. Layken passed an open bottle of coke to Sara Beth. "For you, Mrs. Martin."

She took a sip, then rubbed her nose. "It tastes good, but fizzes in my nose."

He laughed and took a final swig from his bottle, then set it in the rack for empties.

On the sidewalk, three doors down, a commotion drew Layken's attention and a gasp from Sara Beth.

"Help! Help me!" Homer Williams stumbled out the front door of the bank. "We've been robbed."

Frozen in place, Layken stared at his father-in-law. What little hair Williams had was sticking up in all directions, and his face a bright shade of red.

Before Layken could react, a tall, slender man dashed down the sidewalk, knocking an elderly woman off her feet. A shot fired into the air created pandemonium, as folks darted inside buildings to escape impending violence.

Layken drew in a sharp breath. "Shit!"

Earl headed straight toward them, brandishing the smoking pistol, a paper bag secured under his arm.

The man paused for a split second as he neared Layken and Sara Beth.

In one swift move, he grabbed Sara Beth, knocking her bottle of coke onto the sidewalk. He wrapped his free arm around her neck, jerking her off her feet.

Sara Beth screamed and struggled against his hold, her eyes wide with fear. "Layken, help!"

Layken's blood froze in his veins and chills raced down his spine. Earl's crazed and desperate stare was one he'd seen before.

Doubting Earl recognized him from their brief encounter, Layken dropped the packages and put his hands out in front of him. "Whoa. You don't want to do that, mister."

Earl snarled, "The hell I don't. This pretty face is my ticket out of this one-horse town." He waved the gun at Layken. "So back off!" He put the pistol to the side of Sara Beth's head. "Or she gets it."

For once, Layken wished Everton was big enough to have a sheriff. They only had a night watchman who helped keep the riff-raff out, but the closest law officer was in Greenfield.

He held eye contact with Sara Beth, trying to transfer his thoughts to her. *Don't panic. Don't let him see you sweat.*

As she squirmed and twisted, trying to get out of Earl's grip, a tear slipped out of the corner of her eye and a frightened whimper left her constricted throat.

Layken wanted more than anything to knock Earl away from her and pull her into his arms.

But the gun was loaded, and the man was crazy enough to use it. He wouldn't risk Sara Beth's life for anything.

While several of the townsfolk ran to Homer Williams, Layken took advantage of the distraction to pick up the packages from the sidewalk and toss them into the bed of the pickup, as if nothing was out of the ordinary.

Earl followed his every move, then jerked Sara Beth toward the pickup. "Get in," he growled.

Layken opened the door to get inside when Earl kicked it shut. "Not you, asshole. Her. And give me the keys."

There was no way on God's green earth he would stand by and let Earl drive away with Sara Beth. He nonchalantly dug into his pocket and pulled out a key. While he knew it didn't fit the pickup, he could only hope it would buy him a minute of time. One minute was all he needed. Well, that and a bit of luck.

Layken's nerves stretched taut as Homer Williams' wails traveled across the distance. "I've got a scratch on my head. Oh, God, I'm bleeding."

Layken ground his teeth. It took every bit of willpower he had to stay focused on Sara Beth. The man's only daughter was in danger, and all he could think about was a superficial scratch.

Earl shoved her against the side of the pickup and she shrieked.

"Shut up," he roared. He struck her face with the back of his hand.

Sara Beth's head hit the pickup door.

A growl left Layken's throat. He poised, fists clenched, ready to pounce—rage built inside him, longing to be released.

Every muscle tensed. He narrowed his eyes.

His jaw clenched, he prayed for some kind of distraction. All he needed was half a second.

CHAPTER 33

In a flash, Sara Beth twisted to the side, lifted her right foot, and caught Earl directly behind his knee.

The man went down with a thud, followed by a loud curse and a grunt.

That opportunity was exactly what Layken needed. His fist connected with Earl's jaw, and the satisfying crack only fueled his anger. In less than two seconds, he was on top of Earl, pummeling his face with unleashed fury.

He glimpsed Sara Beth's dainty foot kicking Earl's gun out into the street, and pride spread across his chest. His girl was a fighter.

"Get off me." Earl struggled beneath Layken's weight.

"You're a sorry piece of shit. And you slapped my wife. So why should I get off?" Layken growled between clenched teeth as he let his fists fly again, this time landing directly on Earl's ribcage.

"I'll kill you!" Earl thrashed underneath, landing a fist on Layken's jaw.

Layken barely reacted. Adrenaline had him numb to pain, including the one in his side from the still tender ribs. "I don't think so. Your sorry days of stealing and mistreating women and children are over. You're going to spend time behind bars."

Blood oozed from Earl's nose and out of the corner of his cracked lip.

By the time the other townsfolk reached the scene of the fight, Layken had Earl subdued, with his hands pinned above his head.

"Oh, hell." One of the men stepped back. "Looks like that Martin boy has this under control, and he didn't even lose his hat. Jim, go get some rope. We'll make sure the thieving bastard stays put 'til we can get the sheriff over here."

Layken reluctantly got up, dragging Earl to his feet. "Tie him up on the bandstand. I want everyone to see the big bad bank robber."

Earl let loose a wad of spittle toward Layken and missed.

The crowd of men dragged Earl off toward the rock gazebo that sat in the middle of town, a length of rope hanging from one man's shoulder.

"Pete, go call the sheriff. Tell him we caught a bank robber red-handed. We'll take turns standing watch 'til the sheriff gets here. But it'll be tomorrow before he can catch the train over to get him."

"You can't leave me out here all night," Earl twisted his body, trying to get free from the giant of a man holding onto him.

"The hell we can't. It's better than what you deserve, you no good thieving bastard." The town blacksmith kept an iron grip.

The new Mrs. Williams came flying down the street, her hair in curlers and apron flopping. "Homer. Homer. Are you okay? I heard."

Homer Williams thrust out his chest. "I'm fine, honey. Just a little scratch. But we got him." He pointed toward Earl.

Sara Beth laid a hand on Layken's arm, and he promptly wrapped it around her waist. "You okay?"

She nodded, rubbing her jaw where a red handprint formed. "I think so."

Her body trembled against him. "Don't let Homer Williams get to you. I've never seen a more pitiful excuse for a man than your father," he whispered in her ear.

"I have to agree. But you. You saved me and stopped Earl from getting away."

Layken glanced down at her and tucked a stray strand of hair behind her ear. "I wanted to do more to him, but it's best to let the law handle it." He bent and picked up the paper bag Earl had been carrying under his arm.

With one arm still wrapped protectively around Sara Beth, he reached Homer Williams in a determined stride and thrust the bag toward him. "Here's your money."

Homer blustered. "Well, if it ain't my long-lost daughter. Don't you two look cozy?"

"We're married, Father. Remember?" Sara Beth's words held an icy sting. "You need to thank Layken for stopping the robber and getting your money back."

Layken tipped his hat to the new Mrs. Williams and focused on Homer's red face. "No thanks necessary. Only doing what any real man would."

"Sara Beth, aren't you even going to ask me if I'm okay?" Homer whined.

"Father, I can see you're fine. You have a minor scratch. I'm sure your new wife will tend to it."

Layken took Sara Beth's hand and led her back to the pickup without a backward glance. He didn't miss the tremble that ran through her. No doubt, the shock and adrenaline brought on by the attack were wearing off.

Once she climbed in, he closed her door and hurried to the driver's side. The quicker they got out of town, the better.

Sara Beth gave in to the after-effects of the attack and sank into the seat, her head in her hands. Silent sobs shook her shoulders.

"You're okay, Sara Beth. It's over." Layken's gentle words drifted across the small space between them.

"I'm...sss-ssorry."

"No apology necessary. You're having a normal reaction to stress."

She swiped at her nose and sat up straighter, glancing at her husband. A purplish bruise was beginning to form on his jaw where Earl's fist had connected. "What about you? I see a bruise forming."

Layken rubbed his jaw. "It's nothing. I'm happy it all went down the way it did, except for the part about Earl grabbing you." He pulled the pickup over to the side of the road and let the engine idle.

"He could've killed you, and would've if he'd gotten a chance." She wiped her eyes. "Why are we stopping?"

He leaned toward her. "Because there's something I need to say, and I want to look at you while I say it."

She folded her hands on her lap, hardly daring to breathe. Perhaps she'd disappointed him. She was used to that, but somehow the idea of it caused a deeper ache inside her chest. She met his gaze and fought to control her trembling lip. "Okay. I guess just say it." She lifted her chin.

"I want to say I've never been more proud to be your husband than I was back there." His voice grew husky. "You're a fighter, Sara Beth. I hope I'm never on the receiving end of that." A wide grin formed. He held up a hand as she opened her mouth. "Let me finish."

"Go on," she whispered.

"I realized when Earl grabbed you that I would kill for you. I would lay down my own life for you. I've developed some deep feelings for you." He softly touched the red splotch on the side of her face.

She sucked in a breath, and more tears leaked out. "I was so scared for you. Your ribs aren't completely healed yet. I knew Earl was going to hurt you more."

He let out a soft chuckle. "I've fought much bigger and badder men than him. He's a bully and a chicken. I know his kind. I had him. All I needed was half a chance, and that kick behind his knee you gave him was it."

A smile formed behind her tears. "It was all I could think of to do. Uncle Seymour taught me that trick when I was a little girl."

"Right now, I have the strongest urge to wrap my arms around you and hold you. Would you let me do that?" He pinned her with his gaze.

Breaking the intensity of his stare, she opened the pickup door with her free hand. "Yes. I would."

Before she could clear the step, Layken was around the pickup and lifted her down. Her heart did flip-flops as he drew her into the circle of his arms. She laid her cheek against his chest, comforted by the steady beat of his heart in her ear. They stood that way, unmoving for a long minute.

When she raised her head, the desire burning in his eyes brought shivers, even though the day was quite warm.

"I'd like it if you'd kiss me."

A soft growl left Layken's throat. "You don't have to ask me twice."

He lowered his head and softly pressed his lips to hers.

While the kiss was gentle, the sincerity of it went all the way to her toes.

How would she ever get used to the idea of someone genuinely caring for her? Or even accept that she was worthy?

Layken held her tight for another few seconds. "As long as I'm living and breathing, no one is going to hurt you again. I give you my word."

His shirt muffled her reply. "You're a good man, and I'm glad my father forced me to marry you."

"So am I." He released her, took a step back, then brought both her hands to his lips and kissed each. "Let's go home." The words came out gruff.

Immediately feeling a loss as he stepped away, she said, "I know Tab will be relieved to hear that Earl has been caught, that it's over and he is safe."

He waited until she was seated back in the pickup before he closed her door, then returned to the driver's side.

She spared a glance, only to meet his smoky blue-gray eyes boring into hers. "Thank you."

"For?"

"For caring."

"Sara Beth, I do care. And I won't lie. That feeling is growing stronger each day. But I don't want to put any pressure on you or make you feel like you need to respond any certain way. Whatever we have, I want it to grow on its own, not forced like our marriage was."

"What I feel for you is real, and not out of obligation as your wife, or repayment for your kindness."

"That's good enough." He shifted into gear and let off the clutch.

A part of her wanted to scoot across the seat to reclaim the closeness. Yet another part said to stay where she was.

She reached up and touched her lips where his kiss had been gentle and sweet.

Yet, the passion in his eyes told her much more than the kiss did.

Her husband had needs, and she would look forward to being his wife in every way someday.

But only when it was right.

Layken deserved that.

She deserved that.

CHAPTER 34

An excited mama dog and an equally excited little boy holding the bunny ran to greet Sara Beth and Layken before the pickup rolled to a complete stop in front of the farmhouse.

What a big difference between the eager face in front of her and the terrified one Sara Beth had discovered at the tree house in the forest.

She gave Layken a reassuring glance before opening the pickup door. "Looks like everyone here is okay." She took Cuddles from Tab. "You did a good job of looking after things, and we brought you something."

Layken followed with the packages. "Let's go inside. We have something to tell you, ace."

The boy frowned, and his shoulders drooped. "You ain't making me go away, are you?"

Sara Beth's heart broke. She put a hand on Tab's shoulder. "Oh, heavens no. In fact, we have some good news."

Tab squinted. "What happened to your face, Mr. Layken?"

"Well, that's part of what we have to tell you." He held the screen door, and they filed into the living room. Uncle Seymour joined them from the kitchen.

"We were starting some dinner. You kids hungry?" The old man wiped his hands on his overalls.

Sara Beth put a hand on her hip. "Uncle Seymour. You didn't have to do that."

Seymour patted her on the back. "No trouble. Happy to. Just a pot of soup. Of course, it's nothing fancy like you make. Besides, Tab helped."

Sara Beth hugged him. "Thank both of you."

Layken stood next to the fireplace. "Take a seat, everyone. We have some things to discuss."

Sara Beth stole a sideways glance at her husband. He'd filled out some since she'd been feeding him, and she admired his muscular physique, remembering the comfort of his arms around her, and the tingles his kiss brought. She gave him a wan smile as he focused his attention on Tab.

"First of all, Tab, you never have to worry about Earl finding you or hurting you or your family ever again. We caught him red-handed robbing the bank in town."

Tab let out a loud gasp. "You caught him?"

Sara Beth stroked Cuddles. "You shoulda seen Mr. Layken, Tab. He fought Earl, and then the men in town tied him up to wait for the sheriff to come and get him tomorrow."

"That's where you got the bruise on your jaw?" Tab screwed up his face.

"Yep. That's it, but you should see Earl. He looks a lot worse."

"Well, good! I'm glad you gave the bastard what for."

Sara Beth cleared her throat. "Language, Tab."

He ducked his head. "Sorry, Miss Sara Beth."

Layken chuckled. "It's okay. You get a free pass this one time. But there's more." He handed the packages to Sara Beth. "We got you a few things."

Tears misted the boy's eyes. "For me?"

"For you." Sara Beth untied the twine, laid the clothes on the coffee table, and then handed him the new shoes. "And I got some material to make you a few more things."

"But how could you afford all of this?" Tab's voice cracked.

"It wasn't much, really." Layken caught Sara Beth's gaze and winked.

"I'll make it up to you, Mr. Layken. I promise I'll work hard."

Sara Beth stood and pulled the boy into a hug. "We know you will, Tab. And we appreciate all you do. Don't worry. Mr. Layken assured me we could afford these, and you needed them."

Seymour pushed to his feet. "This calls for a celebration. After supper, we need to have some music out on the porch." He mussed Tab's hair. "And you get your first harmonica lesson."

"I do believe that's a good idea, Seymour." Layken twirled his hat between his hands. "There's something else we need to talk about, Tab. Your mother and brother and sister."

Tab swiped at his nose. "What about them?"

"Sara Beth and I are going over to Greenfield tomorrow and see if we can talk them into coming here. I know this isn't much, but at least your family would all be together. Maybe you could share your bedroom with your brother until I could get something else built."

Uncontrollable sobs shook the young boy's shoulders. "You mean it, Mr. Layken? Can I go with you to Greenfield? That is, if you're sure Earl's really not going to show up."

"I can assure you the men in Everton will make sure Earl doesn't get away. They're gonna take turns guarding him, and then the sheriff will lock him up behind iron bars. No one can get out of those."

Sara Beth hoped Layken spoke the truth. She shuddered, imagining what kind of revenge on them all Earl might extract should he get away.

Tab ran to Layken and threw his arms around his waist. "I can't thank you enough, sir."

Layken cleared his throat and patted the child's back. "Okay. How about we finish the evening chores and get ready for supper? You might want to try on your new clothes."

"Mr. Layken's right. We need to make sure they fit." Sara Beth patted his back. "Why don't you go try them on so we can see?"

Tab straightened and wiped his tears. "Yes, ma'am." He picked up the clothes and disappeared into the bathroom.

"How about you wash up while you're in there?" Sara Beth called out.

A muffled reply acknowledged he'd heard her.

"Seymour, let's me and you go tend to the evening chores." Layken winked at Sara Beth. "We've got an evening of celebrating to do."

Her mind relived the velvet touch of Layken's earlier kiss. She had to wonder if his comment held a hidden meaning. Her pulse quickened as she made a beeline for the kitchen. She grabbed her apron off the nail by the door, humming a tune she loved to play on her thumb piano.

She had precisely enough chocolate and time left to stir up another cake.

A few hours later, Tab lay on his cot in the loft with a full tummy, holding his new harmonica with a smile on his face. He lay flat, still dressed in his new clothes, despite the heat. He touched the crisp new fabric as if to make sure it was still real.

His new boots sat under his cot, ready for his feet to slide into come morning. They all fit perfectly.

He shuddered at the memories that clouded his young mind. The last two years had been hard. The beatings, being locked in the stifling dark pantry, and listening to Earl beat on his mother were images and sounds time couldn't erase.

But squatting on the deserted Martin farm had turned out to be the beginning of good things for him and maybe his whole family.

Should he dare to hope all the bad times were over?

He pictured his mother's face, alight with joy, when Earl was no longer a threat, and they could all be together again.

It didn't matter if they had to bunk up. At least they'd be safe.

And someday he'd pay Layken Martin back for his kindness.

Excitement kept him awake way past his normal bedtime. Tomorrow held promise. Tomorrow held new beginnings for his little family. Even at twelve, he felt like a man. He couldn't wait for his body to catch up to his mind.

And when he got grown, he was going to always be kind like Mr. Layken and when the time came, he'd look for a wife exactly like Miss Sara Beth.

Finally, around midnight, he dozed, only to be awakened a short time later by Sadie's frantic barking.

Something was wrong. He could feel it. His skin prickled despite the heat. He eased off his cot and inched toward the opening that overlooked the house and Sara Beth's garden.

Movement in the shadows caught his eye.

"No, it can't be," he muttered. "I must be dreaming." He pinched his arm, and the immediate sting told him he was indeed awake.

He instantly recognized the tall, thin man, and the glow of the cigarette in his mouth, as he slinked through the shadows toward the barn. His heart stopped.

Sadie barked louder, snarling and snapping her teeth.

Earl kicked at her and let out a low curse. Sadie dodged his foot, and even though she backed off, she still growled and bared her teeth.

Tab balled his fists. If he hurt Sadie, he'd kill him. He glanced around the small space for anything he could use as a weapon.

He prayed that the commotion would wake Mr. Layken, and he'd come to investigate. Or maybe Uncle Seymour heard it.

But what if they didn't? The responsibility rested on his thin shoulders to protect these people who had become as close as any family.

An acrid odor reached the boy's nose.

Kerosene.

Earl's intent became clear. He was going to burn them out.

Tab had to stop him. But how? He reached for the ceramic dog sitting on top of the box next to his cot. Maybe he could knock him out if he could throw it hard enough.

He crawled to the edge of the loft for a better view, poised, waiting.

Earl sprinkled kerosene across the hay and into the empty stalls.

Anger overtook fear. He wouldn't let him destroy the only good thing he'd found.

Another movement from outside the barn drew his attention back to the opening.

Sara Beth stood in the kitchen door.

Layken hitched up his pants, running across the yard barefoot, with his rifle tucked under one arm. "Stay back, Sara Beth. Stop right there, mister," he yelled as he cocked the gun.

Tab held his breath.

Earl jerked toward the voice and tossed the kerosene can over his shoulder. "Whatcha gonna do about it this time, farmer? The whole damn place'll go up in flames before you can get off a shot."

Sadie lunged through the opening and grabbed Earl's pant leg. He shook his leg and sent her tumbling across the floor.

Layken skidded to a stop, and Tab crawled back to the edge of the loft. If only he could get a clear view. He gripped the ceramic piece tighter, hoping to distract Earl long enough for Mr. Layken to get to him.

He held his breath as Layken laid down the rifle and put his hands out in front of him. "Whoa, now. Let's talk about this."

"I want the boy," Earl snarled. "Ain't leavin' 'til I get him."

"What boy? I've told you before, there's no boy here. You need to get gone, and I'll forget you ever showed up here."

Earl cackled. "You really think I'm that big of a fool, farmer?"

Out of the corner of his eye, Tab spied Uncle Seymour slinking along the wall, getting closer to Earl's back.

The boy had to help. He stood and yelled out, "Come and get me, Earl, if you think you're big enough."

Earl jerked his gaze upward. "There you are, you little shit." He moved toward the ladder. "You're comin' with me."

"No, I ain't." Tab backed up. "You can't make me."

Earl took a long drag from his cigarette and the ash turned red. "You really want me to burn this place down?"

Sadie barked furiously as Layken eased forward while Uncle Seymour came from the other side. Just a little bit more time, and they'd have him.

Too late!

Earl started up the ladder and dropped the cigarette behind him.

What happened next was a flash. Tab first tossed the ceramic dog toward Earl and missed. Then he grabbed the lantern from its perch and flung it at Earl's head the minute his beady, black eyes appeared.

The blow sent him reeling downward as flames licked at the walls.

Tab let out a piercing scream when Layken tackled Earl. Uncle Seymour grabbed a nearby blanket in an attempt to quell the flames.

Hard, furious punches flew as Layken tangled with the man for the second time.

CHAPTER 35

Dressed only in her gown, Sara Beth dashed out the back door, grabbed the one garden hose they owned, and sprinted toward the barn, yelling at the top of her lungs, "Tab, get out! Quick!"

She had no way of knowing if Layken was okay, but the fire was spreading, gobbling up the weathered dry wood like a hungry monster. Each new board crackled as the flames devoured it, sending sparks into the sky.

Everything they were working so hard to save and build was turning to ash in front of her eyes. It took all her effort to keep her knees from buckling.

With the hose turned on full force, she sprayed a stream of water blindly toward the barn.

Everyone had to get out of there.

Human life was the one thing they couldn't replace.

Two boots hit the ground beside her, and she glanced up to see Tab tossing the box of books from the barn loft. She moved over in time to avoid being hit. "Leave it all, Tab. Get out of there."

The hose jerked her back, halting her progress. It wasn't long enough to go any farther.

Oh, God! What could she do?

"Uncle Seymour, Layken," she screamed. "Get out! Now! Please."

Her hands trembled, and she jumped when a loud crash came from inside the structure, sending a new spray of sparks into the night air.

She only breathed a tiny sigh of relief when Tab's slight frame appeared in the opening, illuminated by the flames.

But then he turned around and went back inside.

"Tab!" *What was he doing?* "Tab! Layken! Uncle Seymour! Get out." She lifted the water hose high over her head to make the spray go closer to the building.

Finally, Tab appeared, carrying Sadie under one arm and the barn cat under the other. He set the animals down and ran toward her, coughing and crying, his face covered with soot. "Miss Sara Beth. We have to help 'em."

She thrust the water hose into the boy's hands. "Keep this pointed toward the barn."

"What are you going to do? You can't go in there. What if you get burned?"

"I have to help. Keep the water spraying."

With her heart pounding, she turned back toward the house, running as fast as her legs could carry her. Inside, she jerked the bedspread off her bed and dashed back out.

After dipping it into the water trough, she wrapped it around herself, covering her nose and mouth, and charged into the barn.

The intense heat reached through the wet layers, pushing her back. Thick smoke made it near to impossible to see, but the noise of a struggle and loud punches and grunts led her to Layken.

When she reached him, he motioned her back and coughed. "I've got him. Get back out."

"Uncle Seymour?" The roar of the angry flames almost drowned out her words and sucked all the oxygen out of her lungs.

"Go, Sara Beth. Now!" Layken's sternness spurred her into action.

As she turned, her foot caught on the edge of a plow, and she fell headlong, the bedspread tangled around her legs.

Layken let out a curse, delivered a final blow to Earl, knocking him unconscious, then grabbed her and slung her over his shoulder while he dragged Earl behind him.

Sara Beth sobbed. "Uncle Seymour. We have to help him."

Tab threw down the water hose and dashed toward them as Layken put her down gently. "I'll get Seymour. Stay here with Tab." He snatched the rifle from where he'd dropped it earlier and thrust it into Tab's hands. "Keep Earl covered, and shoot the bastard if he wakes up, son." He squeezed the boy's shoulder. "I mean it. Don't hesitate for a second."

"Don't worry, Mr. Layken. I'll shoot him." The boy spread his legs for more balance and let out a ragged cough into his shirtsleeve. He put the gun to his shoulder, squinting one eye, while he pointed the weapon directly at Earl's still form.

"Please be careful." Sara Beth thrust the still-damp bedspread toward Layken. Her knees knocked together so hard she could barely stay on her feet. Her lungs burned from the short time she'd been in the barn, so she could only imagine what Layken's must feel like. Yet, he'd go back in to save Uncle Seymour. And if he didn't, she would.

She glanced toward Tab. The heavy rifle dwarfed the boy, and for a minute she questioned Layken's judgment in giving Tab such a responsibility. No matter. If worse came to worse, she'd help Tab.

Her heart broke as she stared at the old structure that was beginning to cave in on itself. Her hands shook violently. *Oh, God! Uncle Seymour had to be okay.*

She couldn't bear to lose her dearest friend, or God forbid that he was injured and trapped inside.

In a flash, Layken ripped off a long strip from the bedspread and wrapped it around his face.

But before he could make it back inside, the old man limped around the corner of the barn from the back side, carrying a burlap sack.

Sara Beth rushed to meet him, throwing her arms around him. Relief left her weak. "Uncle Seymour! Are you okay?"

He patted her on the back. "I'm okay, little girl," he rasped.

"How did you get out?" Her voice shook as hard as her hands.

At that moment, another crash came from inside as part of the roof collapsed, followed by an explosion that shook the ground. It took all of her strength to stay on her feet.

"Broke through the back wall with an ax." He dropped the bag onto the ground. "Managed to get most of my stuff."

Layken put an arm around her shoulders and shook Seymour's hand.

Earl groaned and tried to roll over, then attempted to raise up, letting out a string of curses followed by a severe rattling coughing attack.

Layken pushed him back with his foot. "Don't even try it, you sonofabitch." He motioned to Tab to give him the rifle, then pressed it hard into Earl's back. "I'd as soon shoot you as look at you." He motioned to the others. "Get around front where it's safer."

With Earl's face pressed into the ground, his muffled protests went unheard.

Good!

Sara Beth tugged at Tab's sleeve. "Let's go."

Tab threw his small arms around Sara Beth's waist, burying his face in her nightclothes, while he let out a heart-wrenching sob. "I'm so sorry, Miss Sara Beth. It's my fault Earl came here."

Sara Beth kneeled down to hug the boy as smoke burned her eyes and lungs. She attempted to clear her throat. "Don't say that, Tab. Earl is an evil man, and Mr. Layken stopped him from robbing the bank yesterday, so he was out for revenge." She smoothed back his hair. "You're a very brave boy. But don't you ever scare me like that again. We could always replace your things."

"No, ma'am. I wasn't gonna let no fire burn up my new shoes and books." Sadie let out a short bark and licked his face. The boy let go of Sara Beth, sat on the ground, and pulled the dog onto his lap. "And I wasn't gonna let Earl hurt Sadie or any of you." He looked up. "But the barn is a goner."

Sparks flew through the night air, a few landing near the house.

Uncle Seymour stepped forward. "Hurry it up, Sara Beth. Take the boy and animals around front." He picked up the water hose. "I'll make sure the house don't catch fire."

Panic rose in Sara Beth's throat again. She hadn't considered that it could spread to the house. No way could she simply sit by and watch, and from the look on Tab's face, neither could he.

She stayed rooted and made eye contact with Layken. She gasped at the blood running through black soot down the side of his face. His hair stuck up at odd angles, and some of it appeared to be singed off.

As if he could read her mind, he said softly, "I'm okay, Sara Beth. We can tend to me later."

Forcing a calm she didn't feel, she squared her shoulders and asked, "What can I do to help?"

Tab stepped forward, raising his chin. "Me too, Mr. Layken. What can I do?"

"I'd feel better if you and Tab were farther away."

She met his gaze. "And I'd feel a mite better if I was pitching in to help."

Layken raked a hand through his disheveled hair and blew out a sigh. "We can't save the barn. It'll burn itself out. But maybe if we can keep this side of the house wet, we stand a better chance of turning the fire. Find buckets and start tossing water onto the ground and the house."

"I know where buckets are." Tab ran off toward the garden.

"Once I'm satisfied Earl can't get loose, then I'll pitch in as well. Sara Beth, can you go in the house and bring me anything you can find? The rope was all in the barn, so maybe leather."

She nodded and darted inside. With her heart racing and the glow from the flames reflecting on the windows, she jerked open dresser drawers and grabbed every strip of leather she could find.

Acrid smoke mixed with despair filled the air and evaporated into the water Uncle Seymour sprayed onto the roof of the house.

With the belts in hand, she raced through the house and back to Layken, where she handed them to him.

Earl struggled against Layken's hold. Raw hatred emanated from the man.

Once Layken had that situation under control, she grabbed one of the buckets Tab had retrieved and started making trips from the water trough toward the house.

Her legs ached, and rocks dug into her bare feet. But it didn't matter. Nothing mattered but saving what they could.

She could only imagine what Layken must be feeling, watching angry, licking flames destroy the tractor and everything inside the barn.

Earl was lucky that Layken didn't kill him outright.

Once Layken had Earl's hands and feet tied securely, he stuffed a rag into the man's mouth and gave him one last hard kick.

Then he joined Sara Beth, taking the bucket from her.

"We need to form a brigade. You stay by the trough and refill the buckets when Tab brings them back."

She nodded, glad for the reprieve to give her feet and legs a break.

Hot, enraged flames lit up the night sky. Soon, the sun would begin to chase the darkness away. Daylight would reveal the extent of the destruction, and Sara Beth dreaded seeing it.

How could Layken stay so calm when everything he worked so hard to save was being destroyed? He had to be falling apart inside.

But his demeanor was deadly focused and calm.

Perhaps that's what the military trained him to do in the face of disaster.

Filling bucket after bucket, she dipped water from the trough until it was nearly empty. She shoved back a loose strand of hair. Her shoulder and arm muscles screamed at the exertion, but none of that mattered. She had to refill the trough somehow. She gauged the distance to the water pump.

Seymour kept the one water hose busy sending a stream of water onto the roof.

She wanted to sink down into the dirt and give in to exhaustion, but for her husband's sake, she wouldn't.

Smoke swirled around the small band of warriors as if taunting them. She imagined the fire laughing at their feeble attempt to save what they could from the beast.

Headlights shone through the darkness, and the crunch of wheels on the driveway grabbed her attention.

Within minutes, Mr. and Mrs. Grover ran around the side of the house.

"We saw the flames and heard the explosion," Mr. Grover said. "Got here as soon as we could."

Mrs. Grover laid a chubby hand on Sara Beth's shoulder. "Oh, you poor thing. What can we do to help?"

Layken wanted to let out a whoop but instead shook Mr. Grover's hand. "I can't thank you enough, sir. The barn is totally gone, so we're focused on trying to save the house. Any help is appreciated. Looks like the water trough is about empty. Could you help me refill it?"

"It's a damn shame when fires come. We're helpless to fight it out here in the country. At least in town, they have a fire truck." Without another word, Mr. Grover grabbed one end of the almost empty trough while Layken grabbed the other, and together, they moved it closer to the pump.

Mrs. Grover wrung her hands. "Oh, dear Lord. This is awful." Then she spied Earl trussed up on the ground like a pig and whirled to face Layken. "Don't tell me this man set the fire."

"Yes, ma'am. I'm afraid he did, but he won't be setting any more. In fact, he's going to be behind bars for a long time. He tried to rob the bank in Everton yesterday."

She threw her hand over her mouth. "Well, I'll be." She moved closer to Earl and gave him a swift kick. "You ought to be ashamed of yourself."

Earl attempted to kick her back while the gag in his mouth muffled a string of curses. His eyes flashed with hatred.

Layken bent over in a coughing fit. He'd best diffuse that situation before it got worse. Once he caught his breath, he wiped his watering eyes with the back of his hand. "Mrs. Grover, maybe you and Sara Beth could go inside and put some coffee on to boil. She's exhausted, and we've got this under control out here."

"Of course." The matronly lady motioned to Sara Beth. "Come on, dear. Let the menfolk tend to this."

Layken didn't miss the plea in Sara Beth's eyes, but he shook his head. "Go on, Sara Beth. We're gonna to need a stout cup of coffee when this is over." He wanted to drop everything and wrap his arms around her, comfort her, and tell her everything would be all right. But now wasn't the time. And would it really be okay?

What did he have left to offer her?

Everything but the house was gone, and it could still catch. How would he continue to raise crops without a tractor? For once, he wished he'd parked it outside the barn.

He refused to let himself look at what was left of the old barn his grandfather had originally built. Renewed anger arose in him, and for two cents, he'd put a bullet through Earl's head and end his miserable life. But he was no murderer. He wouldn't stoop to Earl's level.

His gaze landed on Sara Beth. She attempted to smooth back her hair with a shaky hand as she followed Mrs. Grover toward the back door. Black soot covered her arms and left streaks on her face. But she was beautiful, and she was strong. And she was his wife.

The fact that she'd fought valiantly beside him did not go unnoticed.

Maybe she was truly thinking of this place as her home, too.

The loss of the barn would set him back. There was no denying that.

But with his makeshift family's help, he wouldn't let it defeat them.

The same fighting spirit that lived in his ancestors' hearts and minds lived in him. He'd rebuild if it took him a lifetime.

Yet, would Sara Beth be willing to stick with him if she wasn't bound by the bargain?

CHAPTER 36

Daylight found a tired and bedraggled group surveying the extent of the damage. Even though the adults had bathed and put on clean clothes, the unyielding odor of charred wood and smoke, along with layers of ash, still lingered in every nook and cranny. Tab refused to take off his new clothes, proudly proclaiming they weren't dirty.

But they'd saved the house. That was one bright spot. And no one was seriously injured, not even sweet Sadie, who had bravely alerted them to the intruder.

Mr. and Mrs. Grover had left as the sun rose, with Earl tossed in the back of their pickup truck, intent on delivering him to the sheriff in Greenfield. Grateful wasn't a big enough word to describe how much Layken appreciated their help. Someday, he'd have the opportunity to repay their kindness. He looked forward to that day.

His father had instilled in him the value of neighbors helping neighbors. When he was a boy about Tab's age, a group of farmers came together to help a man who'd fallen ill harvest his crop. The farming community turned it into a celebration, with the women cooking while the men worked.

Sara Beth, Tab, and Seymour stood with him in the morning silence, disturbed only by hens blissfully clucking, goats bleating, and birds chirping. The remains of the barn still smoldered, leaving only the metal skeleton of the tractor and some farm implements to mock him.

The remains resembled a war zone and Layken shook off a distant memory of burned-out buildings the soldiers had left behind with no hesitation and little remorse.

His heart sank lower with each breath. It was all too much. Then there was the issue of Tab's mother and siblings that remained. With each subsequent realization, the weight on his shoulders grew. Recovery would not come easy.

Sara Beth slipped a small hand into his. "I know it's bad, but we all survived. Things can be rebuilt or replaced."

He glanced at her and sighed. "Of course, you're right. But I sure didn't expect this kind of a setback. Now saving the farm looks next to impossible with no tractor to work the fields." The slight squeeze she gave his hand spoke volumes.

Seymour rubbed his forehead. "Once it cools down, we'll see what, if anything, we might salvage. Maybe it's not as bad as it looks."

"Reckon so."

Tab sidled next to him, Sadie close by. "Mr. Layken, I'm sorry I brought this kind of trouble to you. Earl never would've come if not for me."

Layken placed a hand on the boy's shoulder. "Son, Earl would've come, anyway. He wanted revenge for what happened yesterday. It's not your fault, so get that out of your head."

"Still." Tab sniffled. "It's awful." Sadie whined, and he leaned down to bury his face in her fur.

"Hey, we owe this little dog a big thank you for alerting us. If she hadn't barked, no tellin' what other damage Earl could've done." Layken released Sara Beth's hand and kneeled beside the dog. When he stroked her distended stomach, he pulled back in alarm at the tightness. "Tab, I think we need to make Sadie a bed. Her puppies are coming soon."

Sara Beth gasped. "How can you tell?"

"Her stomach is contracting hard. She's in labor."

"I'll fetch something for her." Sara Beth turned back toward the house.

"Will she be okay, Mr. Layken?" Tab hugged the dog harder.

"She'll be fine. Animals instinctively know what to do." He ruffled the boy's hair. "How about you go with Sara Beth and fix her a nice bed on the front porch where we can keep an eye on her?"

Tab jumped to his feet, and Sadie followed him around the corner of the house.

Layken turned to Seymour. "I can't thank you enough for helping so much." After all, the old man was no spring chicken. "I know you must be plumb give out."

"I'm okay, sir. Sure hate this for you."

"For us, Seymour. We're all in this together."

"I s'pose that's true."

"We'll figure out sleeping arrangements for everyone before dark."

"That's the least of my worries. Was glad to save most of my belongings. I can sleep pert near anywhere."

"You and Tab might have to share the front porch for a bit. Or you can take my bedroom, and I'll stay on the porch with the boy. I'm sure worried about Tab's mama and her kids, though. Didn't look like she'd been eatin' much when I was over there."

"Yes, sir. Had them on my mind too. Don't worry about me. The porch'll do me fine, and I don't mind sharing with the boy. Gives me a chance to keep an eye out for him."

Layken met the old man's gaze. "You're a good man, Seymour."

"Takes one to know one." Seymour shuffled his feet. "Where do we start?"

"Can't do much 'til everything cools down. Want to walk with me to take a look at the peanuts?"

The earlier rain had perked up the plants, and they were growing. Yet, they would need regular water. Would it be enough? And how would he harvest them without a tractor?

So many unanswered questions.

So much loss.

How much more could a man take?

Sara Beth gazed through the open window at Layken and Uncle Seymour as they trudged across the pasture toward the field. Layken's usually straight shoulders drooped, no doubt beneath the weight of the burden they carried.

Her heart crumbled, and she blinked back hot tears.

If he gave up, what would become of her? The bargain made with her father would be null and void when he repossessed the farm. While guilt washed over her at the selfish thought, it was honest.

Still...he was her husband. Of course, he could end the marriage.

The very idea of returning to her father's house strangled her. She'd rather build a treehouse and live in the forest the way Tab had.

She rummaged through the hall closet and pulled out a threadbare blanket. It would make a soft bed for Sadie.

Tab called out. "Miss Sara Beth, where are you?"

She poked her head around the corner and held out the blanket. "Here. I found this for Sadie. Let's get her all fixed up."

Worry clouded the youngster's eyes. "I don't want anything bad to happen to Sadie."

"Let's not create worries we don't need. We'll get her settled and let nature take its course."

She followed Tab out to the porch. Sadie watched them with curiosity reflected in her wide brown eyes. "I think we need to find something to prop the screen door open with so Sadie can get out if she needs to. Can you look for a big stick or rock while I fix her bed?"

"Yes, ma'am."

The boy dropped the blanket and took off, running toward the tree line.

Sara Beth fluffed the blanket in one corner of the porch, then called to the dog. "Come on, Sadie." She patted the side of her leg. "Nothing to be afraid of." The dog wagged her tail but didn't budge. Instead, she turned and followed Tab.

Taking advantage of the quiet moment, Sara Beth stretched her tired back muscles and smoothed her hair. The past twelve hours had been the most exhausting of her entire life. While the smoke had all but dissipated, her lungs still weighed heavy, and she coughed into the crook of her arm. Layken was inside the barn longer and breathed more of the smoke. As if in response, a dry rasping hack carried across the distance between the house and the peanut field.

They all needed rest, but that didn't appear to be possible anytime soon. While she waited for Tab, she dropped onto the porch swing and closed her eyes.

The next thing she knew, Tab was shaking her. "Wake up, Miss Sara Beth. Wake up. Sadie threw up. She's sick."

Sara Beth jerked awake. She couldn't have drifted off for more than five minutes. "It's okay, Tab. She's getting ready." She rubbed her burning eyes. "We need to coax her onto the porch, then leave her to do her job."

Tab swiped at a tear that escaped and whistled to Sadie. "Come, Sadie." He squatted and called again.

Sadie slinked up the porch steps, pausing at the top.

"She's most likely never been inside, Tab. That's why we need to keep the door propped open, so she knows she's not trapped."

The boy glanced up at her with wide eyes. "I sure do know what that feels like."

Sara Beth's heart twisted, leaving a hard knot in her stomach. Yes, sadly enough, he knew that feeling all too well.

Tab moved toward the blanket and patted it. "Here, Sadie. This is for you."

The dog glanced from the boy to Sara Beth and inched forward, finally putting a paw on the blanket.

"Okay, Tab. Let's leave her now."

"Are you sure?" Tab's fear echoed in his voice.

The child had lost so much in his short years of living. "I'm sure, son." She pushed up from the swing and wrapped an arm around his shoulders. "Let's you and me go check on Cuddles and the chickens." Maybe he wouldn't worry so much if she could keep him busy.

He reluctantly followed her into the house with several backward glances at the dog.

Sadie whined, but plopped down on the blanket. That was as good as they could hope for. The rest would be up to nature.

"Cuddles is on my bed, Tab. Want to go get him?"

The boy nodded and dashed down the hallway. He returned in seconds with his face buried in the bunny's fur. "Why is Cuddles so soft?"

Sara Beth chuckled. "Because he's a rabbit, and God made him that way."

"Is that why you are so soft, too?"

A flush crept up her neck. She'd never considered how she might appear to the boy. Mainly, she wanted him to feel kindness and acceptance.

She cleared her throat. "I suppose so."

"I like soft. I remember when my mama felt soft and warm…before we lost my daddy."

"Tab, don't think we've forgotten about your mother. We haven't. We've had a minor setback. But I will talk with Mr. Layken after supper, and we'll make a plan."

"One time, we lived in a tent." The boy scrunched up his face. "That was, 'til Earl came along and moved us into the house. I liked the tent better."

An idea sparked inside Sara Beth. "Do you suppose your mother still has that tent?"

He shrugged his shoulders. "Dunno."

She'd talk with Layken. If Mrs. Chesson still owned the tent, that would provide instant housing for the family.

One thing she knew for sure. Her husband would not turn away anyone in need. Even in the face of devastation, he still considered others.

It didn't take much to imagine what her father's response to Tab's family would be. How could she possibly have his cold blood flowing through her veins? She couldn't be more opposite.

The next thought stopped her in her tracks. What if he wasn't her father?

A sudden burning desire to know washed over her, along with the need for a heart-to-heart talk with the man who'd been her one stability in life since she could remember.

Only Uncle Seymour would know the truth.

But would he tell her?

CHAPTER 37

Layken and Seymour trudged back across the pasture toward the house. Worry about how quickly the ground had dried since the rain ate at Layken's gut while the relentless mid-day sun beat down on his back. He had to keep watering the crop somehow. It wouldn't be easy, but what in life was these days?

The only ease he'd found recently was in his blossoming partnership with Sara Beth. Her quiet, steady presence helped fortify the days and give him the determination to keep trying.

"Seymour, what do you think of the probability of more rain anytime soon?"

The old man rubbed his whiskered chin and cast an eye toward the clear blue sky. "Slim to none, I'd say."

"Unfortunately, I agree. We have to get water on the crop one way or another. The only option I can see is to haul water in the back of the pickup."

"How about we load the water trough in the back of the truck and haul it that way?"

"That would work, too. It would make for fewer trips to the creek to refill it." Layken stuck his hands in his pockets, wincing at the tenderness of the skin raw from the fire. "All I know is I have to make this crop, no matter what it takes."

"Yes, sir. I understand what's at stake. One time back in Mississippi, we had to haul water in buckets to the fields. I rigged up a pulley system where we could roll the buckets back and forth with someone on each end."

"That's an idea. Even watering from the trough. I'll give that some thought. I know Sara Beth and Tab will help, too."

"You know, sir, that boy has been a godsend. It's been many a year since I've been around a young'un, and it's surely given these old bones a boost."

Layken nodded. "He's a good kid. Strong, too."

When they reached the house, Sara Beth met them in the yard with glasses of sweet tea. "Thirsty?"

When he sought her gaze, she blushed and looked down.

"Mighty thirsty now that you mention it." He let his hand linger on hers longer than necessary and relished the softness, thankful she'd suffered no burns.

Seymour accepted the glass. "Always thoughtful."

"How's Sadie?" Layken took a long drink.

"Settling in. We propped the screen door open so she can come and go from the porch. I had a hard time convincing Tab she would be okay to leave her on her own."

"They've gotten attached to each other for sure. Where is he?"

"I've got him weeding the garden. Had to keep him busy."

Seymour handed back the half-empty glass. "I'll mosey on and help him." He headed toward the garden.

Layken sought Sara Beth's gaze and motioned toward the back door. "Let's go to the kitchen. Need to talk about some things."

Sara Beth fell in step beside him. "Tab told me something that might help with his mama and the other kids."

"Good. I'm fresh out of ideas."

When they reached the back door, he held it open and placed a hand on the small of her back. The smell of beans cooking took him back to his childhood. Oh, the many times he'd come barreling through the door to be greeted by that delicious aroma. Sara Beth's cooking rivaled his mother's and maybe even outdid it in some ways. She knew her way around a kitchen. "Smells like home in here."

Sara Beth flashed a tired smile. "It is home, Layken."

"Thank goodness we still have a roof over our heads." He pulled out a chair and motioned for her to join him.

She picked up Cuddles, who hopped across the floor toward her. Once seated, she met his gaze. "Tab told me they used to live in a tent before Earl came along. It got me to thinkin' that maybe if Mrs. Chesson still has that tent, we could pitch it next to the house."

Layken ran a hand through his hair, noting the singed odor that followed. "That would be a true miracle. I'm too worn out to go over today, but I say we pay her a visit tomorrow."

"I'd like that. Tab wants to go. What do you think?"

"He should go. He could convince her if she hesitates about moving out here. These hard times mean we all need to pull together."

"I couldn't agree more." She chewed on a fingernail and stroked her bunny's fur. "How are you going to harvest the crop without a tractor?"

His forehead tightened as he wrinkled his brow. "I haven't got that far with thinking it through yet. First, we have to get more water on the peanuts, or there won't be a crop to harvest. Me and Seymour talked about that and came up with a plan."

Sara Beth handed Cuddles to Layken and pushed back her chair, reaching for his empty glass. "Let me refill your tea, then you can explain."

Her petite frame moved with grace across the kitchen. It was almost as if she floated like an angel. Maybe that's what she was. A real live earth angel. How could he have ever believed he could save the farm alone? It now seemed like a lifetime ago when he'd visited the graves of his mother and father and made the solemn vow to keep the land no matter what he had to do.

Funny how things went. Whatever you imagine it will be, you can bet you'll get the exact opposite.

She rejoined him at the table, and he placed a hand on hers as she put the tea in front of him.

He sought her gaze. "Thank you."

"You're welcome." She took Cuddles back and sat down. "Now, tell me your plan and how I can help."

While he outlined the idea, she furrowed her brow and tapped a finger on the tabletop.

"And before we go any further." He paused and drank from the glass. "We need to see where we stand with the money situation. I have to know what we have left. We're gonna to have more mouths to feed."

A yelp from the front porch drew Layken to his feet.

Sara Beth followed close behind, clutching the rabbit. "I hope she's okay."

Sadie raised her head and gave a doleful stare as they both stepped out onto the porch. Three wet and wriggling puppies blindly searched for a food source.

"Looks like she's more than okay." Layken bent down and moved the smallest pup closer to Sadie. The tiny pup quickly found a nipple and latched on. Sadie leaned forward, licked it, then turned her attention to the other two, nudging them with her nose.

"Is she done?" Sara Beth leaned in for a better view, and her breath on his skin brought tiny prickles.

"Let's leave her for now. Who knows? This may be all. Or there could be more." Layken stroked the dog's head.

"Tab's going to be so excited. I'm not sure he's ever had a pet." Sara Beth gave Sadie a comforting pat. Cuddles twisted out of her arms and quickly joined Sadie and the pups, his black nose twitching.

Layken chuckled. "Looks like Cuddles is excited to have some playmates."

"Should I leave him with them?"

"Don't see what it could hurt except the door is propped open, and he might wander out."

The way Sara Beth chewed her bottom lip gave Layken a sudden urge to kiss it. What was happening to him?

He cleared his throat. "Let's get back to what we were doing. I'll fetch the money from my dresser."

Sara Beth scooped up Cuddles. "I'll go tell Tab and meet you back in the kitchen."

The boy's excited whoop echoed through the house, followed by his footsteps as he dashed inside. Layken couldn't help but smile at the enthusiasm.

The transformation from a skittish, shy kid to this outgoing youngster eager to experience life was astonishing.

He only hoped they'd see the same change in the boy's mother and siblings. Getting them moved to the farm was a priority.

Even if Mrs. Chesson no longer had the tent, they'd figure out something.

And maybe that plan would work in his favor. If he had to relinquish his bedroom to the woman, where would that put him? On the couch? Or perhaps in Sara Beth's bed.

That musing brought a surge of excitement that overrode all the stress of the fire and losing the tractor.

He quickly tucked it away. Now wasn't the time for such pondering.

Gathering the remaining money from his dresser drawer, he stuck it in his pocket. He quickly calculated in his head what they'd spent. There should still be around a hundred dollars, but it wouldn't hurt to know for sure. He regretted the doctor's expenses they'd had, but nothing he could change. Every penny he'd spent had been necessary to his way of thinking.

Somehow, they'd make it all work.

Because that's what people like them did.

War and the hard times that followed forced folks to come together and help one another.

Perhaps that was the only good thing that came out of it all, besides keeping America free.

He hurried back through the house in time to see Tab leaning over Sadie, sobbing while Sara Beth and Cuddles watched from inside.

"Tab." Layken leaned against the door frame and slipped an arm around Sara Beth's slender waist. "You okay, son?"

The youngster glanced up, tears streaking down his face. "I'm so happy. Sadie's gonna be a good mama."

"Yes, she is. Now, how about we leave her to tend her babies?"

Sara Beth added. "You can check on her again in a while."

Tab reluctantly came back inside, swiping at his face and nose with his shirtsleeve. "I never had a dog before, Mr. Layken. And Sadie's my dog."

"She loves you, that's for sure. And she knows you love her, too."

"And now I'll have puppies to play with." He scrunched up his face. "Wonder if the puppies will like me."

Layken tousled the boy's hair while Sara Beth hugged him. "I'm sure they will."

While it meant more mouths to feed, the joy the dog and her pups had brought to this child who had suffered and lost so much was worth everything.

He'd figure it out.

Damned if Layken hadn't gone from being totally alone in the world to a makeshift family he'd protect with his life, and now a dog and a litter of puppies to boot.

And if things worked out, he'd have Tab's mother, brother, and sister living with them by sundown tomorrow.

If sheer determination counted for anything, he'd rebuild the barn and turn this faltering farm into a profitable venture.

Honestly, he couldn't imagine doing anything different in life.

There was nowhere else he wanted to be, even with the obstacles the fire had presented.

They'd make magic working together as a team—his little family.

And eventually, he and Sara Beth would figure out how to turn this forced partnership into a marriage.

That is, if it was what she wanted.

Somehow, her soft touches and sweet smiles told him she did.

CHAPTER 38

Sara Beth arose before the sun came up the following day and tiptoed through the house with Cuddles tucked under one arm. She peeked out the front door and had to smile at the sight of Tab sleeping on the blanket next to Sadie, one arm thrown across her while the three pups nestled against her.

Layken had moved back into his bedroom, giving his bed on the porch to Uncle Seymour, whose snores rattled the walls.

A warmth spread across her chest. She had people who cared about her and depended on her. People who treated her with respect. People she loved looking after.

After she and Layken had counted the remaining money, they'd made a new budget that would include feeding extra mouths. They could make it until the crop came in if they were careful. It would help that the garden would soon start yielding.

Recalling her conversation with Uncle Seymour after everyone else had gone to bed last night, her heart soared. It took some convincing, but he finally told her the truth.

The truth is, little girl, your mama was already pregnant with you before she married Homer Williams. She was desperate to provide for you. Living a nomad lifestyle was no way to raise a young'un, especially as a single woman. And that's all you'll get out of me. I promised.

And while it thrilled her to know she didn't have the cold-hearted blood of Homer Williams in her veins, it raised more questions that Uncle Seymour refused to answer. Maybe someday he'd tell her more. But for now, it mattered little.

Moving into the kitchen, she softly hummed a tune while she started coffee boiling and mixed up flour, lard, baking soda, and water for biscuits. She covered the heavy crock bowl with a damp cloth for the dough to rest until it went into the oven.

Next, she eased the back door open and grabbed the milk bucket and egg basket.

She put Cuddles down and stared at the remains of the barn in the early morning red dawn. It had finally stopped smoldering and now lay in a heap of ashes and half-burned pieces of wood that jutted out at grotesque angles. The image of The Tower card in the tarot deck crossed her mind. If only she'd pulled cards, maybe she could have seen this coming. But she'd been too busy.

While she still had some heaviness in her chest from all the smoke, what she felt went beyond anything physical. Her heart broke for Layken. He tried so hard, only to have the rug pulled from under his feet. And yet he put on a brave face for them.

She stepped inside the chicken coop, scattering grain across the ground. The hens responded with soft clucking as they hopped down from their nests, voluntarily relinquishing their eggs.

It took no time to fill her basket, and she stepped back out, slipping the hasp over the metal loop, securing the wire door.

She then corralled a mama goat and coaxed her into standing still with feed so she could milk her.

With enough eggs and milk for a hearty breakfast, she picked up her bunny and headed back inside. She paused on the back step and cast a glance at the rosy glow of the sunrise peeking over the tops of the trees. The serene setting contrasted harshly with the burned remains of the barn.

"Good morning,"

Layken's deep voice made her jump. "Morning. Sleep well?"

"I think I died when my head hit the pillow. You?"

She leaned down to put Cuddles on the floor and set the eggs and milk on the counter. "The same. I was exhausted."

Layken pulled out a chair and dropped into it. "We've got a busy day ahead. Once we tend to the chores, we'll go on into Greenfield. I need to stop by the sheriff's office and talk to him about what happened here with Earl, and then we'll pay Tab's mother a visit."

With his hair freshly combed and face shaved, Sara Beth discreetly admired his handsome features. The still-wet hair was beginning to curl over his shirt collar, and the tiny lines that crinkled around his eyes when he smiled had her heart quickening. This man was her husband. And they were growing closer and more comfortable with each other.

She'd do anything to help him and make life easier. "We should pick up a few more staples to tide us over. I made a list last night." She pulled a folded piece of paper from her pocket and handed it to him.

While he looked it over, she poured coffee and set it in front of him.

He glanced up. "Thank you. I can't think of anything else to add. You've covered everything." He handed it back to her, and she tucked it away.

Uncle Seymour appeared in the doorway, wiping sleep from his eyes and pulling his suspenders onto his shoulders. "Mornin'. Sure smells good in here."

Sara Beth motioned toward the well-worn, blue-speckled enamel coffee pot. "Coffee's ready. I'm making biscuits, gravy, and eggs this morning."

"I swear to goodness, you're going to make this old man fat." He tweaked the end of her nose and reached for a cup.

She bent down to light the oven. "Not the way you work, Uncle Seymour. I'm glad you rested."

"Slept like a baby. That boy's still dead to the world, curled up next to his dog."

"I say let him sleep as long as he needs to. Poor thing was exhausted."

Layken sipped from his cup. "Going into Greenfield to try and get the boy's mother. Do you want to ride along, Seymour?"

"Nah. Don't need a thing in town. I'll stick around here and watch after things. I can start gathering up the rubble." He lumbered across the wooden floor and pulled out a chair. "Sure do hope you can convince his mama to come with you."

"So do I. And if I don't miss my guess, she won't hesitate too much when she sees Tab and how well he's doing."

Sara Beth kneaded the biscuit dough, then reached for the wooden rolling pin that had belonged to Layken's mother. How often Nancy Martin must have used that same rolling pin to prepare food for her family. She touched the kitchen tool with reverence for a brief moment, then rolled out the dough before cutting perfect circles using a glass.

She slid the biscuits into the warm oven.

The possibility of having more children around made her heart happy. Tab had shared that his brother was six, and his sister was only four. How sad that the children would probably not even remember their father. And no telling how frightened they'd be of Uncle Seymour and Layken after seeing Earl's violence.

She'd do her best to make them all feel safe and welcomed.

Tab sat in the middle between Layken and Sara Beth as Layken nosed the pickup toward Greenfield. With so much work to be done, he intended to get back to the farm as quickly as possible.

Tab all but bounced up and down on the seat. His excitement was contagious. Beyond any shadow of a doubt, he couldn't wait to see his mother.

Layken hoped the boy wouldn't be too disappointed if she refused to come with them. They'd deal with that if it happened.

He caught Sara Beth's gaze over Tab's head and winked. The sun leaving gold streaks in her dark hair and the instant blush on her cheeks made her even prettier.

Tab leaned over Sara Beth and stared out the window at the passing scenery.

"When was the last time you rode in a car, Tab?" Layken made a left turn at the intersection.

"My daddy had a car. He used to take us for picnics. But that was a long time ago."

"You like looking out the window, don't you?"

"Yes, sir. I sure do."

The boy was practically sitting in Sara Beth's lap at this point.

"Sara Beth, how about you scoot over here by me and let Tab have the window seat before he smushes you?"

She let out a giggle. "Let's switch, Tab."

Once she moved over, Layken draped an arm around her shoulders. He liked having her close. He'd take every opportunity he could get.

Tab hung his head out the window.

Layken whispered, "I think he's enjoying the ride."

"I'd say so." Sara Beth kept her voice low. "There's something I want to tell you, but I don't want Tab to hear." She pulled at a loose thread on her blouse.

"I don't think he can hear a thing right now but the wind." He accelerated the pickup.

"I had a heart-to-heart with Uncle Seymour last night. He confirmed what I've always felt. Homer Williams is not my blood father." She chewed her bottom lip. "Finding that out made me happy."

Layken scanned her face for any signs of shock or dismay. Her sparkling brown eyes and gently folded hands on her lap only reflected peace. "I can see it didn't upset you."

"Not in the least. Somehow, I always knew."

"Does he know?"

"Uncle Seymour wouldn't say."

Tab pulled himself back inside the pickup. "Are we getting close, Mr. Layken? I can't wait to see my mama."

"It's not too much farther, son. And remember, I have to stop by the sheriff's office first."

"Oh, yeah." His face fell. "What if they let Earl go?"

Sara Beth took the boy's hand. "That will not happen. No one robs a bank and gets away with it. And that's not even counting what he did at the farm. So, stop your worrying. He's going away for a long time."

"But he escaped once." The boy's mouth set in a grim line. "I hope I'm all growed up if he ever comes back. He'll never touch any of us again." He squinted one eye to emphasize his words.

Layken had to admire the boy's determination. "You may be an old man by the time he gets out of prison."

"I'll never get too old to kill him."

Layken caught Sara Beth's worried glance. "Now, Tab, don't talk like that, especially around your mama."

"Okay, sir. I won't. I promise. Are we almost there?" He leaned out the window again.

"Almost."

The stop at the sheriff's office didn't take long. Layken signed papers, pressing charges against Earl for arson and assault to be added to the bank robbery charge. The sheriff shook his hand and reassured him Earl would be going up the river for a long time.

Back in the pickup, he asked Sara Beth, "Do we want to go talk to Tab's mama or stop by the store first?"

"I think we need to go talk to Mrs. Chesson. If she needs to pack some things, we could go to the store to give her some time."

It amazed him at how practical Sara Beth was in making any decision. Each day gave him a new reason to admire his wife. He nodded. "Let's go then. Ready, Tab?"

"Yes, sir." The boy sat up straight, his chin up. Layken grinned when Tab spit on his hands and slicked back his hair, then straightened his clothes.

When he turned onto Maple Street, Tab was barely inside the pickup. As they neared the house, he hollered, "Mama. Mama. It's me, Tab."

Sara Beth tugged at his overalls. "Come back inside, son. You don't want to scare your mother."

He sat on the edge of the seat, his left foot bouncing against the floorboard.

When Layken pulled into the driveway and killed the engine, Tab didn't wait a second longer. He flung open the pickup door and ran to the house.

Mrs. Chesson stepped out onto the decaying front porch, shielding her eyes against the sun. "Tab? Is that you?"

He flung his arms around his mother's waist, sobbing. "Yes. It's me, Mama."

Layken held the door for Sara Beth, and they quietly approached the woman. He took off his hat. "Mrs. Chesson, remember me?"

She smiled through tears. "Yes. I sure do. You've brought my boy home to me."

He put a hand on Sara Beth's back. "And this is my wife, Sara Beth."

Sara Beth smiled. "It's so nice to meet you, ma'am."

"You too." She swung her gaze back to Layken. "You know it ain't safe for Tab here."

"Can we go inside?" Layken needed to get them away from the neighbors' prying eyes.

"Of course." Mrs. Chesson wiped at her tears and hugged Tab closer. "I have to warn you, it ain't much to look at."

"We don't care." Sara Beth placed a hand on the frail woman's shoulder. "We only want to talk to you."

The minute they walked through the door, two miniature replicas of Tab ran toward him, then stopped short when they spied Layken and Sara Beth.

"It's okay, children. These are our friends." Mrs. Chesson extracted Tab's arms from around her waist. "Son, go play with your brother and sister for a minute while we talk."

She waited until the children disappeared into the next room, then turned to her company. "Would you have a seat? I'd offer you some refreshment, only I ain't got a thing to offer."

Sara Beth stepped forward with a warm smile. "It's okay, Mrs. Chesson. Please don't apologize. We didn't come for refreshments."

Layken cleared his throat. "I don't know if you've heard, but Earl is in jail and facing a long sentence for bank robbery and arson."

Her hand fluttered to her throat, and she let out a slight moan. "Oh, Lord. I didn't know. I wondered why he didn't come home."

"Listen, we're going to get right to the point." Layken twirled his hat between his hands. "Sara Beth and I want to bring you and your children to our farm to live. Would you consider that? We could all help each other."

"You mean it? You want me and my kids to come to your farm?" All color drained from her face, and she sat on the edge of a straight-backed chair.

"Yes. We mean it. Do you rent this house?"

"Earl rented it, and the landlord has been by every day for weeks, threatening to throw us out. Lord knows when he last paid the man." She rubbed a hand across her forehead. "Didn't know where we would go."

"Ma'am." Sara Beth crossed the room and kneeled in front of her. "Tab said you used to live in a tent. Do you, by chance, still have it?"

She nodded, her eyes filling with unshed tears. "It's out back."

"Then is it okay if we bring it? We have a small place on the farm but could pitch the tent next to the house. We can promise you it would be safe, and you would have food."

The woman only nodded and sat as if frozen.

Sara Beth got to her feet. "Then, if you will pack up what you want to bring, we're going to go to the store and then come back to get you and the children."

Layken stepped forward. "Show me where the tent is, and I'll load it."

Mrs. Chesson pushed to her feet and pointed toward the back door of the shotgun house.

Sara Beth started to follow him.

"I can get it, Sara Beth. Will you go talk to Tab?"

"Of course."

That had all gone easier than Layken had imagined. It was no surprise to learn Earl hadn't paid the rent.

The poor woman's worry and desperation were etched in the lines on her face.

As his father had done, helping others to survive during the Great Depression, he would now do for this woman and her children.

The land could help heal deep grief and wounds. It offered a new life.

It was worth fighting to keep. He hadn't forgotten.

He'd battle with everything he had to save it, as it had saved him and many others who'd come before.

He tossed the tent into the back of the pickup and hurried to get Sara Beth.

Now, they had a new mission.

CHAPTER 39

Half past noon, Layken pulled off the blacktop road onto the dirt lane that led to his farm. Mrs. Chesson sat next to the door, holding four-year-old Ellen on her lap, while Sara Beth occupied the space next to him. The child had put up a fuss, wanting to ride in the back of the pickup with her two brothers, but Layken had been relieved when her mother insisted the child ride up front with her.

He'd trusted that the boys would be safe enough in the back, but kept an eye on them in the rearview mirror.

As he neared the house, several vehicles sat parked at various angles.

Sara Beth gasped and leaned forward, putting one hand on the dashboard.

"What in tarnation?" Layken steered around a vehicle halfway blocking the road.

"I don't know." Sara Beth pointed. "But I see Mr. and Mrs. Grover's pickup."

He glanced at Sara Beth. "Can you help Mrs. Chesson and the young'uns while I see what's going on?"

Tab's mother leaned forward. "I'd appreciate it if you'd call me Mildred, not Mrs. Chesson. It's so formal."

"Of course, Mildred." Sara Beth put a hand on the frail woman's arm. "And please call us Layken and Sara Beth."

Layken parked the pickup and stepped out. Confident his wife would take care of getting Tab's mother settled in, he followed the sounds of men's voices, hammers, and saws.

Seymour met him with a wide grin. He took off his hat and wiped the sweat from his brow. "Can you believe this?"

"What's going on?"

"These are your neighbors. The Grovers gathered 'em up. They came to help. Never seen anything like it." He pointed toward the house. "And there's a whole group of women in the kitchen. They brought a bunch of fixin's with 'em. Couldn't wait for you to get back to see all this."

"I'll be damned." Layken's throat constricted. He prayed he'd be able to speak as he strode to where seven men worked together, removing burned pieces of wood and shoveling rubble into piles. "Gentlemen."

The men paused and straightened.

Mr. Grover stepped forward. "Son, this here is Arthur, Jake, Paul, Ralph, Frank, and Albert. They volunteered to help get this mess cleaned up."

Layken shook each man's hand, fighting to hold back tears. "I cannot thank you enough for what you're doing."

The one named Arthur stepped forward. "It's an awful thing that happened here. We've all had hard times. I knew your mom and dad. Fine folks, they were. Your dad helped me out more than once. It's what neighbors do."

Jake pointed to Mr. Grover. "When Henry here told us what happened, we had to come on over. I live about ten miles down the road toward Ash Grove. I knew your folks, too. Your dad brought us some beef during the Depression. It sure helped feed my family."

Layken attempted to swallow past the lump lodged in his throat, yet his voice came out as a croak. "I will repay your kindness. And that's a promise." He picked up a shovel, thankful for a chance to hide his emotions. The men returned to working side-by-side.

That so many would drop what they were doing and pitch in to help a virtual stranger touched him down to his very core. Sure, they'd known his folks, but they didn't know him from Adam. He tried to place any of the men in his growing-up memory, but had never paid much attention to his father's friends and acquaintances. He'd taken so much for granted, including the sacrifices his folks had made for him and others.

A new appreciation for them welled up inside, along with unshed tears that stung behind his eyelids.

With each scoop of the shovel, the weariness that had settled deep in his bones evaporated, only to be replaced with renewed vigor and determination.

He would save this farm or die trying.

Sara Beth got out of the pickup behind Mildred as Tab jumped over the side.

Excitement shone in the child's eyes, and his cheeks glowed rosy-red from riding in the back of the vehicle. "What are all these people doing here, Miss Sara Beth?"

"I haven't the foggiest idea, but I'll find out."

He scrunched up his face. "I wanna introduce everyone to Sadie and the puppies." He motioned to his little brother, Daniel, and sister, Ellen. "Come on, y'all. We have a dog, and her name is Sadie. Mama, you come too." He tugged on his mother's arm. "Please. And we have a bunny you can hold and pet. Is it okay if I show Cuddles to them, too, Miss Sara Beth?"

Sara Beth put a hand on his shoulder. "Yes, of course. Don't be too rough with the pups. Then I need for you and your brother to get the tent out." She turned to Mildred. "Do you know how to pitch it?" She certainly hoped so, because she didn't have the faintest idea.

Mildred nodded. "I know how. I'll need a little help."

"Help I can give. I don't know the first thing about how to set it up. Let me go talk to Mrs. Grover, then I'll be back."

Tab opened the tailgate and helped his little brother down, then squared his shoulders. "I can help Mama, Miss Sara Beth. Looks like you've got lots to tend to."

She gave him a quick hug. The pride and determination that showed in the little boy trying to be a man tugged at her heart. "Thank you, Tab. Yes. I need to go see what's going on, but then I can help. I also need to ask Mr. Layken exactly where he wants the tent. If you can unload things, that would be great."

The children took off running, with Mildred struggling to keep up while throwing furtive glances over her shoulder as if she expected the devil himself to jump out and grab her.

It broke Sara Beth's heart to see the deep-rooted and lingering fright, even though they'd repeatedly assured her that Earl couldn't hurt her ever again. Like it had been with Tab, it may take some time for her to feel safe. And also, like Tab, maybe in time, she'd even find a way to smile again.

Sara Beth hurried around the house to the back door, where she was greeted with chatter among several women.

Before she could open the door to go inside, one lady said, "Well, I never put any stock in the rumors they spread around in town about the poor girl being a witch. That's nothing more than a bunch of mean-spirited gossip. Everybody knows there ain't no such thing as witches, anyway."

Another woman chimed in. "A shy girl. And she was different, especially after her mother died. But if I had to live with Homer Williams, I'd be shy and different too. Never had any use for that man. Glad the menfolk have to deal with him, not me."

Sara Beth plastered on a smile and opened the screen door. "Ladies." Everywhere she looked, there were piles of vegetables, jars of canned goods, pie makings, a steaming pot on the stove, and the smell of fresh coffee boiling.

The women stopped what they were doing and murmured greetings, a couple of them blushing at the realization that Sara Beth had most likely overheard their conversation.

Mrs. Grover took charge. "Sara Beth, these are friends of mine. I've known these women for years. They're all neighbors. While the menfolk are helping clean up the mess from the fire, we thought we'd cook up a feast for them."

Sara Beth's hand flew to her mouth. "Oh my! You are all too kind."

"Pffssh." Mrs. Grover waved her away. "We've got this if you need to do something else."

"Actually, we brought a woman and her children with us from Greenfield. They're going to be staying for a while. I don't suppose any of you know how to pitch a tent?"

Two women wiped their hands on their aprons and nodded. "I'm Agnes, and this is Berta. We both know how to pitch a tent. Done it many times. Lived in 'em while we built our houses."

Mrs. Grover motioned around the room. "That over there at the cabinet is Louise. Next to her is Opal, then this is Freda and Gertie."

Sara Beth nodded at each one. "Don't expect me to remember your names. But please know I am deeply moved by your generous outpouring of love and help. Layken has been through so much."

Mrs. Grover touched her arm. "He has, but so have you, my dear. When our men suffer, so do we. Now, run along and do what you need to. We've got this under control."

Tears threatened to fall as Sara Beth turned to go back out the door. The kindness of these people overwhelmed her in every way. It was how she'd always believed people should be...The way her mother had described the Gypsy communities, and how, as outcasts of society, they stuck together and survived the worst life threw at them.

Living in the country was indeed different from town life, even one as small as Everton. Out here, people loved and respected the land and were quick to lend a helping hand.

Agnes and Berta followed her, Agnes taking the lead. "Don't you worry none. We'll have the tent up in no time. We'll wait here on the steps while you find out where we're putting it. Needed a breath of fresh air, anyway."

"Thank you. I'll be right back." Sara Beth headed toward Layken, shielding her eyes against the relentless sun. With soot-blackened hands, he threw his shovel over his shoulder and strode toward her. The emotion that filled his eyes and face opened the dam of tears she'd been holding back.

"Can you believe this?" Layken pointed toward the men. "They willingly stopped their lives and came to help."

Sara Beth motioned toward the kitchen. "And there's a slew of women in there cooking up a feast. It's like nothing I've ever seen." She swiped at her tears and sniffed.

"Don't cry." Layken reached out to wipe away a stray tear and left a streak of soot across her cheek. "Oh, sorry." He pulled a handkerchief out of his pocket. "Didn't mean to get your face dirty."

She held her breath as he gently wiped away the soot. Something about that simple and innocent action reminded her so much of her mother and the many times she'd done the same thing. New tears formed. "I'm not sad. Just overwhelmed."

"Yeah, me too." He cleared his throat.

She met his gaze. "Two of the women say they can help Mildred pitch her tent. Where should we put it?"

He pointed to the side of the house, away from the work area. "Let's put it over there and up by the front corner of the house."

She nodded. "That's all I needed." She turned to walk away when his soft voice stopped her.

"You sure that's all you need? If I wouldn't get your clothes all dirty, I'd hug you real tight, 'cause I think you need that."

She smiled through her tears. "That would be real nice. I'll take you up on that offer later when you aren't covered with soot and ashes." With her heart beating in double time, she hurried to join the two women waiting for her on the back porch steps.

Layken was getting bolder in outwardly showing affection—the way she'd always imagined a real husband would do.

And with each passing day, the desire to return that, in the way a true wife would, swelled.

Her cheeks grew hot, and her breath shallow as her thoughts wandered to the bedroom she occupied alone.

Would Layken eventually share it with her?

Did she want him to?

What would it be like to sleep next to him?

The bold imaginings frightened her, while at the same time, she found them exhilarating.

One thing she knew for certain—Layken would treat her with kindness and a gentle hand.

And he'd be patient with her while she learned how to be a wife.

Thank the stars above, Homer Williams had forced her out of his house and into this marriage.

Somehow, she had to believe that maybe her mother had a hand in it from beyond the grave, if that was even possible. Oh, the many questions she'd ask if only she could talk to her.

She tucked away the musings and hurried to help their house guests.

For now, she'd hold her chin high and be what Layken needed her to be.

Together, they'd rebuild what they'd lost and give back to the land that provided so much.

CHAPTER 40

By the time the sun set, the men had scraped clean the area the barn had once occupied, leaving only piles of rubble to show it ever existed. They'd had stacked salvageable farm implements under a tree. The plows, although blackened, were still usable.

The biggest loss besides the structure itself was the tractor. Two men hooked onto it with ropes and pulled it away using one of their trucks.

And now everyone was gone. It was as if a whirlwind had passed through.

Layken leaned back against the sofa, fighting to keep his eyes open. Every muscle ached. While he wanted nothing more than to collapse into bed, he needed some alone time with Sara Beth. Watching her work alongside the other women throughout the day fueled his admiration for her. Besides, he'd promised her a squeeze-tight hug.

Mildred Chesson and the three children huddled around the radio. Tab had carried the three pups inside, and each child held one while Sadie kept a close watch through the screen door.

Cuddles hopped over to the children, then onto Mildred's lap. It was as if the rabbit could sense when someone needed soothing soft fur to stroke.

Layken's weariness evaporated as he watched the blended souls, both human and animal. He had a tribe. Maybe not by blood, but family just the same. And every ounce of instinctive protectiveness he possessed arose in him.

Seymour had moved out onto the porch, no doubt exhausted as well. He worked hard and never asked for anything. He thanked his lucky stars again that the old man's love for Sara Beth had prompted him to come to the farm.

Sara Beth shuffled from the kitchen and dropped onto the sofa beside him with a wide smile. "That's a sweet sight." She pointed to Mildred and the children.

"It is." He let out a contented sigh. "There's nothing better than a mother and children safe and reunited." Visions of sad faces in war-ravaged areas crossed his mind. Maybe this was a way to make up for things he wasn't allowed to do over there—wrongs he couldn't right.

"I agree. It's turned out better than I imagined."

Leaning forward, he raked a hand through his hair. "Sara Beth, would you walk with me if you're not too tired?"

"Of course."

He stood and stretched. "Folks, we'll be back. Enjoy the radio."

No one even turned around. They simply nodded that they'd heard him.

Pointing toward the kitchen, he placed a hand on the small of her back. "Let's go out that way."

The oppressive summer night air clung to his skin like dewdrops on a morning rose as he guided Sara Beth across the property toward the creek. A full moon lit the worn path.

"Today's been quite a day." He slid an arm around her slender waist.

She glanced up at him. "It has. The way the people all came together to help us was overwhelming, to say the least."

"It sure made me do a lot of thinking. I took so much for granted living here with my folks. I never paid much attention to the things they did to help others. But now I want to keep that alive."

"I wish I could have known your mom and dad. I know they were wonderful people." Her eyes glowed in the moonlight. "They raised a good son."

Layken helped her over a protruding tree root. "I don't know about that, but I made a vow today to be a better man—to honor them." When they reached the creek bank, he pointed to a large rock that jutted over the water. "This used to be one of my favorite places to sit and think and to fish."

"It's perfect."

He jumped up on the rock, then held out his hand, which she accepted. "Let's sit. I need to tell you some things."

Crickets and cicadas chirped their constant songs, and the thick brush along the creek rustled as night animals foraged for their next meal. In the distance, a lone owl hooted, drawing a response from one farther down, while the stream trickled over rocks with a calm, steady rhythm.

This was his home, his land.

Sara Beth settled beside him with a deep sigh. "It's so peaceful here, like nothing bad or evil has ever touched it."

"Yet, it has. My ancestors fought tooth and nail for it, and many shed their blood." He reached for her hand, intertwining their fingers, her softness soothing his calloused skin. "But today, it was like something new awakened in me. A new appreciation for the people who love it, and the land's strength and ability to always provide what we need to survive."

"That's almost poetic. But I agree. The women who helped Mildred set up their tent went back to their farms and returned with bedding. And that's not to mention the feast they all put together. I've never seen such generosity."

A lump in his throat left him struggling with a reply. "I made it a point to try and remember all the names of the men working with me." He stared out into the night. "One of them said they know a man over in Walnut Grove tearing down an old barn so he can build a new one. He offered to ask if I could help in exchange for the lumber. And Henry Grover suggested I borrow his tractor when it's time to harvest the peanuts, since it's off season for them."

When Sara Beth squeezed his hand, it dulled his awareness of everything around him except her. The fresh floral scent of her hair, the softness of her breath, and the relaxed way she leaned into him overtook all his senses.

"Unexpected blessings, like getting Mildred and the children here with us. When I first found Tab living in that treehouse, I never imagined that he'd learn to trust us in such a short time, and then wind up with his whole family here. My heart breaks for that woman. It'll take a while before she can relax and let herself live again."

Layken tucked a stray hair behind her ear. "If anyone can help her find her way, it's you, Sara Beth. I've never known a more gentle soul."

Tears glistened in her eyes when she glanced up. "I'm nothing special."

"I beg to disagree. I never imagined when Homer Williams forced us to marry what a great gift he was giving to me." He tugged her closer as if he couldn't stand for even an inch to separate them. His voice grew husky. "I'm falling in love with you, Sara Beth. I know you may not stay here once my debt is paid, and I won't ask you to. But I would regret it forever if I didn't say what I feel."

She gasped, and tears wet her cheeks. "Layken, there's truly nowhere I want to go. Sure, I once thought I wanted to go to the big city where there are so many things I've never experienced, but if it means leaving this farm and you, it no longer holds any attraction."

"You don't know what it means to hear you say that." He gulped in a breath of night air and blew it out. "May I kiss you?"

Her glistening eyes said it all as she turned her face upward. He lowered his head to claim her soft lips.

When he broke the kiss, she dropped her head onto his shoulder. "I want to be a real wife to you, but I don't know how."

"There's nothing to know, Sara Beth. When you're ready, you'll invite me into your bed. It's as natural as breathing."

"How will I know when I'm ready?"

A chuckle started in his chest and erupted in his throat. "Like I said, it's as natural as breathing. You need to trust that I'll never force myself on you. If you want to be my wife in that way, it will be up to you to tell me."

"I wish my mother was here." Her voice barely above a whisper, Layken heard her loud and clear.

"I understand."

She pushed herself upright and folded her hands on her lap. "Have you been with many women?"

"A few. Mostly when I was overseas. Never really had a serious girlfriend."

"But you're so handsome." She looked away, and he could almost make out the flush on her cheeks. "And good and kind. Why?"

"Don't know, really. Guess I never met the right girl." He picked up a tiny rock and tossed it into the creek. "That is until you."

Turning to face him, she brushed his cheek with a slender finger, leaving a trail of warmth. "It feels like I've known you forever. So much has happened, both good and bad. Hard to believe it's only been a few weeks since my fath…Homer made me come here."

"Best thing that ever happened to me." He rubbed a thumb over the back of her hand. "And, I mean it."

"You can kiss me again, if you want."

"I want." He drew her close, loving the warmth of her softness against him. She awakened desires in him—Ones he could not deny.

The exhilaration of her confession left a tingle up and down his spine.

She wanted to be his wife.

It was more than he'd dared to hope for.

And he'd wait. Wait until she was ready.

Even if it took years, he'd be patient.

The intensity of her kiss told him he wouldn't have to wait long.

CHAPTER 41

Life settled in on the Martin farm, and the next few weeks found Layken, Sara Beth, and their makeshift family toiling from daylight to dark. They all joined in to tend the garden, take care of the chickens and goats, and haul water to the peanuts. The plants flourished in the rich soil despite the relentless sun.

Sara Beth had gone with Layken to talk to the farmer about tearing down the man's barn in exchange for the lumber. Before they left, the farmer's wife had loaded them down with fresh vegetables from their garden, claiming they had way more than they could use.

Seymour and Tab had agreed to accompany Layken daily to help make the project move faster.

Each time they returned, tired and dirty, the pickup groaned under another load of lumber, which they stacked in neat piles according to the size of the boards. It was a slow, tedious process, but still, a way to rebuild. It didn't escape Sara Beth's notice that Layken never complained. He met each day with hopeful expectations and a fresh cup of her coffee.

As Sara Beth spent more time with Tab's mother, she found she enjoyed her company. While the older woman had seemed frail and timid, she was proving to possess more strength than what first met the eye. And slowly but surely, the worry wrinkles smoothed out across Mildred's forehead.

One sweltering afternoon, she and Mildred worked side-by-side in the kitchen, snapping fresh green beans the farmer's wife had given them and preparing them for canning while Ellen and Daniel played with the puppies on the porch. Their giggles echoed through the house like a healing balm.

"You have no idea how much I appreciate your help, Mildred. I've never canned anything in my life. I'm sure I would have messed this up good, if not for you."

"I grew up on a farm in Arkansas, and we had to learn how to can as soon as we were tall enough to reach the cabinet." She ran water over the bowl of beans she'd snapped.

"If you don't mind me asking, do you still have family there? How did you get to Missouri?"

"Far as I know, I still have family around Little Rock. We don't stay in touch. With nine kids, they were glad to see one gone. I married Tab's father, and we moved to Springfield." A sob caught in her throat, and she sagged against the counter. "I've made such a mess of things since Andrew died. He was a good man and a hard worker until his lungs gave out." Her voice lowered to a whisper. "He loved me and the children."

Sara Beth laid a hand on the woman's arm. "I'm so sorry. Don't feel bad about choices you make when the reasons are right."

"It's so hard to get past the mistakes. I feel like such a fool." She gazed through the kitchen window. "But my children are happy here, and I'm finding a certain peace on this farm."

"It seems to have that effect on everyone. Layken loves this land, and crazy as it sounds, it loves back."

Mildred wiped her brow. "I don't mean to be nosy, but how did you meet Layken? You seem so suited to one another."

While Sara Beth explained the situation that forced them together, she thought about the conversation she and Layken had that evening by the creek when he'd admitted he was falling in love with her. There'd been no more time to talk and only stolen moments alone.

With so much work to be done and so many people around, those times were scarce.

Still, she couldn't stop thinking about what it would mean to become Layken's wife in every sense of the word.

"Can I ask you a personal question, Mildred?"

"Yes." The older woman wiped her hands on a towel and faced Sara Beth.

Suddenly shy, Sara Beth wouldn't meet her intense gaze. "Well, it's just that...I haven't actually been with Layken yet. I don't know the first thing about being intimate with a man. I'm embarrassed to even talk about it. But with my mother gone, I have no one." Her voice trailed off.

A broad smile covered Mildred's face. "Child, nothing is more beautiful than a man and woman who love each other coming together that way. It's the most natural thing in the world. There's nothing for you to know other than you love your man and want to please him."

Sara Beth chewed her bottom lip and busied her hands again. "But what if I'm a disappointment?"

"Oh, honey. There isn't a man alive that would be disappointed in you. There's three things a man thinks about, and while I don't mean to be crude, I'll be frank. They think about sex, food, and providing for their families. That's how simple they are."

"Layken has so much weighing on his shoulders. Surely he must think about more."

Mildred cocked an eyebrow. "Maybe. Guess that'll be for you to find out." She motioned toward a large cooking pot. "Let's get some water boiling and blanch these beans."

Sara Beth pondered the woman's words. They mirrored what Layken had said about intimacy being as natural as breathing.

Her pulse quickened, and her face flushed.

When would she know it was the right time?

Desire burned in Layken's eyes when they were alone. And that lit a fire in her belly. Did that mean it was right?

Oh, God, if only she knew.

Layken hurried home that evening with another load of lumber and a few splinters in his hands. But he was excited. Word had spread about a big celebration in Everton, including live music and a street dance. He wanted to treat his makeshift family to some well-deserved fun.

Plus, he hadn't forgotten about the rainbow hair ribbon Sara Beth was saving for a special occasion.

And while they hadn't had the opportunity to talk much over the past couple of weeks, he treasured the moments they'd spent alone. He relished her softness when she leaned into him and the honesty with which she returned his kisses.

He pushed the old pickup a little harder as he considered the fact he'd never put a ring on her hand. A plan formed as he drove.

When he reached the farm, he hurried inside ahead of Tab and Seymour.

"Sara Beth," he called out. "Where are you?"

"Kitchen." She poked her head around the door frame. "Everything okay?"

"More than okay. We're going into town soon as supper's over."

She stepped through the doorway. "Why are we going to town so late in the day?"

He took long strides toward her and twirled her around. "We're going to town for a celebration. Everton is having a big shindig with live music and street dance, and I want to take you. Hell, I want everybody to come."

"Oh." She giggled. "That sounds like fun."

Seymour stepped inside with Tab lingering on the porch to pet Sadie and the pups with his brother and sister. "What's all the commotion in here?"

"We're all going to town, Uncle Seymour. Layken's taking us all." She wriggled out of Layken's grasp. "I'll go tell Mildred."

Seymour slapped his pant leg with his hat. "Well, that'd be mighty fine."

Layken headed down the hallway. "Let's get that lumber unloaded, then we gotta get spiffed up." He called over his shoulder, "And, Sara Beth, don't forget to wear your new hair ribbon. This is a special occasion."

She laughed. "I won't forget."

It didn't take long to unload the day's haul. Layken hummed a tune and tapped his foot while he shaved.

As soon as he finished in the bathroom, he hurried to his bedroom and opened his top dresser drawer. A small decorative wooden box lay nestled in one corner beneath handmade dresser scarves.

He opened the box and fought back unbidden tears at seeing his mother and father's wedding rings. Tonight, he'd put the small gold band on his wife's finger...if she'd accept it.

Slipping it into his pocket, he dressed in his Sunday best.

Throughout supper, he couldn't take his eyes off Sara Beth. Her cheeks had a rosy glow and her eyes twinkled as conversation flew around the table, along with laughter and teasing among the children.

Everyone had caught hold of the excitement.

Hard times weren't over by a long shot, but they could all use a brief reprieve.

After the women cleared the table, Mildred carted the children off, and Seymour headed out back.

Layken carried the last of the dishes to the sink while Sara Beth put food away in the icebox. He caught her by the waist and pulled her close. "You go get gussied up. I'm doing dishes."

"I can help. It won't take long to change clothes and brush my hair."

"Go." He released her and pointed toward the hallway. "I will do the dishes. Maybe some of these splinters will come out of my fingers in the dishwater."

She laughed. "Fine. I'll be back in no time."

He stared out the kitchen window at the dusky sky. Tonight would be a new beginning. He had lumber for a new barn and the use of Mr. Grover's tractor temporarily.

And he had growing feelings for his wife that he'd never expected to happen.

They all loaded into the pickup in less than half an hour. Uncle Seymour rode in the back with the two boys, leaving Layken, Sara Beth, Mildred, and Ellen up front.

He cranked the engine and pointed the truck toward Everton. Even the old pickup seemed excited and raring to go.

Once he shifted into third gear, he put an arm around Sara Beth's shoulders, and she leaned closer. Her soft pink dress, dotted with tiny rosebuds, matched the soft floral scent of her hair. He loved it when she brushed her long brown hair and left it hanging down. He fingered the silky softness. "That ribbon looks mighty pretty in your hair."

She giggled. "I feel like a princess all dressed up for the ball."

Mildred leaned forward, gripping Ellen tighter. "I can't remember the last time I went to a dance. It was long before Andrew died."

"We all deserve a little fun. What's the saying about hard work and no play?" Layken reached the blacktop and sped up.

"All work and no play makes Jack a dull boy," Sara Beth quoted.

"That's it. We don't want to be like Jack. Time to kick up our heels a little." The ring, although small, burned a hole in Layken's pocket. He couldn't wait to put it on Sara Beth's finger, to make her his real wife.

When they reached Everton, fiddle, guitar, and banjo music drifted across the way. Bursts of laughter filled the air. It seemed everyone for miles around had turned out for the celebration. He had to meander down a side street to find a parking place.

The children hopped out of the pickup, laughing and poking at each other. Seymour climbed down and laid a hand on Tab's arm. "You're the man of your house now, so be a good example for your brother and sister."

"Yes, sir." He straightened his clothes. "Daniel, Ellen, hold my hands. Wouldn't want you to get run over."

Layken shot Seymour a grin, then looped his arm through Sara Beth's, and they all made their way toward the rock bandstand in the middle of the street.

As they neared the crowd of people, Seymour spotted an old friend and broke away from the group. The children spied free home-made ice cream and made a beeline for it while Mildred hurried to keep up with them.

Layken tugged Sara Beth closer. "I do hope you'll dance with me, Mrs. Martin."

"It would be a pleasure, Mr. Martin."

He pulled her into the group of dancers, and they weaved their way through the crowd to the edge. His arms fit around her slender body perfectly, their hands intertwined, as she followed his steps to the rhythm of the waltz.

She held her body stiff. "It's been a long time since I've danced. Not sure I remember how."

"Relax. You've got rhythm flowing through your veins." He didn't suppress a grin when she softened and moved closer. "See. That's better already."

After two songs, he mopped his brow and tugged her out of the dance area. "Let's find some refreshment."

At a nearby table, a gray-haired woman offered cold sweet tea for a nickel.

A man approached Layken. "Say, aren't you that Martin boy that caught that bank robber here a while back?"

"Yes, sir. That would be me." He nodded toward Sara Beth. "This is my wife."

The man squinted. "Oh yeah. You're Homer Williams' daughter. I remember you. Say, would you two want a little shot of moonshine?"

Layken glanced at Sara Beth. "What do you think? Want to try some moonshine?"

She raised her chin. "I don't know. Never had any. Is it bitter?"

The man offered a snaggle-toothed grin. "Little girl, it tastes like Mama's apple pie."

At Sara Beth's nod, Layken said, "Reckon we'll take a bit of your moonshine."

The man retrieved a pint jar from behind the iced tea table. "No better in this county. Good and cold, too."

Layken paid the man fifty cents, took the small jar, and then moved on down the street. A man in striped overalls stood on the sidewalk, juggling four balls in the air. A group of children gathered around him, cheering him on. "How about I try to find you a cold Coca-Cola? Might need it after you take a sip of this." He held up the moonshine.

Her eyes sparkled in the streetlights. "Oh, I'd love that. Maybe I'll get to enjoy it this time."

"I can guarantee no one is going to knock anything out of your hands." He unscrewed the jar lid, took a sip, and then wiped his mouth with the back of his hand and handed it to her. "It's good."

She took a tiny taste, then a larger gulp. "It is surprisingly good. It does taste like apple pie, but it's making my eyes water."

Layken chuckled, threw back another swig, screwed the lid back on, and clutched her hand. "Come on. Let's go check out everything. Looks like a county fair."

Now to find the right moment to give her the ring.

CHAPTER 42

A warm flush filled Sara Beth's cheeks as the moonshine burned its way to her stomach. Or maybe it was Layken's powerful arms holding her so close she could feel his heart beating. Either way, she'd never felt more alive.

She smiled and waved to townspeople she recognized, although most turned away with no response.

Layken tugged her hand. "Come on. I see the Cokes."

Following him through the crowd, she raised her chin and lifted her shoulders. She was Mrs. Layken Martin, and it didn't matter what any of these people thought of her.

Layken attempted to trade the remaining moonshine for two cokes. Sara Beth held back a giggle as he skillfully negotiated. With a wide smile and wink, he handed her a cold Coca-Cola. "For you, my dear."

She did a half-curtsy. "Thank you, kind sir." She turned up the bottle, savoring the sweet coldness.

They turned away as the man called out, "Bring those empty bottles back when you finish."

Layken waved. "Sure thing."

They sipped their Cokes and strolled hand in hand past a display of carved wooden art pieces.

It was much quieter at this end of the street.

She gasped when Layken tugged her into the surrounding cloak of darkness and kissed her. "People will see," she whispered.

"Let them." He set his Coke bottle down, pulled something from his pocket, and went down on one knee. "Sara Beth, I want you to be my wife, my real wife in every way. Would you consider wearing this ring? It was my mother's."

"Oh." Tears clouded her vision for an instant. She placed her right hand on his shoulder to steady herself, set her bottle next to his, and kneeled in front of him. "I would be honored to wear your mother's ring, Layken. Truly honored, but you don't have to do this."

He stood and gathered her in his arms. "I know I don't. I want to."

Her hand trembled as he slid the ring onto her finger.

She held it up. "It's simple and beautiful."

"Exactly like you." He smoothed back her hair.

"I don't know what to say."

He pressed a kiss to her temple. "Just know this ring seals my commitment to you and to our lives together." He cleared his throat. "That is…if it's what you want."

She struggled to swallow past the lump in her throat as she lifted her face toward his, touched by his tender sincerity. "It is what I want. I can't imagine being anywhere else but with you on our farm."

"Our farm. I love those words." He drew her closer. "That means more to me than anything. It's as much yours as mine, and we will own it outright again someday."

When his lips met hers, she tingled from head to toe. This was the beginning of a new life. She'd never be alone again.

He broke the kiss, leaned down, and retrieved their refreshments. "Here. Maybe someday you'll get to drink a whole one uninterrupted."

She took a sip, then laughed as he drained his bottle. "Maybe. But this was a good interruption." The cool metal of the ring against her finger contrasted with the hot summer night air. "Thank you, Layken. This means more than you can know. I will be a good wife to you." Try as she might, she couldn't help staring at it. While it was a simple band, it carried a huge promise, and all but took her breath away. Butterflies took up residence in her stomach.

Layken hooked his arm through hers. "If I doubted it for a minute, that ring wouldn't be on your finger." He ran a thumb along her jawline. "Let's go find the others."

They hadn't said the words yet, but somehow their hearts knew. Love was growing between them, much like the peanuts were growing in the field.

Sara Beth sipped her drink while they strolled back toward the hub of noise and activity, letting the cool liquid soothe her jittery nerves. Sure, they had lots of hard work ahead of them, but it didn't matter. They'd already proven what they could accomplish together.

She emptied her bottle as they rounded a corner back onto the main street, and let out a gasp when she came face-to-face with Homer Williams and his new wife.

Layken drew her nearer as if to protect her from any hurt the man might throw at her. His closeness gave her courage. "Homer. Mrs. Williams." While she knew the words dripped ice, she didn't care. This man meant nothing to her.

"Homer? Really, daughter. You no longer call me father."

Fighting against rising anger, she kept her voice calm. "I no longer call you father since it would be a lie. You are, in fact, not my father."

Surprise registered on his face, then quickly turned to a snarl. "What are you implying, Sara Beth? I raised you, gave you a good life."

"That you did, but I know the truth now, and I'm happy your hateful, tainted blood doesn't flow through my veins."

Homer blustered. "Is that the thanks I get for giving you my name? You were a bastard child and now you're nothing but an ungrateful bitch, exactly like your mother." He raised his hand to strike her.

Layken growled low. "I wouldn't do that if I was you, sir."

He glanced at Layken as if seeing him for the first time, then spat venomous words. "Good riddance to both of you." He took his wife's arm. "Come along, my dear. We don't have to put up with such disrespect."

As he hurried down the sidewalk, he threw back over his shoulder. "You still owe me, and don't you forget it because I won't."

"You'll get your damn money. Don't you welch on our bargain." Layken gripped her tighter. "You okay?"

While her legs wobbled, she was more than okay on the inside. "Fine. Felt good to stand up to the bully."

"I'm proud of you." He grinned widely. "Remind me to never get on your bad side."

She laughed, shaking off the tension from the confrontation. "I don't think you have anything to worry about."

They deposited their empty bottles, and he steered her toward the dancers.

The golden band reflected in the streetlights. She couldn't wait to show Mildred and Uncle Seymour. It was like she'd just gotten married. Only this time, it was for real.

When she spied Mildred with Tab clumsily attempting to dance with her, Sara Beth pointed. "Look."

"That's a sight for sore eyes." Layken twirled her around, and they moved closer to the two. When they reached them, Layken tapped Tab on the shoulder. "My turn."

Sara Beth laughed as Tab stumbled toward her. "I'll try not to step on your toes, Miss Sara Beth."

"Here. Follow my lead." She counted out loud. "One, two, three, one, two, three."

Tab struggled to keep up. "I'm not very good at this."

"Oh, but you will be. And someday, when you want to ask a girl to dance, you'll be the best dancer around."

She gazed around the crowd, caught Layken's eye, and shivered in the oppressive night heat when he grinned and winked.

It was nearing midnight when the tired group loaded back into the pickup and Layken pointed it toward the farm. Sara Beth sighed with contentment.

"That was the most fun I've had in years, Layken." Mildred held a sleepy Ellen. "Thank you. Not only for tonight, but for taking us in, giving us a safe place to live." She hesitated and cleared her throat. "And for giving my boy back to me."

"My pleasure, ma'am. Tab is a big help around the farm, and so are you. We're happy you're with us."

Sara Beth held up her hand. "Look, Mildred. Layken gave me his mother's ring tonight." She giggled. "It feels like we're really married now."

"Well, ain't that something?" Mildred admired the ring. "New beginnings for all of us."

Those words echoed in Sara Beth's head as Layken drove.

Truly, a new start. She was free of Homer Williams for good. She had a husband who loved her.

And if she was completely honest, she'd fallen in love with Layken in such a gradual progression there wasn't a way to pinpoint a specific moment.

They pulled onto the dirt lane leading to the farmhouse, and Ellen's quiet snores filled the pickup.

Layken parked the truck. "Stay where you are, Mildred. I'll carry Ellen for you."

The kindness and consideration her husband showed never ceased to touch Sara Beth on a deep level. He could have rejected everyone who had come to his door, starting with Uncle Seymour. But he didn't. He embraced them all.

Once everyone was settled, Sara Beth took Layken's hand, and together, they switched off lights throughout the house.

And, as both Mildred and Layken had promised, she knew in her heart of hearts the time was right.

Ignoring the unspoken question in Layken's eyes, her heart beat triple time as she led her husband toward her bedroom.

Life loomed big and hopeful ahead.

They'd rebuild what they'd lost and save this ancestral farm for future generations to come.

The land would continue to provide, as it always had.

What began as a beggar's bargain had turned into a king's ransom, for Layken had won a queen.

ABOUT JAN SIKES

Jan Sikes writes compelling and creative stories from the heart. She openly admits that she never set out in life to be an author, although she's been an avid reader all her life. But she had a story to tell. Not just any story, but a true story that rivals any fiction creation. She brought the entertaining true story to life through fictitious characters in an intricately woven tale that encompasses four books, accompanying music CDs, and a book of poetry and art. And now, Jan Sikes can't put down the pen. She continues to write fiction in a variety of genres, and has published many award-winning short stories and novels.

Jan is an active blogger, a devoted fan of Texas music, and a grandmother of five. She resides in North Texas. For more, visit JanSikes.com.

Fresh Ink Group

Independent Multi-media Publisher

Fresh Ink Group / Push Pull Press

Voice of Indie / GeezWriter

Hardcovers

Softcovers

All Ebook Formats

Audiobooks

Podcasts

Worldwide Distribution

Indie Author Services

Book Development, Editing, Proofing

Graphic/Cover Design

Video/Trailer Production

Website Creation

Social Media Marketing

Writing Contests

Writers' Blogs

Authors

Editors

Artists

Experts

Professionals

FreshInkGroup.com

info@FreshInkGroup.com

Twitter: @FreshInkGroup

Facebook.com/FreshInkGroup

LinkedIn: Fresh Ink Group

Guntersville

The White Rune Series

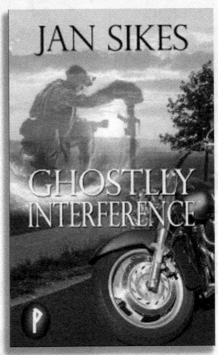

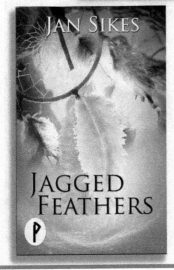

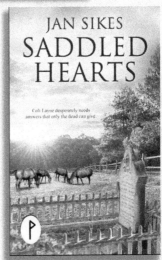

True Story Series

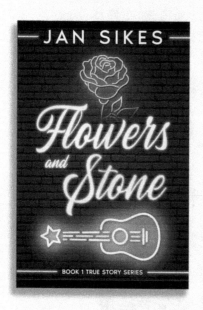

Shorts by Jan Sikes

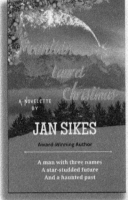

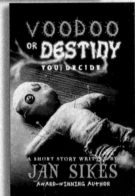

More by Jan Sikes

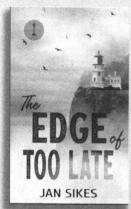

Music by Rick Sikes

Download/Stream
Everywhere

Printed in the USA
CPSIA information can be obtained
at www.ICGtesting.com
LVHW020854220324
775213LV00001B/157